Christmas
Around the Fire

Christmas Around the Fire

Stories, Essays, & Poems for the Season of Christ's Birth

Edited by Ryan N. S. Topping

TAN Books
Charlotte, North Carolina

Copyright © 2019 Ryan N. S. Topping

All rights reserved. With the exception of short excerpts used in critical review, no part of this work may be reproduced, transmitted, or stored in any form whatsoever without the prior written permission of the publisher.

Scripture quotations are from the Revised Standard Version of the Bible—Second Catholic Edition (Ignatius Edition), copyright © 2006 National Council of the Churches of Christ in the United States of America. Used by permission. All rights reserved.

Excerpts from the English translation of the Catechism of the Catholic Church for use in the United States of America © 1994, United States Catholic Conference, Inc. Libreria Editrice Vaticana. Used with permission.

Passages from papal documents, encyclicals, and addresses Copyright © Libreria Editrice Vaticana unless otherwise noted. All rights reserved.

Permission to reprint The Christmas Gift granted by Madonna House Publications, Combermere, Ontario. Original publication Donkey Bells: Advent and Christmas with Catherine Doherty (1994/2000) pp 111-118, madonnahouse.org/publications.

Keeping Christmas Local first appeared in the Imaginative Conservative and is republished with permission of the author.

Cover design by Caroline K. Green

Library of Congress Control Number: 2019937341

ISBN: 978-1-5051-1115-6

Published in the United States by
TAN Books
PO Box 269
Gastonia, NC 28053
www.TANBooks.com

Printed in India

*The Toppings dedicate
this book to the
Sieberts, with thanks
for many happy
Christmases…*

"You shall hold your cherished places in our Christmas hearts, and by our Christmas fires."

—*Charles Dickens*

"God is here, he has not withdrawn from the world."

—*Pope Benedict XVI*

Contents

Introduction IX

Part I: Stories

Leo Tolstoy, Papa Panov's Special Christmas............................ 3

G. K. Chesterton, The Modern Scrooge 9

Charles Dickens, The Spirit of Christmas Past 16

Henry Van Dyke, The First Christmas Tree 39

Stephen Leacock, Merry Christmas 65

The Hegge Cycle, The Annunciation 77

Willa Cather, The Burglar's Christmas 90

Harrison S. Morris, A Christmas Miracle 105

Oscar Wilde, The Selfish Giant 118

Ruth Sawyer, This Was the Christmas 125

Catherine Doherty, The Christmas Gift............................... 137

Henry Van Dycke, The Other Wise Man.............................. 146

Ryan N. S. Topping, A Canadian Christmas 177

Part II: Essays & Poems

Pope Benedict XVI, Advent Calls Us to Silence 187

George MacDonald, That Holy Thing................................. 192

Pope St. John Paul II, Rejoice, The Lord Is Near 193

G. M. Hopkins, Moonless Darkness Stands Between 199

St. Bernard of Clairvaux, Great Is the Lord's Love for Us 200

Ben Jonson, A Hymn on the Nativity of My Saviour 207

Joseph Pearce, Keeping Christmas Local 209

Robert Southwell, The Burning Babe 214

G. K. Chesterton, The Rituals of Christmas 215

Clement Clarke Moore, A Visit From St. Nicholas 221

Hillaire Belloc, A Remaining Christmas 224

G. K. Chesterton, The House of Christmas 235

St. Augustine, A Christmas Sermon 237

Christina Rossetti, The Shepherds Had an Angel 242

Charles Lamb, A Few Words on Christmas 244

Thomas Hardy, The Oxen 248

Charles Dickens, What Christmas Is as We Grow Older 249

John Neale, Good King Wenceslas 256

Charles Dudley Warner, The Burden of Christmas 258

Sara Teasdale, A Christmas Carol 262

Cardinal Newman, Why Do We Need Epiphany? 264

Henry Wadsworth Longfellow, The Three Kings 275

Pope Benedict XVI, Epiphany in a Secular Age 279

Introduction

THIS BOOK was born out of our family's experience of reading together over the holidays. My wife and I often read aloud to each other and to our children. But during the seasons of Advent, Christmas, and Epiphany, when the nights are dark and cold, we devote long evenings to it.

For several years now, our family has shared most of the week between Christmas and New Year's Day with some close friends and their children. After dinner, clean up, baths, prayers, perhaps a play practice and singing, the younger ones are rounded up and tucked into bed and the older ones into some corner or other of the house where we can't hear them. My wife and I have nine children. In our household, bedtime marks the beginning of our "quiet time." It is now that another round of eggnog and brandy is poured, evening crafts and games reappear, a drawing is returned to, and soon will begin one of our favorite Christmas activities—reading aloud.

In the weeks leading up to December 25, the question yearly arises: what to read this year? During these long evenings, we have no time for television, but instead look forward to hearing the voice of a friend or family member read a good story. One Christmas, I decided to put together a list of stories that would suit the leisure and deep joy of this season. The collection you have in your hand grew from that original compilation.

In looking through this volume, you'll find stories, essays, and poems. Some tales are short, others long, some from America, Canada, or England, others from faraway countries and times; some reflections, like the ones by St Augustine and Benedict XVI, provoke deep thought, while others, like those by Tolstoy and G. K. Chesterton, are more whimsical. What unites these selections is that each, in its own way, points us back to the miracle of the Babe in Bethlehem. Just as his birth needed Mary, Joseph, Angels, and also an ox, an ass, and lowly shepherds, so also does the Holy Child's message need our voices—the voices of poets, priests, parents, philosophers, and storytellers to carry his love into our hearts.

May this collection, from our family to yours, help carry that Love into your hearts this Christmas and throughout the year.

PART I

Stories

Papa Panov's Special Christmas

Leo Tolstoy (1828–1910)

"So he did come after all!"

The famed Russian storyteller and novelist Tolstoy describes, in beautifully simple terms, how a poor shoemaker comes, unexpectedly, to meet Christ one Christmas. Tolstoy's tale is inspired by Jesus's saying found in Matthew 25:35: "I was hungry and you gave me food, I was thirsty and you gave me drink, I was a stranger and you welcomed me."

IT WAS Christmas Eve and although it was still afternoon, lights had begun to appear in the shops and houses of the little Russian village, for the short winter day was nearly over. Excited children scurried indoors and now only muffled sounds of chatter and laughter escaped from closed shutters.

Old Papa Panov, the village shoemaker, stepped outside his shop to take one last look around. The sounds of happiness, the bright lights and the faint but delicious smells of Christmas cooking reminded him of past Christmas times when his wife had still been alive and his own children little. Now they had gone. His usually cheerful face, with the little laughter wrinkles behind the round steel spectacles, looked sad now. But he went back indoors with a firm step, put up the shutters and set a pot of coffee to heat on the charcoal stove. Then, with a sigh, he settled in his big armchair.

Papa Panov did not often read, but tonight he pulled down the big old family Bible and, slowly tracing the lines with one forefinger, he read again the Christmas story. He read how Mary and Joseph, tired by their journey to Bethlehem, found no room for them at the inn, so that Mary's little baby was born in the cowshed.

"Oh, dear, oh, dear!" exclaimed Papa Panov. "If only they had come here! I would have given them my bed and I could have covered the baby with my patchwork quilt to keep him warm."

He read on about the wise men who had come to see the baby Jesus, bringing him splendid gifts. Papa Panov's face fell. "I have no gift that I could give him," he thought sadly.

Then his face brightened. He put down the Bible, got up and stretched his long arms to the shelf high up in his little room. He took down a small, dusty box and opened it. Inside was a perfect pair of tiny leather shoes. Papa Panov smiled with satisfaction. Yes, they were as good as he had remembered—the best shoes he had ever made. "I should give him those," he decided, as he gently put them away and sat down again.

PAPA PANOV'S SPECIAL CHRISTMAS

He was feeling tired now, and the further he read the sleepier he became. The print began to dance before his eyes so that he closed them, just for a minute. In no time at all Papa Panov was fast asleep.

And as he slept he dreamed. He dreamed that someone was in his room and he knew at once, as one does in dreams, who the person was. It was Jesus.

"You have been wishing that you could see me, Papa Panov," he said kindly. "Then look for me tomorrow. It will be Christmas Day and I will visit you. But look carefully, for I shall not tell you who I am."

When at last Papa Panov awoke, the bells were ringing out and a thin light was filtering through the shutters. "Bless my soul!" said Papa Panov. "It's Christmas Day!"

He stood up and stretched himself for he was rather stiff. Then his face filled with happiness as he remembered his dream. This would be a very special Christmas after all, for Jesus was coming to visit him. How would he look? Would he be a little baby, as at that first Christmas? Would he be a grown man, a carpenter—or the great King that he is, God's Son? He must watch carefully the whole day through so that he recognized him however he came.

Papa Panov put on a special pot of coffee for his Christmas breakfast, took down the shutters and looked out of the window. The street was deserted, no one was stirring yet. No one except the road sweeper. He looked as miserable and dirty as ever, and well he might! Whoever wanted to work on Christmas Day—and in the raw cold and bitter freezing mist of such a morning?

Papa Panov opened the shop door, letting in a thin stream of cold air. "Come in!" he shouted across the street cheerily. "Come in and have some hot coffee to keep out the cold!"

The sweeper looked up, scarcely able to believe his ears. He was only too glad to put down his broom and come into the warm room. His old clothes steamed gently in the heat of the stove and he clasped both red hands round the comforting warm mug as he drank.

Papa Panov watched him with satisfaction, but every now and then his eyes strayed to the window. It would never do to miss his special visitor.

"Expecting someone?" the sweeper asked at last. So Papa Panov told him about his dream.

"Well, I hope he comes," the sweeper said. "You've given me a bit of Christmas cheer I never expected to have. I'd say you deserve to have your dream come true." And he actually smiled.

When he had gone, Papa Panov put on cabbage soup for his dinner, then went to the door again, scanning the street. He saw no one. But he was mistaken. Someone was coming.

The girl walked so slowly and quietly, hugging the walls of shops and houses, that it was a while before he noticed her. She looked very tired and she was carrying something. As she drew nearer he could see that it was a baby, wrapped in a thin shawl. There was such sadness in her face and in the pinched little face of the baby, that Papa Panov's heart went out to them.

"Won't you come in," he called, stepping outside to meet them. "You both need a warm seat by the fire and a rest."

The young mother let him shepherd her indoors and to the

PAPA PANOV'S SPECIAL CHRISTMAS

comfort of the armchair. She gave a big sigh of relief.

"I'll warm some milk for the baby," Papa Panov said. "I've had children of my own—I can feed her for you." He took the milk from the stove and carefully fed the baby from a spoon, warming her tiny feet by the stove at the same time.

"She needs shoes," the cobbler said.

But the girl replied, "I can't afford shoes, I've got no husband to bring home money. I'm on my way to the next village to get work."

A sudden thought flashed through Papa Panov's mind. He remembered the little shoes he had looked at last night. But he had been keeping those for Jesus. He looked again at the cold little feet and made up his mind.

"Try these on her," he said, handing the baby and the shoes to the mother. The beautiful little shoes were a perfect fit. The girl smiled happily and the baby gurgled with pleasure.

"You have been so kind to us," the girl said, when she got up with her baby to go. "May all your Christmas wishes come true!"

But Papa Panov was beginning to wonder if his very special Christmas wish would come true. Perhaps he had missed his visitor? He looked anxiously up and down the street. There were plenty of people about but they were all faces that he recognized. There were neighbors going to call on their families. They nodded and smiled and wished him Happy Christmas! Or beggars—and Papa Panov hurried indoors to fetch them hot soup and a generous hunk of bread, hurrying out again in case he missed the Important Stranger.

All too soon the winter dusk fell. When Papa Panov next went to the door and strained his eyes, he could no longer make out the passers-by. Most were home and indoors by now anyway. He walked slowly back into his room at last, put up the shutters, and sat down wearily in his armchair.

So it had been just a dream after all. Jesus had not come.

Then all at once he knew that he was no longer alone in the room.

This was not a dream for he was wide awake. At first he seemed to see before his eyes the long stream of people who had come to him that day. He saw again the old road sweeper, the young mother and her baby and the beggars he had fed. As they passed, each whispered, "Didn't you see me, Papa Panov?"

"Who are you?" he called out, bewildered.

Then another voice answered him. It was the voice from his dream—the voice of Jesus.

"I was hungry and you fed me," he said. "I was naked and you clothed me. I was cold and you warmed me. I came to you today in everyone of those you helped and welcomed."

Then all was quiet and still. Only the sound of the big clock ticking. A great peace and happiness seemed to fill the room, overflowing Papa Panov's heart until he wanted to burst out singing and laughing and dancing with joy.

"So he did come after all!" was all that he said.

The Modern Scrooge

G. K. Chesterton (1874–1936)

*"He wanted humanity; he did not
know whether he loved or hated it."*

G. K. Chesterton remains one of the most beloved storytellers, journalists, and apologists in modern times. Chesterton was also a voracious reader and perceptive commentator upon Victorian literature. Here he playfully takes up a theme from Charles Dickens' classic *A Christmas Carol* and recasts it into a contemporary setting.

MR. VERNON-SMITH, of Trinity, and the Social Settlement, Tooting, author of "A Higher London" and "The Boyg System at Work," came to the conclusion, after looking through his select and even severe library, that Dickens's "Christmas Carol" was a very suitable thing to be read to charwomen. Had they been men they would have been forcibly subjected to Browning's "Christmas Eve" with exposition, but chivalry spared the charwomen, and Dickens was funny, and could do no harm. His fellow worker Wimpole would read things like

"Three Men in a Boat" to the poor; but Vernon-Smith regarded this as a sacrifice of principle, or (what was the same thing to him) of dignity. He would not encourage them in their vulgarity; they should have nothing from him that was not literature. Still Dickens was literature after all; not literature of a high order, of course, not thoughtful or purposeful literature, but literature quite fitted for charwomen on Christmas Eve.

He did not, however, let them absorb Dickens without due antidotes of warning and criticism. He explained that Dickens was not a writer of the first rank, since he lacked the high seriousness of Matthew Arnold. He also feared that they would find the characters of Dickens terribly exaggerated. But they did not, possibly because they were meeting them every day. For among the poor there are still exaggerated characters; they do not go to the Universities to be universified. He told the charwomen, with progressive brightness, that a mad wicked old miser like Scrooge would be really quite impossible now; but as each of the charwomen had an uncle or a grandfather or a father-in-law who was exactly like Scrooge, his cheerfulness was not shared. Indeed, the lecture as a whole lacked something of his firm and elastic touch, and towards the end he found himself rambling, and in a sort of abstraction, talking to them as if they were his fellows. He caught himself saying quite mystically that a spiritual plane (by which he meant his plane) always looked to those on the sensual or Dickens plane, not merely austere, but desolate. He said, quoting Bernard Shaw, that we could all go to heaven just as we can all go to a classical concert, but if we did it would bore us.

Realizing that he was taking his flock far out of their depth, he ended somewhat hurriedly, and was soon receiving that generous applause which is a part of the profound ceremonialism of the working classes. As he made his way to the door three people stopped him, and he answered them heartily enough, but with an air of hurry which he would not have dreamed of showing to people of his own class. One was a little schoolmistress who told him with a sort of feverish meekness that she was troubled because an Ethical Lecturer had said that Dickens was not really Progressive; but she thought he was Progressive; and surely he was Progressive. Of what being Progressive was she had no more notion than a whale. The second person implored him for a subscription to some soup kitchen or cheap meal; and his refined features sharpened; for this, like literature, was a matter of principle with him. "Quite the wrong method," he said, shaking his head and pushing past. "Nothing any good but the Boyg system." The third stranger, who was male, caught him on the step as he came out into the snow and starlight; and asked him point blank for money. It was a part of Vernon-Smith's principles that all such persons are prosperous impostors; and like a true mystic he held to his principles in defiance of his five senses, which told him that the night was freezing and the man very thin and weak. "If you come to the Settlement between four and five on Friday," he said, "inquiries will be made." The man stepped back into the snow with a not ungraceful gesture as of apology; he had frosty silver hair, and his lean face, though in shadow, seemed to wear something like a smile. As Vernon-Smith stepped briskly into the street, the man stooped down as if to do up his bootlace. He was, however, guiltless of any such dandyism; and as the young philanthropist stood pulling on his gloves with some particularity, a heavy snowball was suddenly smashed into his face. He was blind for a black instant; then as some of the snow fell, saw faintly, as in a dim mirror of ice or dreamy crystal, the lean man bowing with the elegance of a dancing master, and saying amiably, "A Christmas box." When he had quite cleared his face of snow the man had vanished.

For three burning minutes Cyril Vernon-Smith was nearer to the people and more their brother than he had been in his whole high-stepping pedantic existence; for if he did not love a poor man, he hated one. And you never really regard a labourer as your equal until you can quarrel with him. "Dirty cad!" he muttered. "Filthy fool! Mucking with snow like a beastly baby! When will they be civilized? Why, the very state of the street is a disgrace and a temptation to such tomfools. Why isn't all this snow cleared away and the street made decent?"

To the eye of efficiency, there was, indeed, something to complain of in the condition of the road. Snow was banked up on both sides in white walls and towards the other and darker end of the street even rose into a chaos of low colourless hills. By the time he reached them he was nearly knee deep, and was in a far from philanthropic frame of mind. The solitude of the little streets was as strange as their white obstruction, and before he had ploughed his way much further he was convinced that he had taken a wrong turning, and fallen upon some formless suburb unvisited before. There was no light in any of the low, dark houses; no light in anything but the blank emphatic snow.

He was modern and morbid; hellish isolation hit and held him suddenly; anything human would have relieved the strain, if it had been only the leap of a garotter. Then the tender human touch came indeed; for another snowball struck him, and made a star on his back. He turned with fierce joy, and ran after a boy escaping; ran with dizzy and violent speed, he knew not for how long. He wanted the boy; he did not know whether he loved or hated him. He wanted humanity; he did not know whether he loved or hated it.

As he ran he realized that the landscape around him was changing in shape though not in colour. The houses seemed to dwindle and disappear in hills of snow as if buried; the snow seemed to rise in tattered outlines of crag and cliff and crest, but he thought nothing of all these impossibilities until the boy turned to bay. When he did he saw the child was queerly beautiful, with gold red hair, and a face as serious as complete happiness. And when he spoke to the boy his own question surprised him, for he said for the first time in his life, "What am I doing here?" And the little boy, with very grave eyes, answered, "I suppose you are dead."

He had (also for the first time) a doubt of his spiritual destiny. He looked round on a towering landscape of frozen peaks and plains, and said, "Is this hell?" And as the child stared, but did not answer, he knew it was heaven.

All over that colossal country, white as the world round the Pole, little boys were playing, rolling each other down dreadful slopes, crushing each other under falling cliffs; for heaven is a place where one can fight for ever without hurting. Smith suddenly remembered how happy he had been as a child, rolling about on the safe sandhills around Conway.

Right above Smith's head, higher than the cross of St. Paul's, but curving over him like the hanging blossom of a harebell, was a cavernous crag of snow. A hundred feet below him, like a landscape seen from a balloon, lay snowy flats as white and as far away. He saw a little boy stagger, with many catastrophic slides, to that toppling peak; and seizing another little boy by the leg, send him flying away down to the distant silver plains. There he sank and vanished in the snow as if in the sea; but coming up again like a diver rushed madly up the steep once more, rolling before him a great gathering snowball, gigantic at last, which he hurled back at the mountain crest, and brought both the boy and the mountain down in one avalanche to the level of the vale. The other boy also sank like a stone, and also rose again like a bird, but Smith had no leisure to concern himself with this. For the collapse of that celestial crest had left him standing solitary in the sky on a peak like a church spire.

He could see the tiny figures of the boys in the valley below, and he knew by their attitudes that they were eagerly telling him to jump. Then for the first time he knew the nature of faith, as he had just known the fierce nature of charity. Or rather for the second time, for he remembered one moment when he had known faith before. It was when his father had taught him to swim, and he had believed he could float on water not only against reason, but (what is so much harder) against instinct. Then he had trusted water; now he must trust air.

He jumped. He went through air and then through snow

THE MODERN SCROOGE

with the same blinding swiftness. But as he buried himself in solid snow like a bullet he seemed to learn a million things and to learn them all too fast. He knew that the whole world is a snowball, and that all the stars are snowballs. He knew that no man will be fit for heaven till he loves solid whiteness as a little boy loves a ball of snow.

He sank and sank and sank . . . and then, as usually happens in such cases, woke up, with a start—in the street. True, he was taken up for a common drunk, but (if you properly appreciate his conversion) you will realize that he did not mind; since the crime of drunkenness is infinitely less than that of spiritual pride, of which he had really been guilty.

The Spirit of Christmas Past

Charles Dickens (1812–1870)

*"What was merry Christmas to Scrooge?
Out upon merry Christmas!"*

Here is a selection from what remains the most beloved Christmas novella of all time. We meet many of the colorful and most memorable characters from *A Christmas Carol*: the hoarding Scrooge, his dead business associate Marley, the generous Fezziwigs, and most hauntingly, the Ghost of Christmas Past sent to offer a grasping old man a last chance to make amends.

WHEN SCROOGE awoke, it was so dark, that looking out of bed, he could scarcely distinguish the transparent window from the opaque walls of his chamber. He was endeavouring to pierce the darkness with his ferret eyes, when the chimes of a neighbouring church struck the four quarters. So he listened for the hour.

To his great astonishment the heavy bell went on from six to seven, and from seven to eight, and regularly up to twelve; then stopped. Twelve! It was past two when he went to bed.

THE SPIRIT OF CHRISTMAS PAST

The clock was wrong. An icicle must have got into the works. Twelve!

He touched the spring of his repeater, to correct this most preposterous clock. Its rapid little pulse beat twelve: and stopped.

"Why, it isn't possible," said Scrooge, "that I can have slept through a whole day and far into another night. It isn't possible that anything has happened to the sun, and this is twelve at noon!"

The idea being an alarming one, he scrambled out of bed, and groped his way to the window. He was obliged to rub the frost off with the sleeve of his dressing-gown before he could see anything; and could see very little then. All he could make out was, that it was still very foggy and extremely cold, and that there was no noise of people running to and fro, and making a great stir, as there unquestionably would have been if night had beaten off bright day, and taken possession of the world. This was a great relief, because "three days after sight of this First of Exchange pay to Mr. Ebenezer Scrooge or his order," and so forth, would have become a mere United States' security if there were no days to count by.

Scrooge went to bed again, and thought, and thought, and thought it over and over, and could make nothing of it. The more he thought, the more perplexed he was; and the more he endeavoured not to think, the more he thought Marley's Ghost bothered him exceedingly. Every time he resolved within himself, after mature inquiry, that it was all a dream, his mind flew back, like a strong spring released, to its first position, and presented the same problem to be worked all through, "Was it a dream or not?"

Scrooge lay in this state until the chime had gone three quarters more, when he remembered, on a sudden, that the Ghost had warned him of a visitation when the bell tolled one. He resolved to lie awake until the hour was past; and, considering that he could no more go to sleep than go to Heaven, this was perhaps the wisest resolution in his power.

The quarter was so long, that he was more than once convinced he must have sunk into a doze unconsciously, and missed the clock. At length it broke upon his listening ear.

"Ding, dong!"

"A quarter past," said Scrooge, counting.

"Ding, dong!"

"Half past!" said Scrooge.

"Ding, dong!"

"A quarter to it," said Scrooge.

"Ding, dong!"

"The hour itself," said Scrooge, triumphantly, "and nothing else!"

He spoke before the hour bell sounded, which it now did with a deep, dull, hollow, melancholy ONE. Light flashed up in the room upon the instant, and the curtains of his bed were drawn.

The curtains of his bed were drawn aside, I tell you, by a hand. Not the curtains at his feet, nor the curtains at his back, but those to which his face was addressed. The curtains of his bed were drawn aside; and Scrooge, starting up into a half-recumbent attitude, found himself face to face with the unearthly visitor who drew them: as close to it as I am now to you, and I am standing in the spirit at your elbow.

THE SPIRIT OF CHRISTMAS PAST

It was a strange figure—like a child: yet not so like a child as like an old man, viewed through some supernatural medium, which gave him the appearance of having receded from the view, and being diminished to a child's proportions. Its hair, which hung about its neck and down its back, was white as if with age; and yet the face had not a wrinkle in it, and the tenderest bloom was on the skin. The arms were very long and muscular; the hands the same, as if its hold were of uncommon strength. Its legs and feet, most delicately formed, were, like those upper members, bare. It wore a tunic of the purest white and round its waist was bound a lustrous belt, the sheen of which was beautiful. It held a branch of fresh green holly in its hand; and, in singular contradiction of that wintry emblem, had its dress trimmed with summer flowers. But the strangest thing about it was, that from the crown of its head there sprung a bright clear jet of light, by which all this was visible; and which was doubtless the occasion of its using, in its duller moments, a great extinguisher for a cap, which it now held under its arm.

Even this, though, when Scrooge looked at it with increasing steadiness, was not its strangest quality. For as its belt sparkled and glittered now in one part and now in another, and what was light one instant, at another time was dark, so the figure itself fluctuated in its distinctness: being now a thing with one arm, now with one leg, now with twenty legs, now a pair of legs without a head, now a head without a body: of which dissolving parts, no outline would be visible in the dense gloom wherein they melted away. And in the very wonder of this, it would be itself again; distinct and clear as ever.

"Are you the Spirit, sir, whose coming was foretold to me?" asked Scrooge.

"I am!"

The voice was soft and gentle. Singularly low, as if instead of being so close beside him, it were at a distance.

"Who, and what are you?" Scrooge demanded.

"I am the Ghost of Christmas Past."

"Long past?" inquired Scrooge: observant of its dwarfish stature.

"No. Your past."

Perhaps, Scrooge could not have told anybody why, if anybody could have asked him; but he had a special desire to see the Spirit in his cap; and begged him to be covered.

"What!" exclaimed the Ghost, "would you so soon put out, with worldly hands, the light I give? Is it not enough that you are one of those whose passions made this cap, and force me through whole trains of years to wear it low upon my brow!"

Scrooge reverently disclaimed all intention to offend or any knowledge of having wilfully bonneted the Spirit at any period of his life. He then made bold to inquire what business brought him there.

"Your welfare!" said the Ghost.

Scrooge expressed himself much obliged, but could not help thinking that a night of unbroken rest would have been more conducive to that end. The Spirit must have heard him thinking, for it said immediately:

"Your reclamation, then. Take heed!"

THE SPIRIT OF CHRISTMAS PAST

It put out its strong hand as it spoke, and clasped him gently by the arm.

"Rise! and walk with me!"

It would have been in vain for Scrooge to plead that the weather and the hour were not adapted to pedestrian purposes; that bed was warm, and the thermometer a long way below freezing; that he was clad but lightly in his slippers, dressing-gown, and nightcap; and that he had a cold upon him at that time. The grasp, though gentle as a woman's hand, was not to be resisted. He rose: but finding that the Spirit made towards the window, clasped his robe in supplication.

"I am mortal," Scrooge remonstrated, "and liable to fall."

"Bear but a touch of my hand there," said the Spirit, laying it upon his heart, "and you shall be upheld in more than this!"

As the words were spoken, they passed through the wall, and stood upon an open country road, with fields on either hand. The city had entirely vanished. Not a vestige of it was to be seen. The darkness and the mist had vanished with it, for it was a clear, cold, winter day, with snow upon the ground. "Good Heaven!" said Scrooge, clasping his hands together, as he looked about him. "I was bred in this place. I was a boy here!"

The Spirit gazed upon him mildly. Its gentle touch, though it had been light and instantaneous, appeared still present to the old man's sense of feeling. He was conscious of a thousand odours floating in the air, each one connected with a thousand thoughts, and hopes, and joys, and cares long, long, forgotten.

"Your lip is trembling," said the Ghost. "And what is that upon your cheek?"

Scrooge muttered, with an unusual catching in his voice, that it was a pimple; and begged the Ghost to lead him where he would.

"You recollect the way?" inquired the Spirit.

"Remember it!" cried Scrooge with fervour; "I could walk it blindfold."

"Strange to have forgotten it for so many years!" observed the Ghost. "Let us go on."

They walked along the road; Scrooge recognising every gate, and post, and tree; until a little market-town appeared in the distance, with its bridge, its church, and winding river. Some shaggy ponies now were seen trotting towards them with boys upon their backs, who called to other boys in country gigs and carts, driven by farmers. All these boys were in great spirits, and shouted to each other, until the broad fields were so full of merry music, that the crisp air laughed to hear it.

"These are but shadows of the things that have been," said the Ghost. "They have no consciousness of us."

The jocund travellers came on; and as they came, Scrooge knew and named them every one. Why was he rejoiced beyond all bounds to see them! Why did his cold eye glisten, and his heart leap up as they went past! Why was he filled with gladness when he heard them give each other Merry Christmas, as they parted at cross-roads and bye-ways, for their several homes! What was merry Christmas to Scrooge? Out upon merry Christmas! What good had it ever done to him?

"The school is not quite deserted," said the Ghost. "A solitary child, neglected by his friends, is left there still."

THE SPIRIT OF CHRISTMAS PAST

Scrooge said he knew it. And he sobbed.

They left the high-road, by a well-remembered lane, and soon approached a mansion of dull red brick, with a little weathercock-surmounted cupola, on the roof, and a bell hanging in it. It was a large house, but one of broken fortunes; for the spacious offices were little used, their walls were damp and mossy, their windows broken, and their gates decayed. Fowls clucked and strutted in the stables; and the coach-houses and sheds were over-run with grass. Nor was it more retentive of its ancient state, within; for entering the dreary hall, and glancing through the open doors of many rooms, they found them poorly furnished, cold, and vast. There was an earthy savour in the air, a chilly bareness in the place, which associated itself somehow with too much getting up by candle-light, and not too much to eat.

They went, the Ghost and Scrooge, across the hall, to a door at the back of the house. It opened before them, and disclosed a long, bare, melancholy room, made barer still by lines of plain deal forms and desks. At one of these a lonely boy was reading near a feeble fire; and Scrooge sat down upon a form, and wept to see his poor forgotten self as he used to be.

Not a latent echo in the house, not a squeak and scuffle from the mice behind the panneling, not a drip from the half-thawed water-spout in the dull yard behind, not a sigh among the leafless boughs of one despondent poplar, not the idle swinging of an empty store-house door, no, not a clicking in the fire, but fell upon the heart of Scrooge with a softening influence, and gave a freer passage to his tears.

The Spirit touched him on the arm, and pointed to his younger self, intent upon his reading. Suddenly a man, in foreign garments: wonderfully real and distinct to look at: stood outside the window, with an axe stuck in his belt, and leading an ass laden with wood by the bridle.

"Why, it's Ali Baba!" Scrooge exclaimed in ecstasy. "It's dear old honest Ali Baba! Yes, yes, I know! One Christmas time, when yonder solitary child was left here all alone, he did come, for the first time, just like that. Poor boy! And Valentine," said Scrooge, "and his wild brother, Orson; there they go! And what's his name, who was put down in his drawers, asleep, at the Gate of Damascus; don't you see him! And the Sultan's Groom turned upside-down by the Genii; there he is upon his head! Serve him right. I'm glad of it. What business had he to be married to the Princess!"

To hear Scrooge expending all the earnestness of his nature on such subjects, in a most extraordinary voice between laughing and crying; and to see his heightened and excited face; would have been a surprise to his business friends in the city, indeed.

"There's the Parrot!" cried Scrooge. "Green body and yellow tail, with a thing like a lettuce growing out of the top of his head; there he is! Poor Robin Crusoe, he called him, when he came home again after sailing round the island. "Poor Robin Crusoe, where have you been, Robin Crusoe?" The man thought he was dreaming, but he wasn't. It was the Parrot, you know. There goes Friday, running for his life to the little creek! Halloa! Hoop! Halloo!"

Then, with a rapidity of transition very foreign to his usual character, he said, in pity for his former self, "Poor boy!" and cried again.

"I wish," Scrooge muttered, putting his hand in his pocket, and looking about him, after drying his eyes with his cuff: "but it's too late now."

"What is the matter?" asked the Spirit.

"Nothing," said Scrooge. "Nothing. There was a boy singing a Christmas Carol at my door last night. I should like to have given him something: that's all."

The Ghost smiled thoughtfully, and waved its hand: saying as it did so, "Let us see another Christmas!"

Scrooge's former self grew larger at the words, and the room became a little darker and more dirty. The panels shrunk, the windows cracked; fragments of plaster fell out of the ceiling, and the naked laths were shown instead; but how all this was brought about, Scrooge knew no more than you do. He only knew that it was quite correct; that everything had happened so; that there he was, alone again, when all the other boys had gone home for the jolly holidays.

He was not reading now, but walking up and down despairingly. Scrooge looked at the Ghost, and with a mournful shaking of his head, glanced anxiously towards the door.

It opened; and a little girl, much younger than the boy, came darting in, and putting her arms about his neck, and often kissing him, addressed him as her "Dear, dear brother."

"I have come to bring you home, dear brother!" said the child, clapping her tiny hands, and bending down to laugh. "To bring you home, home, home!"

"Home, little Fan?" returned the boy.

"Yes!" said the child, brimful of glee. "Home, for good and all. Home, for ever and ever. Father is so much kinder than he used to be, that home's like Heaven! He spoke so gently to me one dear night when I was going to bed, that I was not afraid to ask him once more if you might come home; and he said Yes, you should; and sent me in a coach to bring you. And you're to be a man!" said the child, opening her eyes, "and are never to come back here; but first, we're to be together all the Christmas long, and have the merriest time in all the world."

"You are quite a woman, little Fan!" exclaimed the boy.

She clapped her hands and laughed, and tried to touch his head; but being too little, laughed again, and stood on tiptoe to embrace him. Then she began to drag him, in her childish eagerness, towards the door; and he, nothing loth to go, accompanied her.

A terrible voice in the hall cried. "Bring down Master Scrooge's box, there!" and in the hall appeared the schoolmaster himself, who glared on Master Scrooge with a ferocious condescension, and threw him into a dreadful state of mind by shaking hands with him. He then conveyed him and his sister into the veriest old well of a shivering best-parlour that ever was seen, where the maps upon the wall, and the celestial and terrestrial globes in the windows, were waxy with cold. Here he produced a decanter of curiously light wine, and a block of curiously heavy cake, and administered instalments of those dainties to the young people: at the same time, sending out a meagre servant to offer a glass of something to the postboy, who answered that he thanked the gentleman, but if it was the same tap as he had tasted before, he had rather not. Master Scrooge's trunk being by this time tied on to the top of the chaise, the children bade the schoolmaster good-bye right willingly; and getting into it, drove gaily down the garden-sweep: the quick wheels dashing the hoar-frost and snow from off the dark leaves of the evergreens like spray.

"Always a delicate creature, whom a breath might have withered," said the Ghost. "But she had a large heart!"

"So she had," cried Scrooge. "You're right, I will not gainsay it, Spirit. God forbid!"

"She died a woman," said the Ghost, "and had, as I think, children."

"One child," Scrooge returned.

"True," said the Ghost. "Your nephew!"

Scrooge seemed uneasy in his mind; and answered briefly, "Yes."

Although they had but that moment left the school behind them, they were now in the busy thoroughfares of a city, where shadowy passengers passed and repassed; where shadowy carts and coaches battle for the way, and all the strife and tumult of a real city were. It was made plain enough, by the dressing of the shops, that here too it was Christmas time again; but it was evening, and the streets were lighted up.

The Ghost stopped at a certain warehouse door, and asked Scrooge if he knew it.

"Know it!" said Scrooge. "Was I apprenticed here!"

They went in. At sight of an old gentleman in a Welch wig, sitting behind such a high desk, that if he had been two inches taller he must have knocked his head against the ceiling, Scrooge cried in great excitement:

"Why, it's old Fezziwig! Bless his heart; it's Fezziwig alive again!"

Old Fezziwig laid down his pen, and looked up at the clock, which pointed to the hour of seven. He rubbed his hands; adjusted his capacious waistcoat; laughed all over himself, from his shows to his organ of benevolence; and called out in a comfortable, oily, rich, fat, jovial voice:

"Yo ho, there! Ebenezer! Dick!"

Scrooge's former self, now grown a young man, came briskly in, accompanied by his fellow-'prentice.

"Dick Wilkins, to be sure!" said Scrooge to the Ghost. "Bless me, yes. There he is. He was very much attached to me, was Dick. Poor Dick! Dear, dear!"

"Yo ho, my boys!" said Fezziwig. "No more work to-night. Christmas Eve, Dick. Christmas, Ebenezer! Let's have the shutters up," cried old Fezziwig, with a sharp clap of his hands, "before a man can say, Jack Robinson!"

You wouldn't believe how those two fellows went at it! They charged into the street with the shutters—one, two, three—had 'em up in their places—four, five, six—barred 'em and pinned 'em—seven, eight, nine—and came back before you could have got to twelve, panting like race-horses.

"Hilli-ho!" cried old Fezziwig, skipping down from the high desk, with wonderful agility. "Clear away, my lads, and let's have lots of room here! Hilli-ho, Dick! Chirrup, Ebenezer!"

Clear away! There was nothing they wouldn't have cleared

away, or couldn't have cleared away, with old Fezziwig looking on. It was done in a minute. Every movable was packed off, as if it were dismissed from public life for evermore; the floor was swept and watered, the lamps were trimmed, fuel was heaped upon the fire; and the warehouse was as snug, and warm, and dry, and bright a ball-room, as you would desire to see upon a winter's night.

In came a fiddler with a music-book, and went up to the lofty desk, and made an orchestra of it, and tuned like fifty stomach-aches. In came Mrs. Fezziwig, one vast substantial smile. In came the three Miss Fezziwigs, beaming and lovable. In came the six young followers whose hearts they broke. In came all the young men and women employed in the business. In came the housemaid, with her cousin, the baker. In came the cook, with her brother's particular friend, the milkman. In came the boy from over the way, who was suspected of not having board enough from his master; trying to hide himself behind the girl from next door but one, who was proved to have had her ears pulled by her Mistress. In they all came, one after nother; some shyly, some boldly, some gracefully, some awkwardly, some pushing, some pulling; in they all came, anyhow and everyhow. Away they all went, twenty couple at once; hands half round and back again the other way; down the middle and up again; round and round in various stages of affectionate grouping; old top couple always turning up in the wrong place; new top couple starting off again, as soon as they got there; all top couples at last, and not a bottom one to help them. When this result was brought about, old Fezziwig, clapping his hands to stop the dance, cried out, "Well done!" and the fiddler plunged his hot face into a pot of porter, especially provided for that purpose. But scorning rest, upon his reappearance, he instantly began again, though there were no dancers yet, as if the other fiddler had been carried home, exhausted, on a shutter, and he were a bran-new man resolved to beat him out of sight, or perish.

There were more dances, and there were forfeits, and more dances, and there was cake, and there was negus, and there was a great piece of Cold Roast, and there was a great piece of Cold Boiled, and there were mince-pies, and plenty of beer. But the great effect of the evening came after the Roast and Boiled, when the fiddler (an artful dog, mind! The sort of man who knew his business better than you or I could have told it him!) struck up "Sir Roger de Coverley." Then old Fezziwig stood out to dance with Mrs. Fezziwig. Top couple, too; with a good stiff piece of work cut out for them; three or four and twenty pair of partners; people who were not to be trifled with; people who would dance, and had no notion of walking.

But if they had been twice as many: ah, four times: old Fezziwig would have been a match for them, and so would Mrs. Fezziwig. As to her, she was worthy to be his partner in every sense of the term. If that's not high praise, tell me higher, and I'll use it. A positive light appeared to issue from Fezziwig's calves. They shone in every part of the dance like moons. You couldn't have predicted, at any given time, what would become of 'em next. And when old Fezziwig and Mrs. Fezziwig had gone all through the dance; advance and retire, hold hands with your partner, bow and curtsey; corkscrew; thread-the-needle, and back again to your place; Fezziwig cut—cut so deftly, that he appeared to wink with his legs, and came upon his feet again without a stagger.

When the clock struck eleven, this domestic ball broke up. Mr. and Mrs. Fezziwig took their stations, one on either side of the door, and shaking hands with every person individually as he or she went out, wished him or her a Merry Christmas. When everybody had retired but the two 'prentices, they did the same to them; and thus the cheerful voices died away, and the lads were left to their beds; which were under a counter in the back-shop.

During the whole of this time, Scrooge had acted like a man out of his wits. His heart and soul were in the scene, and with his former self. He corroborated everything, remembered everything, enjoyed everything, and underwent the strangest agitation. It was not until now, when the bright faces of his former self and Dick were turned from them, that he remembered the Ghost, and became conscious that it was looking full upon him, while the light upon its head burnt very clear.

"A small matter," said the Ghost, "to make these silly folks so full of gratitude."

"Small!" echoed Scrooge.

The Spirit signed to him to listen to the two apprentices, who were pouring out their hearts in praise of Fezziwig: and when he had done so, said,

"Why! Is it not? He has spent but a few pounds of your mortal money: three or four perhaps. Is that so much that he deserves this praise?"

"It isn't that," said Scrooge, heated by the remark, and speaking unconsciously like his former, not his latter, self. "It isn't that, Spirit. He has the power to render us happy or unhappy; to make our service light or burdensome; a pleasure or a toil. Say that his power lies in words and looks; in things so slight and insignificant that it is impossible to add and count 'em up: what then? The happiness he gives, is quite as great as if it cost a fortune."

He felt the Spirit's glance, and stopped.

"What is the matter?" asked the Ghost.

"Nothing particular," said Scrooge.

"Something, I think?" the Ghost insisted.

"No," said Scrooge, "No. I should like to be able to say a word or two to my clerk just now! That's all."

His former self turned down the lamps as he gave utterance to the wish; and Scrooge and the Ghost again stood side by side in the open air.

"My time grows short," observed the Spirit. "Quick!"

This was not addressed to Scrooge, or to any one whom he could see, but it produced an immediate effect. For again Scrooge saw himself. He was older now; a man in the prime of life. His face had not the harsh and rigid lines of later years; but it had begun to wear the signs of care and avarice. There was an eager, greedy, restless motion in the eye, which showed the passion that had taken root, and where the shadow of the growing tree would fall.

He was not alone, but sat by the side of a fair young girl in a mourning-dress: in whose eyes there were tears, which sparkled in the light that shone out of the Ghost of Christmas Past.

"It matters little," she said, softly. "To you, very little. Another idol has displaced me; and if it can cheer and comfort you in time to come, as I would have tried to do, I have no just cause to grieve."

"What Idol has displaced you?" he rejoined.

"A golden one."

"This is the even-handed dealing of the world!" he said. "There is nothing on which it is so hard as poverty; and there is nothing it professes to condemn with such severity as the pursuit of wealth!"

"You fear the world too much," she answered, gently. "All your other hopes have merged into the hope of being beyond the chance of its sordid reproach. I have seen your nobler aspirations fall off one by one, until the master-passion, Gain, engrosses you. Have I not?"

"What then?" he retorted. "Even if I have grown so much wiser, what then? I am not changed towards you."

She shook her head.

"Am I?"

"Our contract is an old one. It was made when we were both poor and content to be so, until, in good season, we could improve our worldly fortune by our patient industry. You are changed. When it was made, you were another man."

"I was a boy," he said impatiently.

"Your own feeling tells you that you were not what you are," she returned. "I am. That which promised happiness when we were one in heart, is fraught with misery now that we are two. How often and how keenly I have thought of this, I will not say. It is enough that I have thought of it, and can release you."

"Have I ever sought release?"

"In words. No. Never."

"In what, then?"

"In a changed nature; in an altered spirit; in another atmosphere of life; another Hope as its great end. In everything that made my love of any worth or value in your sight. If this had never been between us," said the girl, looking mildly, but with steadiness, upon him; "tell me, would you seek me out and try to win me now? Ah, no!"

He seemed to yield to the justice of this supposition, in spite of himself. But he said with a struggle, "You think not."

"I would gladly think otherwise if I could," she answered, "Heaven knows! When I have learned a Truth like this, I know how strong and irresistible it must be. But if you were free to-day, to-morrow, yesterday, can even I believe that you would choose a dowerless girl—you who, in your very confidence with her, weigh everything by Gain: or, choosing her, if for a moment you were false enough to your one guiding principle to do so, do I not know that your repentance and regret would surely follow? I do; and I release you. With a full heart, for the love of him you once were."

He was about to speak; but with her head turned from him, she resumed.

"You may—the memory of what is past half makes me hope you will—have pain in this. A very, very brief time, and you will dismiss the recollection of it, gladly, as an unprofitable dream, from which it happened well that you awoke. May you be happy in the life you have chosen!"

She left him, and they parted.

"Spirit!" said Scrooge, "show me no more! Conduct me home. Why do you delight to torture me?"

"One shadow more!" exclaimed the Ghost.

"No more!" cried Scrooge. "No more. I don't wish to see it. Show me no more!"

But the relentless Ghost pinioned him in both his arms, and forced him to observe what happened next.

They were in another scene and place; a room, not very large or handsome, but full of comfort. Near to the winter fire sat a beautiful young girl, so like that last that Scrooge believed it was the same, until he saw her, now a comely matron, sitting opposite her daughter. The noise in this room was perfectly tumultuous, for there were more children there than Scrooge in his agitated state of mind could count; and, unlike the celebrated herd in the poem, they were not forty children conducting themselves like one, but every child was conducting itself like forty. The consequences were uproarious beyond belief; but no one seemed to care; on the contrary, the mother and daughter laughed heartily, and enjoyed it very much; and the latter, soon beginning to mingle in the sports, got pillaged by the young brigands most ruthlessly. What would I not have given to one of them! Though I never could have been so rude, no, no! I wouldn't for the wealth of all the world have crushed that braided hair, and torn it down; and for the precious little shoe, I wouldn't have plucked it off, God bless my soul! to save my life. As to measuring her waist in sport, as they did, bold young brood, I couldn't have done it; I should have expected my arm to have grown round it for a punishment, and never come straight again. And yet I should have dearly liked, I own, to have touched her lips; to have questioned her, that she might have opened them; to have looked upon the lashes of her downcast eyes, and never raised a blush; to have let loose waves of hair, an inch of which would be a keepsake beyond price: in short, I should have liked, I do confess, to have had the lightest licence of a child, and yet to have been man enough to know its value.

But now a knocking at the door was heard, and such a rush immediately ensued that she with laughing face and plundered dress was borne towards it the centre of a flushed and boisterous group, just in time to greet the father, who came home attended by a man laden with Christmas toys and presents. Then the shouting and the struggling, and the onslaught that was made on the defenceless porter! The scaling him, with chairs for ladders, to dive into his pockets, despoil him of brown-paper parcels, hold on tight by his cravat, hug him round the neck, pommel his back, and kick his legs in irrepressible affection! The shouts of wonder and delight with which the development of every package was received! The terrible announcement that the baby had been taken in the act of putting a doll's frying-pan into his mouth, and was more than suspected of having swallowed a fictitious turkey, glued on a wooden platter! The immense relief of finding this a false alarm! The joy, and gratitude, and ecstasy! They are all indescribable alike. It is enough that by degrees the children and their emotions got out of the parlour, and by one stair at a time, up to the top of the house; where they went to bed, and so subsided.

And now Scrooge looked on more attentively than ever, when the master of the house, having his daughter leaning fondly on him, sat down with her and her mother at his own fireside; and when he thought that such another creature, quite as graceful and as full of promise, might have called him father, and been a spring-time in the haggard winter of his life, his sight grew very dim indeed.

"Belle," said the husband, turning to his wife with a smile, "I saw an old friend of yours this afternoon."

"Who was it?"

"Guess!"

"How can I? Tut, don't I know." she added in the same breath, laughing as he laughed. "Mr. Scrooge."

"Mr. Scrooge it was. I passed his office window; and as it was not shut up, and he had a candle inside, I could scarcely help seeing him. His partner lies upon the point of death, I hear; and there he sat alone. Quite alone in the world, I do believe."

"Spirit!" said Scrooge in a broken voice, "remove me from this place."

"I told you these were shadows of the things that have been," said the Ghost. "That they are what they are, do not blame me!"

"Remove me!" Scrooge exclaimed, "I cannot bear it!"

He turned upon the Ghost, and seeing that it looked upon him with a face, in which in some strange way there were fragments of all the faces it had shown him, wrestled with it.

"Leave me! Take me back. Haunt me no longer!"

In the struggle, if that can be called a struggle in which the Ghost with no visible resistance on its own part was undisturbed by any effort of its adversary, Scrooge observed that its light was burning high and bright; and dimly connecting that with its influence over him, he seized the extinguisher-cap, and by a sudden action pressed it down upon its head.

The Spirit dropped beneath it, so that the extinguisher covered its whole form; but though Scrooge pressed it down with all his force, he could not hide the light, which streamed from under it, in an unbroken flood upon the ground.

He was conscious of being exhausted, and overcome by an irresistible drowsiness; and, further, of being in his own bedroom. He gave the cap a parting squeeze, in which his hand relaxed; and had barely time to reel to bed, before he sank into a heavy sleep.

The First Christmas Tree

Henry Van Dyke (1852–1933)

*"It was Winfried of England . . .
whom all men called the Apostle of Germany."*

A thrilling tale of friendship, holy zeal, and sacrifice. In this retelling of one of the famed missions of Winfried (later called St. Boniface), we catch a glimpse of both the depravity and nobility of old pagan Europe, and how the Christmas tree became to all Christendom a symbol of hope.

"HIDE ME no cross," cried Winfried, lifting his staff, "for I have come to show it . . ."

Deep in the forests of medieval Germany, Winfried of England—later known as St. Boniface—puts an end to the dark rituals of pagan sacrifice. In this retelling of his conquest over death we see the missionary rescue a young prince, fell an ancient oak sacred to Thor, and give Europe its first Christmas Tree.

The day before Christmas, in the year of our Lord 722.

Broad snow-meadows glistening white along the banks of

the river Moselle; steep hill-sides blooming with mystic forget-me-not where the glow of the setting sun cast long shadows down their eastern slope; an arch of clearest, deepest gentian bending overhead; in the centre of the aerial garden the walls of the cloister of Pfalzel, steel-blue to the east, violet to the west; silence over all,—a gentle, eager, conscious stillness, diffused through the air, as if earth and sky were hushing themselves to hear the voice of the river faintly murmuring down the valley.

In the cloister, too, there was silence at the sunset hour. All day long there had been a strange and joyful stir among the nuns. A breeze of curiosity and excitement had swept along the corridors and through every quiet cell. A famous visitor had come to the convent.

It was Winfried of England, whose name in the Roman tongue was Boniface, and whom men called the Apostle of Germany. A great preacher; a wonderful scholar; but, more than all, a daring traveller, a venturesome pilgrim, a priest of romance.

He had left his home and his fair estate in Wessex; he would not stay in the rich monastery of Nutescelle, even though they had chosen him as the abbot; he had refused a bishopric at the court of King Karl. Nothing would content him but to go out into the wild woods and preach to the heathen.

Through the forests of Hesse and Thuringia, and along the borders of Saxony, he had wandered for years, with a handful of companions, sleeping under the trees, crossing mountains and marshes, now here, now there, never satisfied with ease and comfort, always in love with hardship and danger.

What a man he was! Fair and slight, but straight as a spear

and strong as an oaken staff. His face was still young; the smooth skin was bronzed by wind and sun. His gray eyes, clean and kind, flashed like fire when he spoke of his adventures, and of the evil deeds of the false priests with whom he contended.

What tales he had told that day! Not of miracles wrought by sacred relics; not of courts and councils and splendid cathedrals; though he knew much of these things. But to-day he had spoken of long journeyings by sea and land; of perils by fire and flood; of wolves and bears, and fierce snowstorms, and black nights in the lonely forest; of dark altars of heathen gods, and weird, bloody sacrifices, and narrow escapes from murderous bands of wandering savages.

The little novices had gathered around him, and their faces had grown pale and their eyes bright as they listened with parted lips, entranced in admiration, twining their arms about one another's shoulders and holding closely together, half in fear, half in delight. The older nuns had turned from their tasks and paused, in passing by, to bear the pilgrim's story. Too well they knew the truth of what he spoke. Many a one among them had seen the smoke rising from the ruins of her father's roof. Many a one had a brother far away in the wild country to whom her heart went out night and day, wondering if he were still among the living.

But now the excitements of that wonderful day were over; the hour of the evening meal had come; the inmates of the cloister were assembled in the refectory.

On the dais sat the stately Abbess Addula, daughter of King Dagobert, looking a princess indeed, in her purple tunic, with the hood and cuffs of her long white robe trimmed with ermine, and a snowy veil resting like a crown on her silver hair. At her right hand was the honoured guest, and at her left hand her grandson, the young Prince Gregor, a big, manly boy, just returned from school.

The long, shadowy hall, with its dark-brown rafters and beams; the double row of nuns, with their pure veils and fair faces; the ruddy glow of the slanting sunbeams striking upward through the tops of the windows and painting a pink glow high up on the walls,—it was all as beautiful as a picture, and as silent. For this was the rule of the cloister, that at the table all should sit in stillness for a little while, and then one should read aloud, while the rest listened.

"It is the turn of my grandson to read to-day," said the abbess to Winfried; "we shall see how much he has learned in the school. Read, Gregor; the place in the book is marked."

The lad rose from his seat and turned the pages of the manuscript. It was a copy of Jerome's version of the Scriptures in Latin, and the marked place was in the letter of St. Paul to the Ephesians,—the passage where he describes the preparation of the Christian as a warrior arming for battle. The young voice rang out clearly, rolling the sonorous words, without slip or stumbling, to the end of the chapter.

Winfried listened smiling. "That was bravely read, my son," said he, as the reader paused. "Understandest thou what thou readest?"

"Surely, father," answered the boy; "it was taught me by the masters at Treves; and we have read this epistle from beginning to end, so that I almost know it by heart."

Then he began to repeat the passage, turning away from the page as if to show his skill.

But Winfried stopped him with a friendly lifting of the hand.

"Not so, my son; that was not my meaning. When we pray, we speak to God. When we read, God speaks to us. I ask whether thou hast heard what He has said to thee in the common speech. Come, give us again the message of the warrior and his armour and his battle, in the mother-tongue, so that all can understand it."

The boy hesitated, blushed, stammered; then he came around to Winfried's seat, bringing the book. "Take the book, my father," he cried, "and read it for me. I cannot see the meaning plain, though I love the sound of the words. Religion I know, and the doctrines of our faith, and the life of priests and nuns in the cloister, for which my grandmother designs me, though it likes me little. And fighting I know, and the life of warriors and heroes, for I have read of it in Virgil and the ancients, and heard a bit from the soldiers at Treves; and I would fain taste more of it, for it likes me much. But how the two lives fit together, or what need there is of armour for a clerk in holy orders, I can never see. Tell me the meaning, for if there is a man in all the world that knows it, I am sure it is thou."

So Winfried took the book and closed it, clasping the boy's hand with his own.

"Let us first dismiss the others to their vespers," said he, "lest they should be weary."

A sign from the abbess; a chanted benediction; a murmuring

of sweet voices and a soft rustling of many feet over the rushes on the floor; the gentle tide of noise flowed out through the doors and ebbed away down the corridors; the three at the head of the table were left alone in the darkening room.

Then Winfried began to translate the parable of the soldier into the realities of life.

At every turn he knew how to flash a new light into the picture out of his own experience. He spoke of the combat with self, and of the wrestling with dark spirits in solitude. He spoke of the demons that men had worshipped for centuries in the wilderness, and whose malice they invoked against the stranger who ventured into the gloomy forest. Gods, they called them, and told weird tales of their dwelling among the impenetrable branches of the oldest trees and in the caverns of the shaggy hills; of their riding on the wind-horses and hurling spears of lightning against their foes. Gods they were not, but foul spirits of the air, rulers of the darkness. Was there not glory and honour in fighting them, in daring their anger under the shield of faith, in putting them to flight with the sword of truth? What better adventure could a brave man ask than to go forth against them, and wrestle with them, and conquer them?

"Look you, my friends," said Winfried, "how sweet and peaceful is this convent to-night! It is a garden full of flowers in the heart of winter; a nest among the branches of a great tree shaken by the winds; a still haven on the edge of a tempestuous sea. And this is what religion means for those who are chosen and called to quietude and prayer and meditation.

"But out yonder in the wide forest, who knows what storms

are raving to-night in the hearts of men, though all the woods are still? who knows what haunts of wrath and cruelty are closed tonight against the advent of the Prince of Peace? And shall I tell you what religion means to those who are called and chosen to dare, and to fight, and to conquer the world for Christ? It means to go against the strongholds of the adversary. It means to struggle to win an entrance for the Master everywhere. What helmet is strong enough for this strife save the helmet of salvation? What breastplate can guard a man against these fiery darts but the breastplate of righteousness? What shoes can stand the wear of these journeys but the preparation of the gospel of peace?"

"Shoes?" he cried again, and laughed as if a sudden thought had struck him. He thrust out his foot, covered with a heavy cowhide boot, laced high about his leg with thongs of skin.

"Look here,—how a fighting man of the cross is shod! I have seen the boots of the Bishop of Tours,—white kid, broidered with silk; a day in the bogs would tear them to shreds. I have seen the sandals that the monks use on the highroads,—yes, and worn them; ten pair of them have I worn out and thrown away in a single journey. Now I shoe my feet with the toughest hides, hard as iron; no rock can cut them, no branches can tear them. Yet more than one pair of these have I outworn, and many more shall I outwear ere my journeys are ended. And I think, if God is gracious to me, that I shall die wearing them. Better so than in a soft bed with silken coverings. The boots of a warrior, a hunter, a woodsman,—these are my preparation of the gospel of peace.

"Come, Gregor," he said, laying his brown hand on the

youth's shoulder, "come, wear the forester's boots with me. This is the life to which we are called. Be strong in the Lord, a hunter of the demons, a subduer of the wilderness, a woodsman of the faith. Come."

The boy's eyes sparkled. He turned to his grandmother. She shook her head vigorously.

"Nay, father," she said, "draw not the lad away from my side with these wild words. I need him to help me with my labours, to cheer my old age."

"Do you need him more than the Master does?" asked Winfried; "and will you take the wood that is fit for a bow to make a distaff?"

"But I fear for the child. Thy life is too hard for him. He will perish with hunger in the woods."

"Once," said Winfried, smiling, "we were camped on the bank of the river Ohru. The table was set for the morning meal, but my comrades cried that it was empty; the provisions were exhausted; we must go without breakfast, and perhaps starve before we could escape from the wilderness. While they complained, a fish-hawk flew up from the river with flapping wings, and let fall a great pike in the midst of the camp. There was food enough and to spare! Never have I seen the righteous forsaken, nor his seed begging bread."

"But the fierce pagans of the forest," cried the abbess,— "they may pierce the boy with their arrows, or dash out his brains with their axes. He is but a child, too young for the danger and the strife."

"A child in years," replied Winfried, "but a man in spirit.

And if the hero fall early in the battle, he wears the brighter crown, not a leaf withered, not a flower fallen."

The aged princess trembled a little. She drew Gregor close to her side, and laid her hand gently on his brown hair. "I am not sure that he wants to leave me yet. Besides, there is no horse in the stable to give him, now, and he cannot go as befits the grandson of a king."

Gregor looked straight into her eyes.

"Grandmother," said he, "dear grandmother, if thou wilt not give me a horse to ride with this man of God, I will go with him afoot."

II

Two years had passed since that Christmas-eve in the cloister of Pfalzel. A little company of pilgrims, less than a score of men, were travelling slowly northward through the wide forest that rolled over the hills of central Germany.

At the head of the band marched Winfried, clad in a tunic of fur, with his long black robe girt high above his waist, so that it might not hinder his stride. His hunter's boots were crusted with snow. Drops of ice sparkled like jewels along the thongs that bound his legs. There were no other ornaments of his dress except the bishop's cross hanging on his breast, and the silver clasp that fastened his cloak about his neck. He carried a strong, tall staff in his hand, fashioned at the top into the form of a cross.

Close beside him, keeping step like a familiar comrade, was

the young Prince Gregor. Long marches through the wilderness had stretched his legs and broadened his back, and made a man of him in stature as well as in spirit. His jacket and cap were of wolf-skin, and on his shoulder he carried an axe, with broad, shining blade. He was a mighty woodsman now, and could make a spray of chips fly around him as he hewed his way through the trunk of a pine-tree.

Behind these leaders followed a pair of teamsters, guiding a rude sledge, loaded with food and the equipage of the camp, and drawn by two big, shaggy horses, blowing thick clouds of steam from their frosty nostrils. Tiny icicles hung from the hairs on their lips. Their flanks were smoking. They sank above the fetlocks at every step in the soft snow.

Last of all came the rear guard, armed with bows and javelins. It was no child's play, in those days, to cross Europe afoot.

The weird woodland, sombre and illimitable, covered hill and vale, table-land and mountain-peak. There were wide moors where the wolves hunted in packs as if the devil drove them, and tangled thickets where the lynx and the boar made their lairs. Fierce bears lurked among the rocky passes, and had not yet learned to fear the face of man. The gloomy recesses of the forest gave shelter to inhabitants who were still more cruel and dangerous than beasts of prey,—outlaws and sturdy robbers and mad were-wolves and bands of wandering pillagers.

The pilgrim who would pass from the mouth of the Tiber to the mouth of the Rhine must trust in God and keep his arrows loose in the quiver.

The travellers were surrounded by an ocean of trees, so vast, so full of endless billows, that it seemed to be pressing on every side to overwhelm them. Gnarled oaks, with branches twisted and knotted as if in rage, rose in groves like tidal waves. Smooth forests of beech-trees, round and gray, swept over the knolls and slopes of land in a mighty ground-swell. But most of all, the multitude of pines and firs, innumerable and monotonous, with straight, stark trunks, and branches woven together in an unbroken flood of darkest green, crowded through the valleys and over the hills, rising on the highest ridges into ragged crests, like the foaming edge of breakers.

Through this sea of shadows ran a narrow stream of shining whiteness,—an ancient Roman road, covered with snow. It was as if some great ship had ploughed through the green ocean long ago, and left behind it a thick, smooth wake of foam. Along this open track the travellers held their way,—heavily, for the drifts were deep; warily, for the hard winter had driven many packs of wolves down from the moors.

The steps of the pilgrims were noiseless; but the sledges creaked over the dry snow, and the panting of the horses throbbed through the still air. The pale-blue shadows on the western side of the road grew longer. The sun, declining through its shallow arch, dropped behind the tree-tops. Darkness followed swiftly, as if it had been a bird of prey waiting for this sign to swoop down upon the world.

"Father," said Gregor to the leader, "surely this day's march is done. It is time to rest, and eat, and sleep. If we press onward now, we cannot see our steps; and will not that be against the word of the psalmist David, who bids us not to put confidence in the legs of a man?"

Winfried laughed. "Nay, my son Gregor," said he, "thou hast tripped, even now, upon thy text. For David said only, 'I take no pleasure in the legs of a man.' And so say I, for I am not minded to spare thy legs or mine, until we come farther on our way, and do what must be done this night. Draw thy belt tighter, my son, and hew me out this tree that is fallen across the road, for our campground is not here."

The youth obeyed; two of the foresters sprang to help him; and while the soft fir-wood yielded to the stroke of the axes, and the snow flew from the bending branches, Winfried turned and spoke to his followers in a cheerful voice, that refreshed them like wine.

"Courage, brothers, and forward yet a little! The moon will light us presently, and the path is plain. Well know I that the journey is weary; and my own heart wearies also for the home in England, where those I love are keeping feast this Christmas-eve. But we have work to do before we feast to-night. For this is the Yuletide, and the heathen people of the forest are gathered at the thunder-oak of Geismar to worship their god, Thor. Strange things will be seen there, and deeds which make the soul black. But we are sent to lighten their darkness; and we will teach our kinsmen to keep a Christmas with us such as the woodland has never known. Forward, then, and stiffen up the feeble knees!"

A murmur of assent came from the men. Even the horses seemed to take fresh heart. They flattened their backs to draw the heavy loads, and blew the frost from their nostrils as they pushed ahead.

The night grew broader and less oppressive. A gate of brightness was opened secretly somewhere in the sky. Higher and higher swelled the clear moon-flood, until it poured over the eastern wall of forest into the road. A drove of wolves howled faintly in the distance, but they were receding, and the sound soon died away. The stars sparkled merrily through the stringent air; the small, round moon shone like silver; little breaths of dreaming wind wandered across the pointed fir-tops, as the pilgrims toiled bravely onward, following their clew of light through a labyrinth of darkness.

After a while the road began to open out a little. There were spaces of meadow-land, fringed with alders, behind which a boisterous river ran clashing through spears of ice.

Rude houses of hewn logs appeared in the openings, each one casting a patch of inky shadow upon the snow. Then the travellers passed a larger group of dwellings, all silent and unlighted; and beyond, they saw a great house, with many outbuildings and inclosed courtyards, from which the hounds bayed furiously, and a noise of stamping horses came from the stalls. But there was no other sound of life. The fields around lay naked to the moon. They saw no man, except that once, on a path that skirted the farther edge of a meadow, three dark figures passed them, running very swiftly.

Then the road plunged again into a dense thicket, traversed it, and climbing to the left, emerged suddenly upon a glade, round and level except at the northern side, where a hillock was crowned with a huge oak-tree. It towered above the heath, a giant with contorted arms, beckoning to the host of lesser trees. "Here," cried Winfried, as his eyes flashed and his hand lifted his heavy staff, "here is the Thunder-oak; and here the cross of Christ shall break the hammer of the false god Thor."

Withered leaves still clung to the branches of the oak: torn and faded banners of the departed summer. The bright crimson of autumn had long since disappeared, bleached away by the storms and the cold. But to-night these tattered remnants of glory were red again: ancient bloodstains against the dark-blue sky. For an immense fire had been kindled in front of the tree. Tongues of ruddy flame, fountains of ruby sparks, ascended through the spreading limbs and flung a fierce illumination upward and around. The pale, pure moonlight that bathed the surrounding forests was quenched and eclipsed here. Not a beam of it sifted through the branches of the oak. It stood like a pillar of cloud between the still light of heaven and the crackling, flashing fire of earth.

But the fire itself was invisible to Winfried and his companions. A great throng of people were gathered around it in a half-circle, their backs to the open glade, their faces toward the oak. Seen against that glowing background, it was but the silhouette of a crowd, vague, black, formless, mysterious.

The travellers paused for a moment at the edge of the thicket, and took counsel together.

"It is the assembly of the tribe," said one of the foresters, "the great night of the council. I heard of it three days ago, as we passed through one of the villages. All who swear by the old gods have been summoned. They will sacrifice a steed to the god of war, and drink blood, and eat horse-flesh to make them strong. It will be at the peril of our lives if we approach them. At least we must hide the cross, if we would escape death."

"Hide me no cross," cried Winfried, lifting his staff, "for I have come to show it, and to make these blind folk see its power. There is more to be done here to-night than the slaying of a steed, and a greater evil to be stayed than the shameful eating of meat sacrificed to idols. I have seen it in a dream. Here the cross must stand and be our rede."

At his command the sledge was left in the border of the wood, with two of the men to guard it, and the rest of the company moved forward across the open ground. They approached unnoticed, for all the multitude were looking intently toward the fire at the foot of the oak.

Then Winfried's voice rang out, "Hail, ye sons of the forest! A stranger claims the warmth of your fire in the winter night."

Swiftly, and as with a single motion, a thousand eyes were bent upon the speaker. The semicircle opened silently in the middle; Winfried entered with his followers; it closed again behind them.

Then, as they looked round the curving ranks, they saw that the hue of the assemblage was not black, but white,—dazzling, radiant, solemn. White, the robes of the women clustered together at the points of the wide crescent; white, the glittering byrnies of the warriors standing in close ranks; white, the fur mantles of the aged men who held the central palace in the circle; white, with the shimmer of silver ornaments and the purity of lamb's-wool, the raiment of a little group of children who stood close by the fire; white, with awe and fear, the faces of all who looked at them; and over all the flickering, dancing radiance of the flames played and glimmered like a faint, vanishing tinge of blood on snow.

The only figure untouched by the glow was the old priest, Hunrad, with his long, spectral robe, flowing hair and beard, and dead-pale face, who stood with his back to the fire and advanced slowly to meet the strangers.

"Who are you? Whence come you, and what seek you here?"

"Your kinsman am I, of the German brotherhood," answered Winfried, "and from England, beyond the sea, have I come to bring you a greeting from that land, and a message from the All-Father, whose servant I am."

"Welcome, then," said Hunrad, "welcome, kinsman, and be silent; for what passes here is too high to wait, and must be done before the moon crosses the middle heaven, unless, indeed, thou hast some sign or token from the gods. Canst thou work miracles?"

The question came sharply, as if a sudden gleam of hope had flashed through the tangle of the old priest's mind. But Winfried's voice sank lower and a cloud of disappointment passed over his face as he replied: "Nay, miracles have I never wrought, though I have heard of many; but the All-Father has given no power to my hands save such as belongs to common man."

"Stand still, then, thou common man," said Hunrad, scornfully, "and behold what the gods have called us hither to do. This night is the death-night of the sun-god, Baldur the Beautiful, beloved of gods and men. This night is the hour of darkness and the power of winter, of sacrifice and mighty fear. This night the great Thor, the god of thunder and war, to whom this oak is sacred, is grieved for the death of Baldur, and angry with this people because they have forsaken his worship. Long is it since an offering has been laid upon his altar, long since the roots of his holy tree have been fed with blood. Therefore its leaves have withered before the time, and its boughs are heavy with death. Therefore the Slavs and the Wends have beaten us in battle. Therefore the harvests have failed, and the wolf-hordes have ravaged the folds, and the strength has departed from the bow, and the wood of the spear has broken, and the wild boar has slain the huntsman. Therefore the plague has fallen on our dwellings, and the dead are more than the living in all our villages. Answer me, ye people, are not these things true?"

A hoarse sound of approval ran through the circle. A chant, in which the voices of the men and women blended, like the shrill wind in the pine trees above the rumbling thunder of a waterfall, rose and fell in rude cadences.

> O Thor, the Thunderer
> Mighty and merciless,
> Spare us from smiting!
> Heave not thy hammer,
> Angry, against us;
> Plague not thy people.
> Take from our treasure

Richest Of ransom.
Silver we send thee,
Jewels and javelins,
Goodliest garments,
All our possessions,
Priceless, we proffer.
Sheep will we slaughter,
Steeds will we sacrifice;
Bright blood shall bathe
O tree of Thunder,
Life-floods shall lave thee,
Strong wood of wonder.
Mighty, have mercy,
Smile as no more,
Spare us and save us,
Spare us, Thor! Thor!

With two great shouts the song ended, and stillness followed so intense that the crackling of the fire was heard distinctly. The old priest stood silent for a moment. His shaggy brows swept down over his eyes like ashes quenching flame. Then he lifted his face and spoke.

"None of these things will please the god. More costly is the offering that shall cleanse your sin, more precious the crimson dew that shall send new life into this holy tree of blood. Thor claims your dearest and your noblest gift."

Hunrad moved nearer to the group of children who stood watching the fire and the swarms of spark-serpents darting upward. They had heeded none of the priest's words, and did not notice now that he approached them, so eager were they to see which fiery snake would go highest among the oak branches. Foremost among them, and most intent on the pretty game, was a boy like a sunbeam, slender and quick, with blithe brown eyes and laughing lips. The priest's hand was laid upon his shoulder. The boy turned and looked up in his face.

"Here," said the old man, with his voice vibrating as when a thick rope is strained by a ship swinging from her moorings, "here is the chosen one, the eldest son of the Chief, the darling of the people. Hearken, Bernhard, wilt thou go to Valhalla, where the heroes dwell with the gods, to bear a message to Thor?"

The boy answered, swift and clear:

"Yes, priest, I will go if my father bids me. Is it far away? Shall I run quickly? Must I take my bow and arrows for the wolves?"

The boy's father, the Chieftain Gundhar, standing among his bearded warriors, drew his breath deep, and leaned so heavily on the handle of his spear that the wood cracked. And his wife, Irma, bending forward from the ranks of women, pushed the golden hair from her forehead with one hand. The other dragged at the silver chain about her neck until the rough links pierced her flesh, and the red drops fell unheeded on her breast.

A sigh passed through the crowd, like the murmur of the forest before the storm breaks. Yet no one spoke save Hunrad:

"Yes, my Prince, both bow and spear shalt thou have, for the way is long, and thou art a brave huntsman. But in darkness thou must journey for a little space, and with eyes blindfolded. Fearest thou?"

"Naught fear I," said the boy, "neither darkness, nor the great bear, nor the were-wolf. For I am Gundhar's son, and the defender of my folk."

Then the priest led the child in his raiment of lamb's-wool to a broad stone in front of the fire. He gave him his little bow tipped with silver, and his spear with shining head of steel. He bound the child's eyes with a white cloth, and bade him kneel beside the stone with his face to the east. Unconsciously the wide arc of spectators drew inward toward the centre, as the ends of the bow draw together when the cord is stretched. Winfried moved noiselessly until he stood close behind the priest.

The old man stooped to lift a black hammer of stone from the ground,—the sacred hammer of the god Thor. Summoning all the strength of his withered arms, he swung it high in the air. It poised for an instant above the child's fair head—then turned to fall.

One keen cry shrilled out from where the women stood: "Me! take me! not Bernhard!"

The flight of the mother toward her child was swift as the falcon's swoop. But swifter still was the hand of the deliverer.

Winfried's heavy staff thrust mightily against the hammer's handle as it fell. Sideways it glanced from the old man's grasp, and the black stone, striking on the altar's edge, split in twain. A shout of awe and joy rolled along the living circle. The branches of the oak shivered. The flames leaped higher. As the shout died away the people saw the lady Irma, with her arms clasped round her child, and above them, on the altar-stone, Winfried, his face shining like the face of an angel.

III

A swift mountain-flood rolling down its channel; a huge rock tumbling from the hill-side and falling in mid-stream: the baffled waters broken and confused, pausing in their flow, dash high against the rock, foaming and murmuring, with divided impulse, uncertain whether to turn to the right or the left.

Even so Winfried's bold deed fell into the midst of the thoughts and passions of the council. They were at a standstill. Anger and wonder, reverence and joy and confusion surged through the crowd. They knew not which way to move: to resent the intrusion of the stranger as an insult to their gods, or to welcome him as the rescuer of their prince.

The old priest crouched by the altar, silent. Conflicting counsels troubled the air. Let the sacrifice go forward; the gods must be appeased. Nay, the boy must not die; bring the chieftain's best horse and slay it in his stead; it will be enough; the holy tree loves the blood of horses. Not so, there is a better counsel yet; seize the stranger whom the gods have led hither as a victim and make his life pay the forfeit of his daring.

The withered leaves on the oak rustled and whispered overhead. The fire flared and sank again. The angry voices clashed against each other and fell like opposing waves. Then the chieftain Gundhar struck the earth with his spear and gave his decision.

"All have spoken, but none are agreed. There is no voice of the council. Keep silence now, and let the stranger speak.

His words shall give us judgment, whether he is to live or to die."

Winfried lifted himself high upon the altar, drew a roll of parchment from his bosom, and began to read.

"A letter from the great Bishop of Rome, who sits on a golden throne, to the people of the forest, Hessians and Thuringians, Franks and Saxons. In nomine Domini, sanctae et individuae Trinitatis, amen!"

A murmur of awe ran through the crowd. "It is the sacred tongue of the Romans; the tongue that is heard and understood by the wise men of every land. There is magic in it. Listen!"

Winfried went on to read the letter, translating it into the speech of the people.

"We have sent unto you our Brother Boniface, and appointed him your bishop, that he may teach you the only true faith, and baptise you, and lead you back from the ways of error to the path of salvation. Hearken to him in all things like a father. Bow your hearts to his teaching. He comes not for earthly gain, but for the gain of your souls. Depart from evil works. Worship not the false gods, for they are devils. Offer no more bloody sacrifices, nor eat the flesh of horses, but do as our Brother Boniface commands you. Build a house for him that he may dwell among you, and a church where you may offer your prayers to the only living God, the Almighty King of Heaven."

It was a splendid message: proud, strong, peaceful, loving. The dignity of the words imposed mightily upon the hearts of the people. They were quieted as men who have listened to a lofty strain of music.

"Tell us, then," said Gundhar, "what is the word that thou bringest to us from the Almighty? What is thy counsel for the tribes of the woodland on this night of sacrifice?"

"This is the word, and this is the counsel," answered Winfried. "Not a drop of blood shall fall to-night, save that which pity has drawn from the breast of your princess, in love for her child. Not a life shall be blotted out in the darkness to-night; but the great shadow of the tree which hides you from the light of heaven shall be swept away. For this is the birth-night of the white Christ, son of the All-Father, and Saviour of mankind. Fairer is He than Baldur the Beautiful, greater than Odin the Wise, kinder than Freya the Good. Since He has come to earth the bloody sacrifice must cease. The dark Thor, on whom you vainly call, is dead. Deep in the shades of Niffelheim he is lost forever. His power in the world is broken. Will you serve a helpless god? See, my brothers, you call this tree his oak. Does he dwell here? Does he protect it?"

A troubled voice of assent rose from the throng. The people stirred uneasily. Women covered their eyes. Hunrad lifted his head and muttered hoarsely, "Thor! take vengeance! Thor!"

Winfried beckoned to Gregor. "Bring the axes, thine and one for me. Now, young woodsman, show thy craft! The king-tree of the forest must fall, and swiftly, or all is lost!"

The two men took their places facing each other, one on each side of the oak. Their cloaks were flung aside, their heads bare. Carefully they felt the ground with their feet, seeking a firm grip of the earth. Firmly they grasped the axe-helves and swung the shining blades.

"Tree-god!" cried Winfried, "art thou angry? Thus we smite thee!"

"Tree-god!" answered Gregor, "art thou mighty? Thus we fight thee!"

Clang! clang! the alternate strokes beat time upon the hard, ringing wood. The axe-heads glittered in their rhythmic flight, like fierce eagles circling about their quarry.

The broad flakes of wood flew from the deepening gashes in the sides of the oak. The huge trunk quivered. There was a shuddering in the branches. Then the great wonder of Winfried's life came to pass.

Out of the stillness of the winter night, a mighty rushing noise sounded overhead.

Was it the ancient gods on their white battlesteeds, with their black hounds of wrath and their arrows of lightning, sweeping through the air to destroy their foes?

A strong, whirling wind passed over the treetops. It gripped the oak by its branches and tore it from the roots. Backward it fell, like a ruined tower, groaning and crashing as it split asunder in four great pieces.

Winfried let his axe drop, and bowed his head for a moment in the presence of almighty power.

Then he turned to the people, "Here is the timber," he cried, "already felled and split for your new building. On this spot shall rise a chapel to the true God and his servant St. Peter.

"And here," said he, as his eyes fell on a young fir-tree, standing straight and green, with its top pointing toward the stars, amid the divided ruins of the fallen oak, "here is the living tree, with no stain of blood upon it, that shall be the sign of your new worship. See how it points to the sky. Call it the tree of the Christ-child. Take it up and carry it to the chieftain's hall. You shall go no more into the shadows of the forest to keep your feasts with secret rites of shame. You shall keep them at home, with laughter and songs and rites of love. The thunder-oak has fallen, and I think the day is coming when there shall not be a home in all Germany where the children are not gathered around the green fir-tree to rejoice in the birth-night of Christ."

So they took the little fir from its place, and carried it in joyous procession to the edge of the glade, and laid it on the sledge. The horses tossed their heads and drew their load bravely, as if the new burden had made it lighter.

When they came to the house of Gundhar, he bade them throw open the doors of the hall and set the tree in the midst of it. They kindled lights among the branches until it seemed to be tangled full of fire-flies. The children encircled it, wondering, and the sweet odour of the balsam filled the house.

Then Winfried stood beside the chair of Gundhar, on the dais at the end of the hall, and told the story of Bethlehem; of the babe in the manger, of the shepherds on the hills, of the host of angels and their midnight song. All the people listened, charmed into stillness.

But the boy Bernhard, on Irma's knee, folded in her soft arms, grew restless as the story lengthened, and began to prattle softly at his mother's ear.

"Mother," whispered the child, "why did you cry out so loud, when the priest was going to send me to Valhalla?"

"Oh, hush, my child," answered the mother, and pressed him closer to her side.

"Mother," whispered the boy again, laying his finger on the stains upon her breast, "see, your dress is red! What are these stains? Did some one hurt you?"

The mother closed his mouth with a kiss. "Dear, be still, and listen!"

The boy obeyed. His eyes were heavy with sleep. But he heard the last words of Winfried as he spoke of the angelic messengers, flying over the hills of Judea and singing as they flew. The child wondered and dreamed and listened. Suddenly his face grew bright. He put his lips close to Irma's cheek again.

"Oh, mother!" he whispered very low, "do not speak. Do you hear them? Those angels have come back again. They are singing now behind the tree."

And some say that it was true; but others say that it was only Gregor and his companions at the lower end of the hall, chanting their Christmas hymn:

> All glory be to God on high,
> And on the earth be peace!
> Good-will, henceforth, from heaven to man,
> Begin and never cease.

Merry Christmas

Stephen Leacock (1869–1944)

"Give me back such days as those, with the old good cheer."

Among the most widely read writers in the first part of the twentieth century, Leacock was a Canadian humorist and satirist. In this playful story, written with the memory of World War I fresh in mind, Father Time and Father Christmas meet a young man and consider the prospects of peace in a world of violence.

"MY DEAR Young Friend," said Father Time, as he laid his hand gently upon my shoulder, "you are entirely wrong."

Then I looked up over my shoulder from the table at which I was sitting and I saw him.

But I had known, or felt, for at least the last half-hour that he was standing somewhere near me.

You have had, I do not doubt, good reader, more than once that strange uncanny feeling that there is some one unseen standing beside you, in a darkened room, let us say, with a dying fire, when the night has grown late, and the October wind sounds low outside, and when, through the thin curtain that we call Reality, the Unseen World starts for a moment clear upon our dreaming sense.

You have had it? Yes, I know you have. Never mind telling me about it. Stop. I don't want to hear about that strange presentiment you had the night your Aunt Eliza broke her leg. Don't let's bother with your experience. I want to tell mine.

"You are quite mistaken, my dear young friend," repeated Father Time, "quite wrong."

"Young friend?" I said, my mind, as one's mind is apt to in such a case, running to an unimportant detail. "Why do you call me young?"

"Your pardon," he answered gently—he had a gentle way with him, had Father Time. "The fault is in my failing eyes. I took you at first sight for something under a hundred."

"Under a hundred?" I expostulated. "Well, I should think so!"

"Your pardon again," said Time, "the fault is in my failing memory. I forgot. You seldom pass that nowadays, do you? Your life is very short of late."

I heard him breathe a wistful hollow sigh. Very ancient and dim he seemed as he stood beside me. But I did not turn to look upon him. I had no need to. I knew his form, in the inner and clearer sight of things, as well as every human being knows by innate instinct, the Unseen face and form of Father Time.

I could hear him murmuring beside me, "Short—short, your life is short"; till the sound of it seemed to mingle with the measured ticking of a clock somewhere in the silent house.

Then I remembered what he had said.

"How do you know that I am wrong?" I asked. "And how can you tell what I was thinking?"

"You, said it out loud," answered Father Time. "But it wouldn't have mattered, anyway. You said that Christmas was all played out and done with."

"Yes," I admitted, "that's what I said."

"And what makes you think that?" he questioned, stooping, so it seemed to me, still further over my shoulder.

"Why," I answered, "the trouble is this. I've been sitting here for hours, sitting till goodness only knows how far into the night, trying to think out something to write for a Christmas story. And it won't go. It can't be done—not in these awful days."

"A Christmas Story?"

"Yes. You see, Father Time," I explained, glad with a foolish little vanity of my trade to be able to tell him something that I thought enlightening, "all the Christmas stuff—stories and jokes and pictures—is all done, you know, in October."

I thought it would have surprised him, but I was mistaken.

"Dear me," he said, "not till October! What a rush! How well I remember in Ancient Egypt—as I think you call it—seeing them getting out their Christmas things, all cut in hieroglyphics, always two or three years ahead."

"Two or three years!" I exclaimed.

"Pooh," said Time, "that was nothing. Why in Babylon they used to get their Christmas jokes ready—all baked in clay—a whole Solar eclipse ahead of Christmas. They said, I think, that the public preferred them so."

"Egypt?" I said. "Babylon? But surely, Father Time, there was no Christmas in those days. I thought ——"

"My dear boy," he interrupted gravely, "don't you know that there has always been Christmas?"

I was silent. Father Time had moved across the room and stood beside the fireplace, leaning on the mantelpiece. The little wreaths of smoke from the fading fire seemed to mingle with his shadowy outline.

"Well," he said presently, "what is it that is wrong with Christmas?"

"Why," I answered, "all the romance, the joy, the beauty of it has gone, crushed and killed by the greed of commerce and the horrors of war. I am not, as you thought I was, a hundred years old, but I can conjure up, as anybody can, a picture of Christmas in the good old days of a hundred years ago: the quaint old-fashioned houses, standing deep among the evergreens, with the light twinkling from the windows on the snow; the warmth and comfort within; the great fire roaring on the hearth; the merry guests grouped about its blaze and the little children with their eyes dancing in the Christmas fire-light, waiting for Father Christmas in his fine mummery of red and white and cotton wool to hand the presents from the yule-tide tree. I can see it," I added, "as if it were yesterday."

"It was but yesterday," said Father Time, and his voice seemed to soften with the memory of bygone years. "I remember it well."

"Ah," I continued, "that was Christmas indeed. Give me back such days as those, with the old good cheer, the old stage coaches and the gabled inns and the warm red wine, the snapdragon and the Christmas-tree, and I'll believe again in Christmas, yes, in Father Christmas himself."

"Believe in him?" said Time quietly. "You may well do that. He happens to be standing outside in the street at this moment."

"Outside?" I exclaimed. "Why don't he come in?"

"He's afraid to," said Father Time. "He's frightened and he daren't come in unless you ask him. May I call him in?"

I signified assent, and Father Time went to the window for a moment and beckoned into the darkened street. Then I heard footsteps, clumsy and hesitant they seemed, upon the stairs. And in a moment a figure stood framed in the doorway—the figure of Father Christmas. He stood shuffling his feet, a timid, apologetic look upon his face.

How changed he was!

I had known in my mind's eye, from childhood up, the face and form of Father Christmas as well as that of Old Time himself. Everybody knows, or once knew him—a jolly little rounded man, with a great muffler wound about him, a packet of toys upon his back and with such merry, twinkling eyes and rosy cheeks as are only given by the touch of the driving snow and the rude fun of the North Wind. Why, there was once a time, not yet so long ago, when the very sound of his sleigh-bells sent the blood running warm to the heart.

But now how changed.

All draggled with the mud and rain he stood, as if no house had sheltered him these three years past. His old red Jersey was tattered in a dozen places, his muffler frayed and ravelled.

The bundle of toys that he dragged with him in a net seemed wet and worn till the cardboard boxes gaped asunder. There were boxes among them, I vow, that he must have been carrying these three past years.

But most of all I noted the change that had come over the face of Father Christmas. The old brave look of cheery confidence was gone. The smile that had beamed responsive to the laughing eyes of countless children around unnumbered Christmas trees was there no more. And in the place of it there showed a look of timid apology, of apprehensiveness, as of one who has asked in vain the warmth and shelter of a human home—such a look as the harsh cruelty of this world has stamped upon the faces of its outcasts.

So stood Father Christmas shuffling upon the threshold, fumbling his poor tattered hat in his hand.

"Shall I come in?" he said, his eyes appealingly on Father Time.

"Come," said Time. He turned to speak to me, "Your room is dark. Turn up the lights. He's used to light, bright light and plenty of it. The dark has frightened him these three years past."

I turned up the lights and the bright glare revealed all the more cruelly the tattered figure before us.

Father Christmas advanced a timid step across the floor. Then he paused, as if in sudden fear.

"Is this floor mined?" he said.

"No, no," said Time soothingly. And to me he added in a murmured whisper, "He's afraid. He was blown up in a mine in No Man's Land between the trenches at Christmas-time in 1914. It broke his nerve."

"May I put my toys on that machine gun?" asked Father Christmas timidly. "It will help to keep them dry."

"It is not a machine gun," said Time gently. "See, it is only a pile of books upon the sofa." And to me he whispered, "They turned a machine gun on him in the streets of Warsaw. He thinks he sees them everywhere since then."

"It's all right, Father Christmas," I said, speaking as cheerily as I could, while I rose and stirred the fire into a blaze.

"There are no machine guns here and there are no mines. This is but the house of a poor writer."

"Ah," said Father Christmas, lowering his tattered hat still further and attempting something of a humble bow, "a writer? Are you Hans Andersen, perhaps?"

"Not quite," I answered.

"But a great writer, I do not doubt," said the old man, with a humble courtesy that he had learned, it well may be, centuries ago in the yule-tide season of his northern home. "The world owes much to its great books. I carry some of the greatest with me always. I have them here ——"

He began fumbling among the limp and tattered packages that he carried. "Look! The House that Jack Built—a marvellous, deep thing, sir—and this, The Babes in the Wood. Will you take it, sir? A poor present, but a present still—not so long ago I gave them in thousands every Christmas-time. None seem to want them now."

He looked appealingly towards Father Time, as the weak

may look towards the strong, for help and guidance.

"None want them now," he repeated, and I could see the tears start in his eyes. "Why is it so? Has the world forgotten its sympathy with the lost children wandering in the wood?"

"All the world," I heard Time murmur with a sigh, "is wandering in the wood." But out loud he spoke to Father Christmas in cheery admonition, "Tut, tut, good Christmas," he said, "you must cheer up. Here, sit in this chair the biggest one; so—beside the fire. Let us stir it to a blaze; more wood, that's better. And listen, good old Friend, to the wind outside—almost a Christmas wind, is it not? Merry and boisterous enough, for all the evil times it stirs among."

Old Christmas seated himself beside the fire, his hands outstretched towards the flames. Something of his old-time cheeriness seemed to flicker across his features as he warmed himself at the blaze.

"That's better," he murmured. "I was cold, sir, cold, chilled to the bone. Of old I never felt it so; no matter what the wind, the world seemed warm about me. Why is it not so now?"

"You see," said Time, speaking low in a whisper for my ear alone, "how sunk and broken he is? Will you not help?"

"Gladly," I answered, "if I can."

"All can," said Father Time, "every one of us."

Meantime Christmas had turned towards me a questioning eye, in which, however, there seemed to revive some little gleam of merriment.

"Have you, perhaps," he asked half timidly, "schnapps?"

"Schnapps?" I repeated.

"Ay, schnapps. A glass of it to drink your health might warm my heart again, I think."

"Ah," I said, "something to drink?"

"His one failing," whispered Time, "if it is one. Forgive it him. He was used to it for centuries. Give it him if you have it."

"I keep a little in the house," I said reluctantly perhaps, "in case of illness."

"Tut, tut," said Father Time, as something as near as could be to a smile passed over his shadowy face. "In case of illness! They used to say that in ancient Babylon. Here, let me pour it for him. Drink, Father Christmas, drink!"

Marvellous it was to see the old man smack his lips as he drank his glass of liquor neat after the fashion of old Norway.

Marvellous, too, to see the way in which, with the warmth of the fire and the generous glow of the spirits, his face changed and brightened till the old-time cheerfulness beamed again upon it. He looked about him, as it were, with a new and growing interest.

"A pleasant room," he said. "And what better, sir, than the wind without and a brave fire within!"

Then his eye fell upon the mantelpiece, where lay among the litter of books and pipes a little toy horse.

"Ah," said Father Christmas almost gayly, "children in the house!"

"One," I answered, "the sweetest boy in all the world."

"I'll be bound he is!" said Father Christmas and he broke now into a merry laugh that did one's heart good to hear. "They all are! Lord bless me! The number that I have seen, and each and every one—and quite right too—the sweetest child in all the world. And how old, do you say? Two and a half all but two months except a week? The very sweetest age of all, I'll bet you say, eh, what? They all do!"

And the old man broke again into such a jolly chuckling of laughter that his snow-white locks shook upon his head.

"But stop a bit," he added. "This horse is broken. Tut, tut, a hind leg nearly off. This won't do!"

He had the toy in his lap in a moment, mending it. It was wonderful to see, for all his age, how deft his fingers were.

"Time," he said, and it was amusing to note that his voice had assumed almost an authoritative tone, "reach me that piece of string. That's right. Here, hold your finger across the knot. There! Now, then, a bit of beeswax. What? No beeswax? Tut, tut, how ill-supplied your houses are to-day. How can you mend toys, sir, without beeswax? Still, it will stand up now."

I tried to murmur my best thanks.

But Father Christmas waved my gratitude aside.

"Nonsense," he said, "that's nothing. That's my life. Perhaps the little boy would like a book too. I have them here in the packet. Here, sir, Jack and the Bean Stalk, most profound thing. I read it to myself often still. How damp it is! Pray, sir, will you let me dry my books before your fire?"

"Only too willingly," I said. "How wet and torn they are!"

Father Christmas had risen from his chair and was fumbling among his tattered packages, taking from them his children's books, all limp and draggled from the rain and wind.

"All wet and torn!" he murmured, and his voice sank again into sadness. "I have carried them these three years past. Look!

These were for little children in Belgium and in Serbia, Can I get them to them, think you?"

Time gently shook his head.

"But presently, perhaps," said Father Christmas, "if I dry and mend them. Look, some of them were inscribed already! This one, see you, was written 'With father's love.' Why has it never come to him? Is it rain or tears upon the page?"

He stood bowed over his little books, his hands trembling as he turned the pages. Then he looked up, the old fear upon his face again.

"That sound!" he said. "Listen! It is guns—I hear them."

"No, no," I said, "it is nothing. Only a car passing in the street below."

"Listen," he said. "Hear that again—voices crying!"

"No, no," I answered, "not voices, only the night wind among the trees."

"My children's voices!" he exclaimed. "I hear them everywhere—they come to me in every wind—and I see them as I wander in the night and storm—my children—torn and dying in the trenches—beaten into the ground—I hear them crying from the hospitals—each one to me, still as I knew him once, a little child. Time, Time," he cried, reaching out his arms in appeal, "give me back my children!"

"They do not die in vain," Time murmured gently.

But Christmas only moaned in answer:

"Give me back my children!"

Then he sank down upon his pile of books and toys, his head buried in his arms.

"You see," said Time, "his heart is breaking, and will you not help him if you can?"

"Only too gladly," I replied. "But what is there to do?"

"This," said Father Time, "listen."

He stood before me grave and solemn, a shadowy figure but half seen though he was close beside me. The fire-light had died down, and through the curtained windows there came already the first dim brightening of dawn.

"The world that once you knew," said Father Time, "seems broken and destroyed about you. You must not let them know— the children. The cruelty and the horror and the hate that racks the world to-day—keep it from them. Some day he will know"—here Time pointed to the prostrate form of Father Christmas—"that his children, that once were, have not died in vain: that from their sacrifice shall come a nobler, better world for all to live in, a world where countless happy children shall hold bright their memory for ever. But for the children of to-day, save and spare them all you can from the evil hate and horror of the war. Later they will know and understand. Not yet. Give them back their Merry Christmas and its kind thoughts, and its Christmas charity, till later on there shall be with it again Peace upon Earth Good Will towards Men."

His voice ceased. It seemed to vanish, as it were, in the sighing of the wind.

I looked up. Father Time and Christmas had vanished from the room. The fire was low and the day was breaking visibly outside.

"Let us begin," I murmured. "I will mend this broken horse."

The Annunciation

The Hegge Cycle Medieval Mystery Play
(ca. fourteenth century)

"That in thy Holy Family fault may be found none."

During the High Middle Ages, the Church rediscovered drama. The medieval "mystery plays" are a cycle of stories, mostly derived from the Bible and Christian tradition, which reenact the central truths of redemption: the creation, fall, flood, exodus, and annunciation, birth, flight to Egypt, ministry, death, and passion of our Lord. In medieval England, specific guilds would sponsor the production of plays to be performed out of doors as pious acts of public entertainment. This merry tradition, brought to a halt by King Henry VIII, was revived in the twentieth century and lives on still.

CONTEMPLATION:

SINCE ADAM and Eve by the serpent fell,
Man for his offence and foul folly
Hath lain in Limbo, as I you tell,
And were worthy to lie therein endlessly.
But then should perish your great mercy,

Good Lord; have on man pity,
Have mind of your prayer said by Isaye [Isaiah]
Let mercy meek be thine highest majesty.
Would God thou would'st break thine heaven mighty
And come down here to earth indeed,
And live therein years three and thirty,
Thy famished folk with thy food to feed;
To staunch their thirst let Thy side bleed.
For else will not be made redemption.
Come visit us in this time of need,
On Thy careful creatures have compassion.
Ah, woe to us! Wretches of wretches we;
For God hath added sorrow to sorrow.
I pray Thee, Lord, Thy souls come see,
How they lie and sob both even and morrow.
With Thy blessed blood from bales them borrow
Thy careful creatures crying in captivity.
Ah, tarry not, gracious Lord, till it be morrow,
Lest the devil take man by his iniquity.
O waters, give to mine eyes such rain
That I may weep both day and night,
To see our brethren in so long pain;
Their mischiefs amend by Thy much might.
As great as the sea, Lord, now is Satan's might;
From our head is fallen the crown;
Man is covered in sin; I cry to Thy sight:
Gracious Lord, gracious Lord, gracious Lord, come down.

**Enter MERCY, JUSTICE, TRUTH and PEACE.
JUSTICE and TRUTH seat themselves.**

TRUTH:
Lord, I am Thy daughter Truth,
That shall last without an end.
And I must testify to man's ruth,
That wretch was to Thee so unkind.
Thy holy will he did abjure;
Thou art his creator and he is Thy creature,
Thou hast loved Truth, it is said evermore,
Therefore in pains let him evermore endure.

MERCY:
O Father of mercy and God of comfort,
Who counsellest us in each tribulation,
Let your daughter Mercy to you resort,
And on man misled have Thou compassion.
Him grieveth full greatly his transgression;
All heaven and earth cry for mercy;
Meseemeth that none should take exception
Their prayers have been offered so specially.

JUSTICE:
Mercy, me marvelleth what you moveth;
You know well I am your sister Justice.
God is rightful and righteousness loveth;
Man offended Him that is endless,

Therefore his endless punishment may never cease;
Also he forsook his maker that made him of clay,
And the devil to be his master he chose.
Should he be saved? Nay, Nay, Nay.

MERCY:
Sister Justice, ye are too vengeful.
Endless sin God endless may restore.
Above all His works God is merciful.
That he forsook God, man always doth deplore;
And though he presumed never so sore,
Yet must thou consider the frailness of mankind.
Learn an ye list, this is Godes lore:
The mercy of God is without an end.

PEACE:
To spare your speeches, sisters, it were fit;
It is not honest in Virtues to be in dissension.
The Peace of God overcometh all wit;
Though Truth and Justice say great reason,
Yet Mercy saith best to my pleasing.
For if man's soul should abide in hell,
Between God and man ever should be division;
And therein might not I, Peace, dwell.
Therefore meseemeth best ye thus accord,
Lest heaven and earth ye should divide:
Put both your sentences unto our Lord,
And in His high wisdom let Him decide.

TRUTH: (rises)
In truth hereto I consent,
I would pray our Lord so it might be.

JUSTICE: (rises)
I, Justice, am well content,
For in Him is very equity.

MERCY:
And I, Mercy, from His counsel will not flee,
Till Wisdom shall have said I shall cease.

PEACE:
Here is God now, here is unity;
Heaven and earth are pleased with Peace.
They hold up hands of supplication.

GABRIEL appears.

GABRIEL:
This is God's word, you shall confess.
Adam died once for his transgression,
That truth and also righteousness
Might be preserved from violation.
Now to restore mercy and peace,
A second Adam must die on earth;
So Codes mercy to man shall not cease,
And the reign of peace shall come to birth.

But he that shall die, ye must know
That in him be none iniquity,
That hell may hold him by no law,
But that he may pass at his liberty.
Find therefore the man that is worthy
His death for man's death to be redemption.
All heaven and earth seek now ye,
That our Lord may fulfill His intention.

TRUTH, JUSTICE and MERCY search and return.

TRUTH:
If Truth, have sought the earth without and within,
And in sooth there can none be found
That is of human birth without sin,
Nor that to death will be bound.

MERCY:
I, Mercy, have run the heavenly region round,
And there is none of that charity
That for man will suffer a deadly wound.
I cannot tell how this shall be.

JUSTICE:
Sure I can find none sufficient,
For servants unprofitable we be each one;
His love needeth to be full ardent
That for man to hell would be gone.

PEACE:
None is there but one that can this do.
Therefore this is Peace's advice,
That we beseech God to give Himself thereto;
For the conclusion in Him of all this lies.

They kneel and pray. After a time the VOICE OF GOD is heard; all the VIRTUES and GABRIEL prostrate themselves

VOICE OF THE FATHER:
From us, God, angel Gabriel, thou shalt be sent
Into the country of Galilee;
To a city called Nazareth be thine intent,
To a maid. Betrothed to a man is she
Of whom the name is Joseph, he
Of the house of David born.
The name of the maid free
Is Mary, of Joachim born.

VOICE OF THE SON:
Say that she is without sin and full of grace,
And that I, the Son of the Godhead, son shall be to her.
Heed thee, that thou arrive apace,
Else we shall before thee be there.
I have so great haste to be made man
In that meekest and pure virgin,
That I may bring to naught what Satan began,

Of all you angels and of men the great ruin.

VOICE OF THE HOLY GHOST:
And if she ask thee how it may be,
Tell her that I, the Holy Ghost, shall work all this.
She shall be overshadowed by our Unity.
In token whereof, her cousin Elizabeth is
Quick with child in her great age, iwis
For to Us there is nothing impossible.
Her body shall be so filled with bliss
That soon shall she think these tidings credible.

GABRIEL: (rising)
In thine high embassy, Lord, I shall go
More speedily than it may be thought.
Behold now, Lord, I go hereto,
I take my flight and bide nought.

The VIRTUES rise and embrace.

PEACE:
Now is the loveday made of us four finally,
And we may live in peace as we did formerly,
Mercy and Truth are met together;
Justice and Peace have kissed each other.

They depart, singing "Mercy and Truth are met together, etc." (Psalm 85).

THE ANNUNCIATION

MARY:
Lord, seven petitions I beseech of you here;
First that I may keep Thy love and Thy law,
The second to love my neighbour as myself dear,
The third, from all that Thou hatest me to withdraw,
The fourth, to do all things that Thou wouldest have done
The fifth, to obey the rulers of Thy temple each one,
The sixth, that all people may serve Thee with awe,
That in Thy holy family fault be none.
The seventh, Lord, I ask with great fear:
That I may see once in my life
That lady that shall Codes Son bear,
That I may serve her with my wits five.
If it please you and with your will doth not strive,
With prayers prostrate for these graces I weep;
O my God, devotion deep in me drive,
That my heart may wake in Thee though my body sleep.

GABRIEL:
Ave Maria, gratia plena, dominus tecum.
Hail, full of grace, God is with thee,
Above all women blessed art thou.

MARY:
Ah, mercy God, this is a marvellous hearing,
In the angel's words I am troubled here.
I wonder what manner is this of greeting;
And also thus highly commended to be

I am most unworthy; I cannot answer,
Great awe and a mighty dread is on me.

GABRIEL:
Mary, in this take ye no dread,
For you have found grace with God almighty.
Ye shall conceive in your womb indeed
A child, the second person of the Trinity.
His name of you JESUS shall be called,
He shall be great, above every sovereign;
And on his father David's throne shall be installed,
Over the house of Jacob endlessly to reign.

MARY:
Angel, I say to you,
In what manner of wise shall this be?
For no man do I know;
I have evermore kept my virginity.

GABRIEL:
The Holy Ghost shall come from above to thee,
And the virtue of the highest o'ershadow thee so.
Therefore that holy child that shall be born of thee,
As Son of God shall all people do him homage.
For witness whereof, your cousin Elizabeth, she
Hath conceived a son in her old age.
This is the sixth month of her childbearing,
Whom to call barren none was sparing.

THE ANNUNCIATION

Mary, come off and haste thee,
And take heed, thou dear,
How the Holy Ghost, blessed He be,
Is waiting for thine answer.
Furthermore, all the blessed spirits of virtue
That are in heaven before God's face,
And all the good livers and true
That are here in this earthly place
And the chosen souls this time of grace
That in Limbo are waiting for rescue,
As Adam and Eve, David and Isaiah,
And many other of good reputation,
All these thine answer desire to hear,
And thine assent to the Incarnation,
In which thou standest as preserver
Of all mankind's salvation.
Give me mine answer now, lady dear,
To all these creatures' comfort.

MARY:
With thy gracious bidding I myself accord,
Bowing down my face with all benignity:
See here the handmaiden of our Lord,
After thy will be it done to me.

GABRIEL: (kneels)
Gramercy, lady free,
Gramercy of your answer full right,

Gramercy of your great humility,
Gramercy, ye lantern of light.

Here the HOLY GHOST descendeth with three beams to our lady; the son of the Godhead next with three beams to the HOLY GHOST; the FATHER GODLY with three beams to the SON; and so enter all three to her bosom.

MARY:
Ah, now I feel you in my body be,
Perfect God and perfect Man,
You take not first one member and then another,
But perfect childhood ye have anon.
Of your handmaiden now have you made your mother,
Without pain, in flesh and bone.
Thus conceived never woman none
That ever was in this life.
O my highest Father on your throne,
It is meet that your Son, now my Son, have a prerogative.

GABRIEL:
Now farewell, turtle, Gods daughter dear,
Fare thee well, God's mother, I do thee honour.
Farewell, God's playfellow and His sister,
Fare thee well, God's chamber and His bower.

THE ANNUNCIATION

MARY:
Farewell, Gabriel, God's messenger express.
I thank you for your travel and your goodness.
I pray you that ye would in your faring
Make it an accustomed occupation
To visit me often in my childbearing;
Your presence is my sweetest comfortation.

GABRIEL:
At your will, lady, so shall it be,
House of the Godhead, so of homage worthy.
I commend me unto you, thou throne of the Trinity,
O meekest maid, now the mother of Jesu;
And as I began, I end, with an AVE new
Enjoined upon heaven and earth. With that, I leave you.

The Burglar's Christmas

Willa Cather (1873–1947)

*"It is a tragic hour, that hour when we are
finally driven to reckon with ourselves."*

One of America's finest writers, Cather is known and beloved for her portraits of the spiritual trials and conquests of noble souls set within the frontiers of the new world in works such as *Death Comes for the Archbishop* (set in New Mexico) and *Shadows on the Rock* (set in Quebec). In the following, Cather describes the awakening of conscience in a Midwestern son whose decisions have rendered his heart cold, but not yet frozen, to the joys and friendship of a mother's love.

TWO VERY shabby looking young men stood at the corner of Prairie avenue and Eightieth street, looking despondently at the carriages that whirled by. It was Christmas Eve, and the streets were full of vehicles; florists' wagons, grocers' carts and carriages. The streets were in that half-liquid, half-congealed condition peculiar to the streets of Chicago at that season of the year. The swift wheels that spun by sometimes threw the slush of mud and snow over the two young men who were talking on the corner.

"Well," remarked the elder of the two, "I guess we are at our rope's end, sure enough. How do you feel?"

"Pretty shaky. The wind's sharp to-night. If I had had anything to eat I mightn't mind it so much. There is simply no show. I'm sick of the whole business. Looks like there's nothing for it but the lake."

"O, nonsense, I thought you had more grit. Got anything left you can hoc?"

"Nothing but my beard, and I am afraid they wouldn't find it worth a pawn ticket," said the younger man ruefully, rubbing the week's growth of stubble on his face.

"Got any folks anywhere? Now's your time to strike 'em if you have."

"Never mind if I have, they're out of the question."

"Well, you'll be out of it before many hours if you don't make a move of some sort. A man's got to eat. See here, I am going down to Longtin's saloon. I used to play the banjo in there with a couple of coons, and I'll bone him for some of his free lunch stuff. You'd better come along, perhaps they'll fill an order for two."

"How far down is it?"

"Well, it's clear down town, of course, way down on Michigan avenue."

"Thanks, I guess I'll loaf around here. I don" feel equal to the walk, and the cars—well, the cars are crowded." His features drew themselves into what might have been a smile under happier circumstances.

"No, you never did like street cars, you're too aristocratic. See here, Crawford, I don't like leaving you here. You ain't good company for yourself to-night."

"Crawford? O, yes, that's the last one. There have been so many I forget them."

"Have you got a real name, anyway?"

"O, yes, but it's one of the ones I've forgotten. Don't you worry about me. You go along and get your free lunch. I think I had a row in Longtin's place once. I'd better not show myself there again." As he spoke the young man nodded and turned slowly up the avenue.

He was miserable enough to want to be quite alone. Even the crowd that jostled by him annoyed him. He wanted to think about himself. He had avoided this final reckoning with himself for a year now. He had laughed it off and drunk it off. But now, when all those artificial devices which are employed to turn our thoughts into other channels and shield us from ourselves had failed him, it must come. Hunger is a powerful incentive to introspection.

It is a tragic hour, that hour when we are finally driven to reckon with ourselves, when every avenue of mental distraction has been cut off and our own life and all its ineffaceable failures closes about us like the walls of that old torture chamber of the Inquisition. To-night, as this man stood stranded in the streets of the city, his hour came. It was not the first time he had been hungry and desperate and alone. But always before there had been some outlook, some chance ahead, some pleasure yet untasted that seemed worth the effort, some face that he fancied was, or would be, dear. But it was not so to-night. The unyielding conviction was upon him that he had failed in everything, had outlived everything. It had been near him for a long time, that Pale Spectre. He had caught its shadow at the bottom of his glass many a time, at the head of his bed when he was sleepless at night, in the twilight shadows when some great sunset broke upon him. It had made life hateful to him when he awoke in the morning before now. But now it settled slowly over him, like night, the endless Northern nights that bid the sun a long farewell. It rose up before him like granite. From this brilliant city with its glad bustle of Yule-tide he was shut off as completely as though he were a creature of another species. His days seemed numbered and done, sealed over like the little coral cells at the bottom of the sea. Involuntarily he drew that cold air through his lungs slowly, as though he were tasting it for the last time.

Yet he was but four and twenty, this man—he looked even younger—and he had a father some place down East who had been very proud of him once. Well, he had taken his life into his own hands, and this was what he had made of it. That was all there was to be said. He could remember the hopeful things they used to say about him at college in the old days, before he had cut away and begun to live by his wits, and he found courage to smile at them now. They had read him wrongly. He knew now that he never had the essentials of success, only the superficial agility that is often mistaken for it. He was tow without the tinder, and he had burnt himself out at other people's fires. He had helped other people to make it win, but he himself—he had never touched an enterprise that had not failed eventually. Or, if it survived his connection with it, it left him behind.

His last venture had been with some ten-cent specialty company, a little lower than all the others, that had gone to pieces in Buffalo, and he had worked his way to Chicago by boat. When the boat made up its crew for the outward voyage, he was dispensed with as usual. He was used to that. The reason for it? O, there are so many reasons for failure! His was a very common one.

As he stood there in the wet under the street light he drew up his reckoning with the world and decided that it had treated him as well as he deserved. He had overdrawn his account once too often. There had been a day when he thought otherwise; when he had said he was unjustly handled, that his failure was merely the lack of proper adjustment between himself and other men, that some day he would be recognized and it would all come right. But he knew better than that now, and he was still man enough to bear no grudge against any one—man or woman.

To-night was his birthday, too. There seemed something particularly amusing in that. He turned up a limp little coat collar to try to keep a little of the wet chill from his throat, and instinctively began to remember all the birthday parties he used to have. He was so cold and empty that his mind seemed unable to grapple with any serious question. He kept thinking about ginger bread and frosted cakes like a child. He could remember the splendid birthday parties his mother used to give him, when all the other little boys in the block came in their Sunday clothes and creaking shoes, with their ears still red from their mother's towel, and the pink and white birthday cake, and the stuffed olives and all the dishes of which he had been particularly fond, and how he would eat and eat and then go to bed and dream of Santa Claus. And in the morning he would awaken and eat again, until by night the family doctor arrived with his castor oil, and poor William used to dolefully say that it was altogether too much to have your birthday and Christmas all at once. He could remember, too, the royal birthday suppers he had given at college, and the stag dinners, and the toasts, and the music, and the good fellows who had wished him happiness and really meant what they said.

And since then there were other birthday suppers that he could not remember so clearly; the memory of them was heavy and flat, like cigarette smoke that has been shut in a room all night, like champagne that has been a day opened, a song that has been too often sung, an acute sensation that has been overstrained. They seemed tawdry and garish, discordant to him now. He rather wished he could forget them altogether.

Whichever way his mind now turned there was one thought that it could not escape, and that was the idea of food. He caught the scent of a cigar suddenly, and felt a sharp pain in the pit of his abdomen and a sudden moisture in his mouth. His cold hands clenched angrily, and for a moment he felt that bitter hatred of wealth, of ease, of everything that is well-fed and well-housed that is common to starving men. At any rate he had a right to eat! He had demanded great things from the world once: fame and wealth and admiration. Now it was simply bread—and he would have it! He looked about him quickly and felt the blood begin to stir in his veins. In all his straits he had never stolen anything, his tastes were above it. But to-night there would be no to-morrow. He was amused at the way in which the idea excited him. Was it possible there was yet one more experience that would distract him, one thing that had power to excite his jaded interest? Good! he had failed at everything else, now he would see what his chances would be as a common thief. It would be amusing to watch the beautiful consistency of his destiny work itself out even in that role. It would be interesting to add another study to his gallery of futile attempts, and then label them all: "the failure as a journalist," "the failure as a lecturer," "the failure as a business man," "the failure as a thief," and so on, like the titles under the pictures of the Dance of Death. It was time that Childe Roland came to the dark tower.

A girl hastened by him with her arms full of packages. She walked quickly and nervously, keeping well within the shadow, as if she were not accustomed to carrying bundles and did not care to meet any of her friends. As she crossed the muddy street, she made an effort to lift her skirt a little, and as she did so one of the packages slipped unnoticed from beneath her arm. He caught it up and overtook her. "Excuse me, but I think you dropped something."

She started, "O, yes, thank you, I would rather have lost anything than that."

The young man turned angrily upon himself. The package must have contained something of value. Why had he not kept it? Was this the sort of thief he would make? He ground his teeth together. There is nothing more maddening than to have morally

THE BURGLAR'S CHRISTMAS

consented to crime and then lack the nerve force to carry it out.

A carriage drove up to the house before which he stood. Several richly dressed women alighted and went in. It was a new house, and must have been built since he was in Chicago last. The front door was open and he could see down the hallway and up the stair case. The servant had left the door and gone with the guests. The first floor was brilliantly lighted, but the windows upstairs were dark. It looked very easy, just to slip upstairs to the darkened chambers where the jewels and trinkets of the fashionable occupants were kept.

Still burning with impatience against himself he entered quickly. Instinctively he removed his mud-stained hat as he passed quickly and quietly up the stair case. It struck him as being a rather superfluous courtesy in a burglar, but he had done it before he had thought. His way was clear enough, he met no one on the stairway or in the upper hall. The gas was lit in the upper hall. He passed the first chamber door through sheer cowardice. The second he entered quickly, thinking of something else lest his courage should fail him, and closed the door behind him. The light from the hall shone into the room through the transom. The apartment was furnished richly enough to justify his expectations. He went at once to the dressing case. A number of rings and small trinkets lay in a silver tray. These he put hastily in his pocket. He opened the upper drawer and found, as he expected, several leather cases. In the first he opened was a lady's watch, in the second a pair of old-fashioned bracelets; he seemed to dimly remember having seen bracelets like them before, somewhere. The third case was heavier, the spring was much worn, and it opened easily. It held a cup of some kind. He held it up to the light and then his strained nerves gave way and he uttered a sharp exclamation. It was the silver mug he used to drink from when he was a little boy.

The door opened, and a woman stood in the doorway facing him. She was a tall woman, with white hair, in evening dress. The light from the hall streamed in upon him, but she was not afraid. She stood looking at him a moment, then she threw out her hand and went quickly toward him.

"Willie, Willie! Is it you?"

He struggled to loose her arms from him, to keep her lips from his cheek. "Mother—you must not! You do not understand! O, my God, this is worst of all!" Hunger, weakness, cold, shame, all came back to him, and shook his self-control completely. Physically he was too weak to stand a shock like this. Why could it not have been an ordinary discovery, arrest, the station house and all the rest of it. Anything but this! A hard dry sob broke from him. Again he strove to disengage himself.

"Who is it says I shall not kiss my son? O, my boy, we have waited so long for this! You have been so long in coming, even I almost gave you up."

Her lips upon his cheek burnt him like fire. He put his hand to his throat, and spoke thickly and incoherently: "You do not understand. I did not know you were here. I came here to rob—it is the first time—I swear it—but I am a common thief. My pockets are full of your jewels now. Can't you hear me? I am a common thief!"

"Hush, my boy, those are ugly words. How could you rob your own house? How could you take what is your own? They are all yours, my son, as wholly yours as my great love—and you can't doubt that, Will, do you?"

That soft voice, the warmth and fragrance of her person stole through his chill, empty veins like a gentle stimulant. He felt as though all his strength were leaving him and even consciousness. He held fast to her and bowed his head on her strong shoulder, and groaned aloud.

"O, mother, life is hard, hard!"

She said nothing, but held him closer. And O, the strength of those white arms that held him! O, the assurance of safety in that warm bosom that rose and fell under his cheek! For a moment they stood so, silently. Then they heard a heavy step upon the stair. She led him to a chair and went out and closed the door. At the top of the staircase she met a tall, broad-shouldered man, with iron gray hair, and a face alert and stern. Her eyes were shining and her cheeks on fire, her whole face was one expression of intense determination.

"James, it is William in there, come home. You must keep him at any cost. If he goes this time, I go with him. O, James, be easy with him, he has suffered so." She broke from a command to an entreaty, and laid her hand on his shoulder. He looked questioningly at her a moment, then went in the room and quietly shut the door.

She stood leaning against the wall, clasping her temples with her hands and listening to the low indistinct sound of the voices within. Her own lips moved silently. She waited a long time, scarcely breathing. At last the door opened, and her husband came out. He stopped to say in a shaken voice,

"You go to him now, he will stay. I will go to my room. I will see him again in the morning."

She put her arm about his neck, "O, James, I thank you, I thank you! This is the night he came so long ago, you remember? I gave him to you then, and now you give him back to me!"

"Don't, Helen," he muttered. "He is my son, I have never forgotten that. I failed with him. I don't like to fail, it cuts my pride. Take him and make a man of him." He passed on down the hall.

She flew into the room where the young man sat with his head bowed upon his knee. She dropped upon her knees beside him. Ah, it was so good to him to feel those arms again!

"He is so glad, Willie, so glad! He may not show it, but he is as happy as I. He never was demonstrative with either of us, you know."

"O, my God, he was good enough," groaned the man. "I told him everything, and he was good enough. I don't see how either of you can look at me, speak to me, touch me." He shivered under her clasp again as when she had first touched him, and tried weakly to throw her off.

But she whispered softly,

"This is my right, my son."

Presently, when he was calmer, she rose. "Now, come with me into the library, and I will have your dinner brought there."

As they went down stairs she remarked apologetically, "I will not call Ellen to-night; she has a number of guests to attend to. She is a big girl now, you know, and came out last winter. Besides, I want you all to myself to-night."

When the dinner came, and it came very soon, he fell upon it savagely. As he ate she told him all that had transpired during the years of his absence, and how his father's business had brought them there. "I was glad when we came. I thought you would drift West. I seemed a good deal nearer to you here."

There was a gentle unobtrusive sadness in her tone that was too soft for a reproach.

"Have you everything you want? It is a comfort to see you eat."

He smiled grimly, "It is certainly a comfort to me. I have not indulged in this frivolous habit for some thirty-five hours."

She caught his hand and pressed it sharply, uttering a quick remonstrance.

"Don't say that! I know, but I can't hear you say it,—it's too terrible! My boy, food has choked me many a time when I have thought of the possibility of that. Now take the old lounging chair by the fire, and if you are too tired to talk, we will just sit and rest together."

He sank into the depths of the big leather chair with the lion's heads on the arms, where he had sat so often in the days when his feet did not touch the floor and he was half afraid of the grim monsters cut in the polished wood. That chair seemed to speak to him of things long forgotten. It was like the touch of an old familiar friend. He felt a sudden yearning tenderness for the happy little boy who had sat there and dreamed of the big world so long ago. Alas, he had been dead many a summer, that little boy!

He sat looking up at the magnificent woman beside him. He had almost forgotten how handsome she was; how lustrous and sad were the eyes that were set under that serene brow, how impetuous and wayward the mouth even now, how superb the white throat and shoulders! Ah, the wit and grace and fineness of this woman! He remembered how proud he had been of her as a boy when she came to see him at school. Then in the deep red coals of the grate he saw the faces of other women who had come since then into his vexed, disordered life. Laughing faces, with eyes artificially bright, eyes without depth or meaning, features without the stamp of high sensibilities. And he had left this face for such as those!

He sighed restlessly and laid his hand on hers. There seemed refuge and protection in the touch of her, as in the old days when he was afraid of the dark. He had been in the dark so long now, his confidence was so thoroughly shaken, and he was bitterly afraid of the night and of himself.

"Ah, mother, you make other things seem so false. You must feel that I owe you an explanation, but I can't make any, even to myself. Ah, but we make poor exchanges in life. I can't make out the riddle of it all. Yet there are things I ought to tell you before I accept your confidence like this."

"I'd rather you wouldn't, Will. Listen: Between you and me there can be no secrets. We are more alike than other people. Dear boy, I know all about it. I am a woman, and circumstances were different with me, but we are of one blood. I have lived all your life before you. You have never had an impulse that I have not known, you have never touched a brink that my feet have not trod. This is your birthday night. Twenty-four years ago I foresaw all this. I was a young woman then and I had hot battles of my own, and I felt your likeness to me. You were not like other babies. From the hour you were born you were restless and discontented, as I had been before you. You used to brace your strong little limbs against mine and try to throw me off as you did to-night. To-night you have come back to me, just as you always did after you ran away to swim in the river that was forbidden you, the river you loved because it was forbidden. You are tired and sleepy, just as you used to be then, only a little older and a little paler and a little more foolish. I never asked you where you had been then, nor will I now. You have come back to me, that's all in all to me. I know your every possibility and limitation, as a composer knows his instrument."

He found no answer that was worthy to give to talk like this. He had not found life easy since he had lived by his wits. He had come to know poverty at close quarters. He had known what it was to be gay with an empty pocket, to wear violets in his button hole when he had not breakfasted, and all the hateful shams of the poverty of idleness. He had been a reporter on a big metropolitan daily, where men grind out their brains on paper until they have not one idea left—and still grind on. He had worked in a real estate office, where ignorant men were swindled. He had sung in a comic opera chorus and played Harris in an Uncle Tom's Cabin Company, and edited a Socialist weekly. He had been dogged by debt and hunger and grinding poverty, until to sit here by a warm fire without concern as to how it would be paid for seemed unnatural.

He looked up at her questioningly. "I wonder if you know how much you pardon?"

"O, my poor boy, much or little, what does it matter? Have you wandered so far and paid such a bitter price for knowledge and not yet learned that love has nothing to do with pardon or forgiveness, that it only loves, and loves—and loves? They have not taught you well, the women of your world." She leaned over and kissed him, as no woman had kissed him since he left her.

He drew a long sigh of rich content. The old life, with all its bitterness and useless antagonism and flimsy sophistries, its brief delights that were always tinged with fear and distrust and unfaith, that whole miserable, futile, swindled world of Bohemia seemed immeasurably distant and far away, like a dream that is over and done. And as the chimes rang joyfully outside and sleep pressed heavily upon his eyelids, he wondered dimly if the Author of this sad little riddle of ours were not able to solve it after all, and if the Potter would not finally mete out his all comprehensive justice, such as none but he could have, to his Things of Clay, which are made in his own patterns, weak or strong, for his own ends; and if some day we will not awaken and find that all evil is a dream, a mental distortion that will pass when the dawn shall break.

A Christmas Miracle

Harrison S. Morris (1856–1948)

*"It was a sore conflict for an unyielding will
like that of the Donna Isabella."*

A traveler through Spain witnesses a Christmas pageant during one Midnight Mass and beholds how the tenderness of an unexpected baby melts the heart of a wounded grandmother. Seeing grace act through another is often the means by which grace works upon ourselves.

YOU HAVE never heard of Alcala? Well, it is a little village nestling between the Spanish hills, a league from great Madrid. There is a ring of stone houses, each with its white-walled patio and grated windows; each with its balcony, whence now and then a laughing face looks down upon the traveller. There is an ancient inn by the roadside, a time-worn church, and above, on the hill-top, against the still blue sky, the castle, dusky with age, but still keeping a feudal dignity, though half its yellow walls have crumbled away.

This is the Alcala into which I jogged one winter evening

in search of rest and entertainment after a long day's journey on mule-back.

The inn was in a doze when my footsteps broke the silence of its stone court-yard; but presently a woman came through an inner door to answer my summons, and I was speedily cast under the quiet spell of the place by finding myself behind a screen of leaves, with a straw-covered bottle at my elbow and a cold fowl within comfortable reach.

The bower where I sat was unlighted save by the waning sun, and I could see but little of its long vista, without neglecting a very imperious appetite. The lattice was covered, I thought, with vine-leaves, and I felt sure, too, that some orange boughs, reaching across the patio wall, mingled with the foliage above my head. But all I was certain of was the relish of the fowl and the delicious refreshment of the cool wine. Having finished these, I lay back in my chair, luxuriating in the sense of healthy fatigue, and going over again, in fancy, the rolling roads of my journey.

I believe I, also, fell into the prevailing slumber of the place, lulled by the soft atmosphere and gentle wine, and might have slept there till morning had a furious sneeze not awakened me with a start. I looked confusedly about in the dusk, but could see nothing save, at last, the tip of a lighted cigarette in the remote depths of the bower. I called out,—

"Who's there?" and was answered, courteously, by a deep, gruff voice in Spanish,—

"It is I, señor, Jose Rosado."

"Are you a guest of 'La Fonda'?" said I, for I had learned that this was the name of the inn, and was a little doubtful whether I had fallen into the hands of friend or foe.

"Ha! ha! ha!" with a long explosion of guttural sounds, was my only answer. Then, after a brightening of the cigarette-fire, to denote that the smoker was puffing it into life, he said,—

"I, señor, am the host."

At this I drew my chair closer, and found, in the thin reflection of the cigarette, a round, bronzed face beaming with smiles and picturing easy good health.

It was winter in Spain, but the scent of flowers was abroad, and the soft, far-off stars twinkled through the moving leaves. What wonder, then, that we fell into talk,—I, the inquiring traveller, he, the arch-gossip of Alcala,—and talked till the moon rose high into the night?

"And who lives in the castle on the hill?" I asked, after hearing the private history of half the town.

"Ah," said mine host, as if preparing to swallow a savory morsel, "there's a bit of gossip; there's a story, indeed!" He puffed away for a minute in mute satisfaction, and then began.

"That is a noble family, the Aranjuez. None can remember in Alcala when there was not a noble Aranjuez living in its castle, and they have led our people bravely in all the wars of Spain. I remember as a boy——"

But, having become acquainted with mine host's loquacity, I broke in with a question more to the point,—

"Who, Señor Jose, lives in the castle now?"

He would have answered without a suspicion of my ruse, had not a bell just then rung solemnly forth, awakening the still night, and arousing Jose Rosado from his comfortable bench, promptly to his feet.

"Come," he said; "that is for the Christmas Mass. I will tell you as we go."

The little inn was lively enough as we emerged from the bower and crossed the court-yard towards the road. The woman who had prepared my supper came forth arrayed in a capulet of white and scarlet, and two younger girls who accompanied her wore veils and long, black robes which fell about their forms like Oriental garments. Two or three men, attendants and hostlers of the place, were also about to start, trigged out in queer little capes and high-crowned hats. All this fine apparel, mine host informed me, was peculiar to Christmas, and I soon found the highway full of peasants in similar garb.

As we got off, Jose Rosado resumed his story, which was brief enough to beguile us just to the church-door.

"You ask me, señor, who lives in the castle now? The Donna Isabella is alone there, now, the only survivor of the noble race, except—except señor," (he laid a peculiar emphasis on the word,) "except a wilful son, whom she has disowned and driven from her house. He is a handsome lad, and married, here in Alcala, the beauty of the town, in spite of his mother's wounded pride. It was a love-match of stolen wooing and secret wedding,—but, ha! ha! we saw it all, knew it all, before even they did themselves. Many an evening have I met them on these roads, billing and cooing like the doves on La Fonda's eaves. They were made by nature for each other, though, and even the rage of the proud Donna Isabella could never part them."

"And do they still live in the town?" I asked.

"Oh, yes," said Jose; "over there in the white house where the olive trees are, at the bottom of the long hill."

I looked in the direction whither he pointed, but I could see little in the dim moonlight save a white wall amid dense shadows.

"And is Donna Isabella a very old lady?" I asked, because very old ladies are often charged with peculiar severity to very young ones.

"No, no, no," said Jose Rosado, with a quick turn of the head to each no. "She's a widow lady of middle age; very proud and very handsome. You shall see her presently, for she has consented to take part in the Christmas play at the church."

As I had come a long journey to see this same Christmas play, my expectation was doubly aroused as we approached the old edifice, whose open belfry and rows of cloisters stood before us at the top of the hill we were ascending.

As we entered, the bells stopped ringing, for it was precisely midnight, and the priest at the altar began to say the Christmas Masses. When he had reached the Gospel, he was interrupted by the appearance of a matron, dressed all in white, who stood at the end of the nave. She was clad like the Madonna, and was accompanied by Joseph, who wore the garb of a mountaineer, with a hatchet in his hand. An officious little officer with a halberd opened the way through the crowd before these personages, and they came solemnly up the aisle towards the chancel, which had been arrayed to represent Bethlehem, the Madonna reciting, as she moved forward, a plaintive song about her homelessness.

Joseph replied cheeringly, and led her under a roof of leaves in the sanctuary, formed in the manner of a stable, in which we could see the manger against the wall. Here she took rest from her journey, while a little crib, wherein lay the Bambino—or waxen image of the Babe—all adorned with ribbons and laces, was brought from the sacristy and placed in the straw at her feet.

As the Madonna passed us, Jose Rosado nudged me, and whispered audibly enough to make the crowd about us turn and stare,—

"Hist! here's the Donna Isabella, señor! She looks like a saint to-night!"

I watched her closely as she went by me, and marked, under the meek expression assumed by the Virgin, a more characteristic one of severe resolution. She was, however, a queenly woman, in the ripest stage of maturity, but she bore herself, in the part she had taken, with a matronly grace something too conscious for the lowly Mary.

As she seated herself on the heap of straw, a little boy in a surplice, representing an angel, with wings of crimped lawn at his shoulders, was raised in a chair, by a cord and pulley, to the very top of the sanctuary arch, where he sang a carol to the shepherds,—

"Shepherds, hasten all
With flying feet from your retreat;
On rustic pipes now play
Your sweetest, sweetest lay;

for"—so ran the song—"Mary and the King of Heaven are in yonder cave."

At this, an orchestra, concealed behind the high altar, set up a tooting from bagpipes, and flute, and violin, which served as a prelude to the appearance of the shepherds, who were concealed in the gallery.

Up they got, with long cloaks and crooked staffs, murmuring their surprise and incredulity at what the angel had said; some pretending to grumble at being awakened from sleep, others anxious to prove the truth of the strange tidings.

Then the angel sang a more appealing ditty still, whereat they were all about ready to advance, when one of their number, of a skeptical turn, urged them to avoid such fanciful matters and give heed to their sheep, who would otherwise become the prey of the wolf.

Hereupon, an old shepherd appeared, who gave three loud knocks with his crook, and denounced those who should disobey the heavenly messenger. The practical man was thus silenced, and they expressed their willingness to go to the manger,—and at the same moment an angel appeared to guide them thither.

They descended from the gallery to the outer porch of the church and knocked loudly at the door, saying, as if to the innkeeper at Bethlehem:

"Pray, good master of the inn,
Open the door and let us in."

But Joseph became alarmed at the approach of such a number of rustics, and inquired who they were. They held a songful colloquy with him; but he continued to refuse them admittance, until an angel again intervened, this time in the form of a tall acolyte from the sanctuary, accompanied by two little angelic choristers. He reassured Joseph, and invited the shepherds to enter and worship the Babe. They came up the aisle flourishing their be-ribboned crooks and singing in praise of the Child, but they were sorely vexed, when they saw the stable, that so humble a place had been found for His shelter. Joseph explained, in several couplets, that no other house would receive them, and the shepherds replied in several others, mingling sympathy and good advice, intended not for Joseph, but for the throng, who listened in religious awe.

After paying due homage to the child and Mary, the shepherds exchanged some more verses with Joseph, and then retired to the other end of the church, singing in chorus as they went.

All these ceremonies had so claimed my attention that I had given scarcely any heed to the Virgin. She was seated humbly in the straw beside the little crib, in which still nestled the Bambino, and, with eyes cast down in maternal thoughtfulness, she was a lovely object there beneath the roof of the leafy stable. She did not appear to notice the actors in the drama; and now, when three young girls, in gayest holiday attire, came forward with distaffs that streamed with bright ribbons, and knelt before her, she reached forth a hand as if to bless them, but kept her eyes turned meekly upon the ground.

As these three girls retired from the manger, another and larger band appeared beneath the gallery opposite the shepherds, singing in sweet voices a salutation to the three who had just left the chancel. These made answer that they had come from the stable where the Saviour was born; and so, in alternate questions and answers, they described all that they had seen. The two groups, having advanced a step or two at each stanza, now met, and went back to the manger together, singing the same air the shepherds had previously sung.

When they arrived at the stable they made their offering, setting up a tent the while, ornamented with plenteous ribbons and flowers, among which blackbirds, thrushes, turtle-doves and partridges fluttered about at the ends of cords to which they were fastened. They brought with them, also, bunches of purple grapes and strings of yellow apples, chaplets of dried prunes and heaps of walnuts and chestnuts. After arranging these rustic offerings, the shepherdesses returned, singing in chorus as they went:

"In Bethlehem, at midnight,
The Virgin mother bore her child.
This world contains no fairer sight
Than this fair Babe and Mary mild.
Well may we sing at sight like this,
Gloria in Excelsis."

I now had another unobstructed view of Donna Isabella, and Jose Rosado's gossip, intensified by her romantic appearance as the Virgin, had given me a deep interest in her every movement.

She reached down into the little crib to lift out the Bambino, and I could plainly see a look of astonishment rise to her face as she started back, both hands held wide apart, as if having encountered something they were unprepared to touch. Then she turned hurriedly to Joseph and whispered a word in his ear, whereupon he too bent with surprise over the little crib. After gazing at it a moment, he reached down and lifted out, not the waxen Bambino, but a sweet young baby that smiled and reached its tiny arms from Joseph towards the white Virgin.

Donna Isabella was visibly affected at this, and took the tender infant into her arms, caressing and soothing it, while it fondled her face and white head-dress.

The audience had now become aware that, instead of the waxen image in the crib, there had been found a living baby, and the impetuous and susceptible minds of the Spanish peasants had jumped at the conclusion that they had witnessed a new miracle. They crowded up to the manger, telling their beads and murmuring prayers, while they pushed and jostled each other madly for a glimpse of the holy infant.

One of the acolytes reached his arms forth to take it from Donna Isabella and bring it to the chancel rail for the crowd to see, but she held it more closely to her bosom, and refused to let it go from her. As she stood there, a tall and stately figure, folded in the white gown of the Virgin and wearing the close head-dress which concealed all save her splendid face, she seemed the creation of some old painter, and the curious crowd of peasants was hushed into admiration by her beauty and her tenderness for the child. She, too, became a part of the strange miracle. The infant Christ had been born anew among them, and lay there in his very mother's arms, an object of mystery and worship. As the silence of wonder ensued, Donna Isabella seemed to collect her startled senses, and looked around her as if expecting the mother of the child to come and claim it. A woman of her resolution was not to be hurried into superstitious follies by some pretty trick or accident. But the little one lay so softly in her arms and reached with such tiny, appealing fingers at her throat, that she began to feel a motherly fondness for it. And, moreover, had it not been sent to her, who was alone now in the great castle on the hill, as a mysterious gift of Providence? Ought she not to feel it a sacred charge, coming as it did, from the very manger, to her arms?

Thus thinking, the Donna Isabella came slowly to the chancel rail, and, holding forth the infant at arms' length, she said:

"Good people of Alcala, my part in the Christmas play is done. The good Lord has sent me this little one to take care of; and here, before you all, I accept the charge and promise to cherish and love it. If any of you know its mother, say that the Donna Isabella has carried it to the castle of Aranjuez, and tell her to follow it there, for where her child is, there the mother should be also." This broke the spell. The silent crowd fell into murmurs and gestures, and each one asked his neighbor where the child belonged. There was no longer any doubt. It was merely a human child; but the mystery of the manger surrounded it with a hallowed interest, and everybody was eager to discover its parents and bear them the good news of its adoption by the great lady.

Now, Jose Rosado was too old a hand, too jolly a host, to be long deceived. He whispered me his views as we stood near the leafy stable, and they were to the effect that the wayward son of the Aranjuez knew more about the child in the manger than any one else thereabouts.

And Jose was right; for, before the bustle of inquiry had quite died away, from out the sacristy door came a young girl wearing a veil and dressed in the long black gown of the Christmas ceremonies. She walked demurely through the crowd, which parted for her with inquiring looks, and, going straight up to the chancel, dropped on her knees before the Donna Isabella. She held down her head and made no motion; but all knew instinctively that she was the mother of the child.

The noble Virgin stooped and raised her head with a loving compassion. She put aside her veil and moved as if to kiss her, but one look at the mother's face turned her kindness into rage. She cried, "What, you?" and overwhelmed at the discovery sank down on the straw of the stable, clasping the child with a firmer hold, as if to shield it from a foe.

It was a sore conflict for an unyielding will like that of the Donna Isabella; but the part she had played in the sacred ceremonies and the surrounding emblems of peace and good-will were softening influences. More potent even than these was the persuasive contact of the little hands which opened and shut in playful touches at her throat. I could see from the varying expressions of her face that she questioned herself. Should she yield? The pride of birth, the disobedience of a youthful son to a mother of her indulgent nature, the stigma of a low connection upon a noble family name—all these things pleaded urgently, No. She looked up vindictively at the gaping congregation, which seemed spellbound in wanton curiosity, wherewith was mingled not a little religious dread. And then, again, she turned her eyes down upon the innocent face beside her bosom, so guileless, to be the cause of such varying passions in the throng about it. No, she could not give it up. All the old maternal instincts were aroused in her, and the firmness of her will was redoubled by the sentiment of love for her grandchild. Was it not her son's child, then, as well as this woman's? Surely, she had a right to keep it, and, glancing up with this last plea for possession on her lips, she saw beside the kneeling wife a new figure, whose presence made her pause and falter.

Only for an instant, however, for a kindlier light came into her clear eyes, and reaching forth the one arm which was free she threw it around her son's neck and kissed him fondly, while the little child which had wrought the change,—a latter-day miracle of broken affections made whole, of bitter wounds healed by the touch of innocence,—lay there between them, striving, with its playful hands, to catch at its mother's bowing head.

As Jose Rosado and I walked homeward through the pale-blue moonlight, we did not say much. I was deeply moved by the touching scene I had beheld; and he was exceedingly reflective.

At last, as we neared La Fonda's vine-run walls, he said:

"Señor, do you think the miracles are all over nowadays?"

"I know not, Señor Jose," I answered; "but there are certainly strange potencies lurking in the depths of a mother's love."

The Selfish Giant

Oscar Wilde (1854–1900)

"'Who hath dared to wound thee?' cried the Giant."

A notorious agnostic, aesthete, and provocateur, the gifted and brilliant Wilde long flirted with Christianity. On his death bed, he was received into the Church. Here we get a glimpse of his abiding love affair with the Child Christ.

EVERY AFTERNOON, as they were coming from school, the children used to go and play in the Giant's garden.

It was a large lovely garden, with soft green grass. Here and there over the grass stood beautiful flowers like stars, and there were twelve peach-trees that in the spring-time broke out into delicate blossoms of pink and pearl, and in the autumn bore rich fruit. The birds sat on the trees and sang so sweetly that the children used to stop their games in order to listen to them. "How happy we are here!" they cried to each other.

One day the Giant came back. He had been to visit his friend the Cornish ogre, and had stayed with him for seven years.

After the seven years were over he had said all that he had to say, for his conversation was limited, and he determined to return to his own castle. When he arrived he saw the children playing in the garden.

"What are you doing here?" he cried in a very gruff voice, and the children ran away.

"My own garden is my own garden," said the Giant; "any one can understand that, and I will allow nobody to play in it but myself." So he built a high wall all round it, and put up a notice-board.

TRESPASSERS
WILL BE
PROSECUTED

He was a very selfish Giant.

The poor children had now nowhere to play. They tried to play on the road, but the road was very dusty and full of hard stones, and they did not like it. They used to wander round the high wall when their lessons were over, and talk about the beautiful garden inside.

"How happy we were there," they said to each other.

Then the Spring came, and all over the country there were little blossoms and little birds. Only in the garden of the Selfish Giant it was still Winter. The birds did not care to sing in it as there were no children, and the trees forgot to blossom. Once a beautiful flower put its head out from the grass, but when it saw the notice-board it was so sorry for the children that it slipped back into the ground again, and went off to sleep. The only people who were pleased were the Snow and the Frost. "Spring has forgotten this garden," they cried, "so we will live here all the year round." The Snow covered up the grass with her great white cloak, and the Frost painted all the trees silver. Then they invited the North Wind to stay with them, and he came. He was wrapped in furs, and he roared all day about the garden, and blew the chimney-pots down. "This is a delightful spot," he said, "we must ask the Hail on a visit." So the Hail came. Every day for three hours he rattled on the roof of the castle till he broke most of the slates, and then he ran round and round the garden as fast as he could go. He was dressed in grey, and his breath was like ice.

"I cannot understand why the Spring is so late in coming," said the Selfish Giant, as he sat at the window and looked out at his cold white garden; "I hope there will be a change in the weather."

But the Spring never came, nor the Summer. The Autumn gave golden fruit to every garden, but to the Giant's garden she gave none. "He is too selfish," she said. So it was always Winter there, and the North Wind, and the Hail, and the Frost, and the Snow danced about through the trees.

One morning the Giant was lying awake in bed when he heard some lovely music. It sounded so sweet to his ears that he thought it must be the King's musicians passing by. It was really only a little linnet singing outside his window, but it was so long since he had heard a bird sing in his garden that it seemed to him to be the most beautiful music in the world. Then the Hail stopped dancing over his head, and the North Wind ceased roaring, and a delicious perfume came to him through the open casement. "I believe the Spring has come at last," said the Giant; and he jumped out of bed and looked out.

What did he see?

He saw a most wonderful sight. Through a little hole in the wall the children had crept in, and they were sitting in the branches of the trees. In every tree that he could see there was a little child. And the trees were so glad to have the children back again that they had covered themselves with blossoms, and were waving their arms gently above the children's heads. The birds were flying about and twittering with delight, and the flowers were looking up through the green grass and laughing. It was a lovely scene, only in one corner it was still Winter. It was the farthest corner of the garden, and in it was standing a little boy. He was so small that he could not reach up to the branches of the tree, and he was wandering all round it, crying bitterly. The poor tree was still quite covered with frost and snow, and the North Wind was blowing and roaring above it. "Climb up! little boy," said the Tree, and it bent its branches down as low as it could; but the little boy was too tiny.

And the Giant's heart melted as he looked out. "How selfish I have been!" he said; "now I know why the Spring would not come here. I will put that poor little boy on the top of the tree, and then I will knock down the wall, and my garden shall be the children's playground for ever and ever." He was really very sorry for what he had done.

So he crept downstairs and opened the front door quite softly, and went out into the garden. But when the children saw him they were so frightened that they all ran away, and the garden became Winter again. Only the little boy did not run, for his eyes were so full of tears that he died not see the Giant coming. And the Giant stole up behind him and took him gently in his hand, and put him up into the tree. And the tree broke at once into blossom, and the birds came and sang on it, and the little boy stretched out his two arms and flung them round the Giant's neck, and kissed him. And the other children, when they saw that the Giant was not wicked any longer, came running back, and with them came the Spring. "It is your garden now, little children," said the Giant, and he took a great axe and knocked down the wall. And when the people were going to market at twelve o'clock they found the Giant playing with the children in the most beautiful garden they had ever seen.

All day long they played, and in the evening they came to the Giant to bid him good-bye.

"But where is your little companion?" he said: "the boy I put into the tree." The Giant loved him the best because he had kissed him.

"We don't know," answered the children; "he has gone away."

"You must tell him to be sure and come here to-morrow," said the Giant. But the children said that they did not know where he lived, and had never seen him before; and the Giant felt very sad.

Every afternoon, when school was over, the children came and played with the Giant. But the little boy whom the Giant loved was never seen again. The Giant was very kind to all the children, yet he longed for his first little friend, and often spoke of him. "How I would like to see him!" he used to say.

Years went over, and the Giant grew very old and feeble. He could not play about any more, so he sat in a huge armchair, and watched the children at their games, and admired his garden. "I have many beautiful flowers," he said; "but the children are the most beautiful flowers of all."

One winter morning he looked out of his window as he was dressing. He did not hate the Winter now, for he knew that it was merely the Spring asleep, and that the flowers were resting.

Suddenly he rubbed his eyes in wonder, and looked and looked. It certainly was a marvellous sight. In the farthest corner of the garden was a tree quite covered with lovely white blossoms. Its branches were all golden, and silver fruit hung down from them, and underneath it stood the little boy he had loved.

Downstairs ran the Giant in great joy, and out into the garden. He hastened across the grass, and came near to the child. And when he came quite close his face grew red with anger, and he said, "Who hath dared to wound thee?" For on the palms of the child's hands were the prints of two nails, and the prints of two nails were on the little feet.

"Who hath dared to wound thee?" cried the Giant; "tell me, that I may take my big sword and slay him."

"Nay!" answered the child; "but these are the wounds of Love."

"Who art thou?" said the Giant, and a strange awe fell on him, and he knelt before the little child.

And the child smiled on the Giant, and said to him, "You let me play once in your garden, to-day you shall come with me to my garden, which is Paradise."

And when the children ran in that afternoon, they found the Giant lying dead under the tree, all covered with white blossoms.

This Was the Christmas

Ruth Sawyer (1880–1970)

"The old priest spoke in humility. . . . 'It is we who have been blind.'"

In this traditional tale of unexpected reversals, a blind, abandoned boy brings to a pious but impervious village one Christmas the shining eyes of faith.

IT WAS midsummer when the great storm came. It swept through the cut in the mountains into the peaceful valley, ripping the roofs off, laying flat the fields of grain, swelling the river to overflowing. The men worked throughout the night to save their herds, their sheep and goats, driving them to high land. When the sickly yellow dawn broke, no life had been lost, and one had been gained. On a rock jutting over the river, a young child was found, crying pitifully.

He was a swarthy, dark-skinned child. Whatever clothes he might have worn, the storm had stripped from him. He was too young to do more than babble a few words and these were in the gypsy tongue. His looks, too, spoke of the Cigani—the gypsies.

It was Father Janovic who found him and brought him to his own cottage, where Mother Janovic was dipping the porridge into bowls for their own children. Her arms reached out to him as mother's arms will for all helpless ones. She wrapped him in a scrap of blanket. She quieted his sobbing and fed him from her own bowl.

"He is of the Cigani. We will not keep him," said Father Janovic.

"He is very little and helpless. And watch his eyes." Mother Janovic passed her hand up and down in front of his face. There was no blinking. She took a candle that still burned and passed it so close that the wick almost singed the long dark lashes. But the eyes remained wide, staring. *"You see?"* said Mother Janovic. *"He is blind. You found him. It is the will of God that we keep him."* And for that one and only time she gathered the blind boy close to her heart and held him there, crooning soft, loving words over him.

The valley dwellers of Serbia are hard-working, honest people, deeply rooted to their land. They do not love the Cigani. They point to the caravans passing through and say: "there go tricksters and thieves. There go the accursed of the earth. Let no man among us give them harborage." But for all their rascally ways the gypsies have some virtues. They can tell amazing fortunes. They have been known to prophesy the great happenings in the world. They are good farriers and potmenders. And their music is beloved by all peoples.

But in that long ago time they were accursed; and the Janovics remembered only this as the blind boy grew older. They called him Marko after their greatest hero—partly in mockery and partly because the boy, like the ancient Marko, loved all small creatures and had a strange way with them. He could call the birds from the woods and they would feed out of his hands. A wounded hare or fox would come whimpering to him for aid. He had tenderness and understanding for all living things. Marking this the Janovic set him at an early age to tend their sheep. Summers he slept with them in the pasture; winters he burrowed under the straw in the shed, holing himself in like a wild creature against the cold. He learned quickly and would have called creature and man alike his brother, had not man despised him.

Because he could not see as other human beings did, he heard what they did not. His fingers and his bare feet soon made him familiar in all the countryside, feeling their way through pasture and woods and along the riverbank. Only along the village road was he a stranger. Six years after the great storm an old shepherd from Dalmatia crossed the pasture and stopped to make himself friendly. He bore a pipe, self-made; discovering the boy's blindness he played tunes on it and gave it into the boy's hands that he might feel out the fashioning of it.

That summer Marko found a young willow and made his own pipe. Before the first frost came, the boy was making music of his own, strange, wild, haunting music. It stirred the hearts of passers-by; it filled the valley dwellers with wonder. Before another summer had passed, tales, hard to believe, were being bandied about among them. Some told how on a gentle night, with the moon full overhead, they had heard the lad piping the lambs and had seen them on their hind legs dancing to the music. Others had seen him pipe the wild hares out of the copses and set them to frolicking in time to a tune as free as the wind.

Mother Janovic did not stint him in his food; but it was ladled out of the big pot, and his bowl was given him to take outside the kitchen. Summers he ate in the pastures; winters in the shed. Only in bitter weather was he bidden inside, to share the warmth of the fire. They were not unkind; only he was set apart from other children, from all humankind. The valley-dwellers made him an outcast from their home and village life.

Do you know what this means—to be cast out from all festivals, all merrymaking? To be forbidden entrance to the church? Only he dared to ask why this should be. *"You are of the Cigani, cursed by all the world. The Church, God, Christ and his blessed Mother are not for you."* Mother Janovic said it without unkindness. Father Janovic said it sternly. But the children taunted him with it so that he gave up waiting for them to depart for church, in all their best clothes; but he listened secretly to the music coming from its door, wide-opened to all but him.

He became a silent boy, save for the music he made and the words he sometimes sang between the pipings. His elders marked this with approval and quoted an old Slav proverb: *"He who preserves silence speaks well."* In lambing time Marko watched over the ewes so well that rarely was a lamb lost. Those that came into the world too feeble to fight for themselves the first few hours, he warmed against his own body, under his tunic. For all his blindness he would have been a happy boy had the people of the valley made him a dweller with them. Yet in an odd way, they were proud of him and stood in awe of his powers to make music and to call wild things to him. They listened stealthily to his songs and pipings; and often a stranger coming into the valley would hear a farmer, ploughing behind his oxen singing:

Harvest and thresh the grain, fill the full measure—Bread for the making, Straw for the baking.
Fathers and mothers and little ones gather—Let bread be broken, let thanks be spoken.

"Tis a good song, a new one to me, From where comes it?" This a man from the north or south would ask; and the farmer would answer: *"Tis only a jingle made by one of our shepherds—a blind boy and not one of us."*

How often Marko heard this! Yet it tied no strings to his pipe, it hung no bitterness across his heart. But he did know sorrow. Every time he turned toward the valley when the church bell rang; every time he listened to a gathering of dancers in the village square, with old Stefan making music on his fiddle the sorrow deepened. But it was worse at Christmas time. To have no part in all the gaiety and beauty of Christ's holy eve and Day—that brought full weight of sorrow.

To lie in the cold and dark of the holy Eve, just before the midnight service and to hear Mother Janovic waking the rest of the children: *"Come Vuk. Come Ivo. Come Draga; we have haste to make."* But never *"Come Marko."* To hear the bustling, the calling of one to another in the cottage; and know he was the outcast, forbidden to have a part in that Christ service; and later to hear the hurrying of feet along the road. That made sorrow a load almost too much to bear. Once, he followed, feeling his way across the barnyard to the road, following the sound of the ringing bell. If he could not enter, he could stand at the door and listen; and coming home he could whisper the part he was forbidden to sing in the carols.

But his feet knew not the valley-road. There were no familiar stones, rises, or hollows to guide him. All was confusion, until, having stumbled off and on again many times, fear came. He turned and somehow stumbled back to the shed. There he lay, shaking with the cold and the fright.

The priest, a kindly man, tried to teach him something of the church, of God and the birth of Christ, so he would not live and die in absolute ignorance. He would stop often when the boy was tending sheep and sit with him for an hour or so, letting the boy ask questions.

"This God—he is the Big King?"

"You may call him that, lad."

"And the Christ, who is the baby in the manger, he is the Small King, Yes?"

"Even so."

"And Mary? She was the Small King's mother—and very holy? Are they in the church yonder?"

"They are in Heaven. Their images only are in the church."

"But if I entered I could feel their faces? I could feel each line until I knew them as I know my sheep."

The Old priest sighed. *"It is the law of the Church. We cannot break it. The people of the valley would not permit it. They have consecrated the church with their vows—even as a bishop of long ago consecrated it with holy water. No Cigani may enter."*

"*And my entering would defile it?*"

"*So they think. When God bade Joseph, Mary and the Child flee to Eygpt, the Cigani—the Eygptians—denied them shelter, food and care. It is a long tale. Sometime I will tell you it.*"

"*For this we are cursed?*"

"*Truely.*"

"*And shall we never have a part of Christmas?*"

"*Short of a miracle, never, my son, never. It is the mark you bear, the mark of the outcast.*"

Marko drew in his breath; slowly he let it out with the words: "*take my hand. Put it on the place where my body bears the mark, and I will cut it out.*" "*It lies not upon your body, my son, but on your soul.*"

There followed a long silence; at last the boy asked his final question: "*Why do you call me 'my son'?*"

The Old priest sighed again: "*Truely, I know not. I am but a simple man.*"

On Christmas day, early, it was the custom for the other boys to gather wood for the great village fire, where sucking pigs would roast all day, turning on their spits. Some one chosen boy would go from house to house and greet each household: "*The Christ is born!*" and the mother scattering a handful of wheat to bring plenty into the house, would answer: "*In truth, He is born!*" The boy would beat the Christ long on the hearth until a great streaming of sparks mounted and he would wish: "*May the Holy Christmas bring as many sheep and goats, pigs and cattle and bees as there are sparks mounting the chimney.*"

Marko wished he might have been that boy just once, to wish plenty on the valley. He wished he might have taken his place, just once, for the feast and had his share of the sucking pigs. But never for him! Had not the priest said it would take a miracle, nothing short of that would lift the curse? Yet, if he could not share the Christmas, worship in church on the Holy Eve, sing the carols, he could make a carol of his own and worship in the shed. That would not be so different from the place the Bethlehem shepherds had come to, to worship the Small King in his manger.

It happened in that year when he was twelve. Father Janovic had marked the years since the great storm in notches with his scythe against an upright of the shed; and Marko, with his fingers checked his age. He had been two or there-abouts when rescued, and there were ten notches. That Holy Eve, a ewe-lamb became tangled in a thorn tree, and being frightened she jumped about so frantically that her leg was broken. Marko tore his tunic to strips, and taking wood bound the leg. Kneeling he lifted her across his shoulders, and holding her fast by her good legs, he bore her to the shed and laid her down in his corner of straw. Then, stretched beside her he talked to her softly, as if she had been kin and human: *"This is the night that Christ was born. We will keep the Christmas, thou and I. Thou shalt hear my carol, made through the long days of ripening wheat. Thou shalt worship with me, here, when stroke of bell rings out from that church we may not enter."*

The ewe lay quietly beside the boy, each warming the other. They slept a little, I think, awoke, and slept again. Then, through the cold of approaching midnight came the voice of Mother Janovic calling her children: *"Come, Vuk. Come Ivo. Come, Draga, we must make haste."* If only she might call one more name, call it joyously: *"Come, Marko."*

But that would never be, short of a miracle. And when had a miracle taken place in the valley here? The blind boy's hand felt for the lamb; his fingers worked in and out of the thick fleece. His other hand held his pipe close. *"Thou knowest it not, small one, but when a human stands in dire need of help—when calamity comes and he needs a friend, a protector, one to be to him as might a brother be, he can ask for such help and it cannot be denied him. That is a law among the Serbian people. Dost thou think that, if I should pray this night—in my great need—that holy ears in Heaven would hear?"*

There came the sound of many feet, brisk and eager feet, young and old. The slow ringing of the bell began, calling all within the valley to come and worship the newborn king.

Marko rose to his knees. Again he spoke to the lamb: *"Small one, I have heard it said that on Christ eve all dumb creatures kneel upon the hour the Christ was born. Canst kneel?"*

As if at his bidding the ewe-lamb shook herself, rose upon her hind legs, even upon the one that had been broken, and bent her forelegs on the straw. Again the blind boy's hand moved comfortably through the thick fleece. He prayed: *"Big king—send someone to sponsor me—one who will speak for me among the valley-folk. For I would be as other boys, welcome at table, called to church by the bell, having a share in worship and the Christ Eve."*

The bell stopped ringing. Marko felt a stirring not far off, feet rustling the straw. Then a strange hand was placed upon his shoulder.

Marko spoke in wonder: *"Can words reach Heaven faster than a bird flies?"*

"Some words can."

"Did the Big King send you to be my sponsor?"

"Perhaps. Perhaps to bear you company, that you need not be alone this Christ Eve."

"Who are you?"

"A boy, even as yourself."

"Blind?"

"Not blind. But are you blind? Think."

"People call me blind, and I would see. I would see the whole world and all it holds."

"No one sees that. But think—in the little piece of world that lies about you, have you not found more beauty than those who see? Do they know the small loveliness of a bird's feather? Do they hear what the wind whispers? Have they caught the song the morning stars sing? And can they put all these things into music and play it on a pipe as you can?"

"But I would see."

"It is not given for any one person in this life to have too much. Have you not seen more with your eyes of faith than those who live by sight. Would you bargain your music away for the power to see only what most humans see? Think."

"I am thinking. This I know. I would see once the face of the Small King."

A hush had fallen on the shed, on the valley, on the whole world. The words Marko heard were barely whispered: *"Put your fingers on my face. Trace every line, slowly, so you will remember."*

Lightly as winter snow the hand of the blind boy touched the face held close to his own—tracing forehead, feeling the wide-set eyes, the rounded cheek, the slender clear-cut nose, the strong molded chin. He nodded, his own face lighting with exaltation as each feature became familiar, possessed. Then he sighed with deep tranquility: *"I will keep the music. I will be a singer for the people of Serbia."*

He put his pipe to his lips and blew the tune for his carol. Between the pipings he sang the words he had made:

This is the Christmas.
To Mary most blessed, Jesus, the Savior, is born.
These are the angel—
Singing through heaven, all curses forgiven this morn.
These are the shepherds.
They seek for the Stranger, they kneel at the manger, to pray.
And I—a blind shepherd -
Give prayer to the Big King, give prayer to the Small King - this day.

The midnight service over, the valley-folk poured out upon the road. A dazzling light filled the sky. It shone over the whole valley. *"It comes from there!"* said one. *"No, from yonder it comes."* said another. Hands pointed everywhere. The Priest, who had shepherded them to the doorway of the church, pointed to Janovic's farm: *"It is there from which it comes."*

He led the way. When they came to the farmyard, they found the small, mean shed bathed in light. No word was spoken. Massed about the low doorway they stood, unbelieving what their eyes told them. For they could see within, kneeling on the straw, the blind boy; and kneeling with him were a small ewe-lamb and one who could only be the Christ. A circle of light shone about his head, making such brightness as the valley-folk had never seen on earth.

All bent their heads as in church worship. The old priest spoke in low humility: *"The miracle. It is we who have been blind. It is upon our heads the curse come home to rest."* And picking up his robe he knelt on the fringe of the straw. The valley folk knelt with him, making no stir in the night. The blind boy piped on, singing his carol over again and again in his great gladness.

There fell three apples from heaven. One for the teller, and one for the listener, and one for all the peoples of the world.

The Christmas Gift

Catherine Doherty (1896–1985)

"Suddenly the front door opened with a wrench, letting in a blast of cold air."

Catherine Doherty was a Russian-born aristocrat who lived through the Communist Revolution. She emigrated to the United States and Canada, eventually to found Madonna House in rural Northern Ontario in the 1940s. The following story is based upon her experience working in Toronto in the 1930s, where she had established the first "Friendship House," a lay apostolate meant to serve the needs of the poor.

OUTSIDE, THE late October evening was dark and stormy. Snow and sleet fell noisily on almost deserted streets. The north wind seemed to take delight in squeezing itself into all the crevices and holes the houses possessed. The big front room of Friendship House was warm and cozy. The Quebec heater roared contentedly, its big belly filled to the top with glowing warm coals. The large kettle on its top sang its happy song invitingly, and reminded everyone that here was nice tea to be had at any time.

Around the large table full of Catholic magazines and newspapers were sitting several workers who had dropped in to get the latest news. Others were wandering around the bookshelves that covered the four walls, inspecting, looking for some good book to take home with them. At a large desk one of the tertiaries was deeply engrossed in writing an article, and the uneven noise of the typewriter blended with the wind and storm and the roaring heater made the place more alive.

From the next room, a kitchen came the clatter of teacups and the subdued laughter of other tertiaries who were preparing a little lunch for the study group, which could be heard occasionally discussing sociology and liturgy. The whole picture was quiet and peaceful.

Suddenly the front door opened with a wrench, letting in a blast of cold air, snow and rain, and the dark figure of a man stood for a moment framed against the outside darkness, almost a part of it. Then, slamming the door with a bang, he riveted his eyes on a large crucifix before which burned dimly a little red votive lamp.

"Another hell-hole of a Christian place!" the man shouted. "Just my luck. I have been thrown out of three tonight, and I am sick, tired, cold and hungry! I was told that there was a communist hall this way, and I had to land here instead."

Quietly, the tertiary who had been typing stood up, a tall figure in a simple brown dress with a silver crucifix gleaming dully in the light. Smilingly, she advanced toward the man and, stretching out her hand, said, "It might be a hell-hole, for we are very poor and have little to offer. It is a Christian place also; but we will not tell you to leave. On the contrary, we welcome you to stay with us as long as you need.

"Forgive our poverty, and share what God in His mercy has seen fit to send us. I am sure He guided you to us; the communist hall is only a few steps down." With these words, she approached the man.

He looked a little bewildered, and then he took a deep breath and collapsed at her feet. Everyone helped to raise him, and he was quickly taken upstairs where a tertiary brother helped him to a warm bath and gave him some dry clothes, for all he had was a jersey, a pair of trousers and some old tennis shoes, and these were soaked.

Clean and warm, he came down to a nice warm lunch prepared quickly for him. But he remained sullen and silent. From the few disjointed sentences he muttered, the tertiaries understood that he was a transient, that he had overstayed his 24-hour city ticket and therefore was not entitled anymore to either food or shelter at the city hostels and had to move on.

Yet, in his flimsy garment, and with the coming Storm, he had tried the private agencies. But they were either full, or had so much red tape attached to their admission that he gave up. And in the last one, he expressed himself rather forcefully and had simply been thrown out.

So he had continued wandering. He was looking for a communist shelter-first, because he called himself a communist, and secondly because he knew that "they wouldn't throw even a dog out in such weather." Without commenting, the tertiaries listened to this short, disjointed yet pitiful tale. They had learned from long and bitter experience that in such cases little would be achieved by words, and more by silence and prayer. Seeing his utter exhaustion, they advised him to go to sleep and discuss things more fully on the morrow.

Tomorrow came. But the man sat sullen and silent in his corner. Only his dark eyes were alive, observing all that was going on. In the light of day, he appeared slight, with an intellectual face, young, not over 30. The tertiaries left him alone all day, and only smiled encouragingly as they passed by.

Toward the evening he stepped up to one of them and wanted to know what was he supposed to do in exchange for his shelter and food. "Nothing," answered the woman.

"Nothing, my friend. You are a guest of St. Francis here; we are only his humble servants. There is nothing you have to do. Just rest and get strong, look for work, or let us look for you.

"Everything in this place belongs to you and your brothers, the 'Christophers' (Christ-bearers) of our great roads. We are only stewards of this place, and our greatest privilege is to help and serve people. If, at any time, you want a part in our lives, and want to help us to help others, let us know and we will find some work for you to do. But there is no obligation of any kind."

The man did not answer, but once again an expression of astonishment and childish bewilderment passed across his face.

Days merged into weeks and still John (he had given no other name and none was asked of him) sat quietly in his corner, a silent listener to all the discussions and conversations that were continually taking place at Friendship House. Intensely he observed how the tertiaries dealt with the many clients of St.

Francis, who came in an endless stream, begging for food, clothing, moral and material help.

Occasionally he smiled a funny, angry, crooked smile when someone would suggest praying for the coffee that was getting low, or asking St. Francis to send coal, which was badly needed. Yet, little by little, as the coffee came and the coal arrived, the smile vanished from his face to be replaced by a puzzled look of concentration, as if he were trying to understand something that eluded his mind.

At the beginning of the third week, he sat before the tertiary's desk and resolutely told her that, since he was a communist, he desired to attend their meetings-and would she object to it?

Sorrowfully, she lifted her face and answered: "No, you can do what you want, John. I will only ask you never to discuss what you hear there with anyone here during my absence. It wouldn't be fair to the others, would it?" He agreed that it would not and that he would not do so.

From that time on, he was often absent half of the day. But he was always home for supper, after which the tertiaries would ask him what he had heard that day at his communist meetings. He would answer and there would start a long discussion, point by point, of the Catholic views as opposed to those of communism. Catholic papers would come out, and books would be piled high on the table, in substantiation of this point or that.

John ceased to be silent. He became the center of all conversations, stimulating others and arguing with them, drawing all present into the fray.

One day, he carried away a bunch of Catholic papers that

dealt with a social question being discussed, and informed everybody at large that he was "taking a few papers to my friends the communists" because "they need broadening out."

"There's a lot of sense to the encyclicals, and they'd better hear some of it." On this remark, he slammed the door and left, leaving everyone a little dizzy at the prospect of a communist teaching the encyclicals of the popes to another group of communists. But the ways of God are incomprehensible to man.

A few days later, on a Sunday, while the tertiaries were bemoaning the absence of one of their group, which made them short-handed for the sale of the Catholic paper at the church door, John cheerfully offered to replace him. A few moments later, John was lustily calling out: "Buy a Catholic paper! Help us to do Catholic Action to offset communist and atheist action!" He whistled a joyful tune on the way home and saw nothing out of the way in his method of action, dismissing all thanks with a "one good turn deserves another."

During that time, John—of his own volition—took in hand the distribution of work to those of the 'Brothers Christopher' who evinced a desire to help. Soon, the house shone like a jewel: windows were polished, floors scrubbed, and the cook wore a happy smile because of some new cheap recipe John had dug up. The dishwashers were through in half the time, thanks to a new soap solution he invented.

Everyone agreed he was efficient, and he smilingly called it his "communist technique." The tertiaries just as smilingly answered that he had "become Catholic after a while."

Once, when the place was empty of visitors and friends, he

asked a tertiary why they devoted their lives to the poor when they all could have good jobs. Why were they living in the slums when their families had lovely homes? Why this simple hospitality—which asked no questions, nor any return? Why this eternal begging for others—so hard and so difficult?

Gently, the tertiary looked into his eyes and slowly answered: "Today's are tragic days when people have forgotten God. And because of that, some who still remember Him have left their homes and friends to live among the needy and poor. They come to help them, to share with them their life of hardship, to atone for the rich who have forgotten their 'brothers and sisters', the poor, who must carry the heavy load which the greed and injustice of their fellow men have thrust upon them.

"Not all are called to a life like this. But those who have this vocation are privileged and rich beyond the dreams of men, for they do it out of love of Christ, whom they see in the poor and downtrodden. It's all really very simple, and so very wonderful."

For a moment both remained silent. Then John told her that he was born a Catholic, and that he had a brother who was a priest. At an early age he had left home and wandered to many places, but he'd always kept his faith—until he began to work for a selfish Catholic employer, whose greed made hundreds of his workers miserable and unhappy. Watching all this, John had lost his faith and had joined the communist party.

As John finished speaking, he suddenly jumped up, grabbed his hat and was gone. That evening, many prayers were said for him, and for the many tired 'lost souls' like him.

Christmas was coming. And in the hustle and bustle of

preparing a little feast for 600 children, and a Christmas dinner for the many Brothers Christopher, the tertiaries forgot about John a little. Besides, they knew he'd found a job and another place to live, and now visited Friendship House rarely.

Christmas Eve came. As everyone was making ready to go to Midnight Mass, John walked in and announced that he had brought a Christmas present to them, but he would give it later. Everyone thanked him, but suggested that he had not worked long enough to allow himself the luxury of buying Christmas presents. John only smiled.

In the rush to get to Mass on time, John was lost sight of. Suddenly, in the church, one of the tertiaries excitedly pointed out to the others a man getting out of the confessional—it was John. Astonished, and glad beyond words, the tertiaries rendered thanks to God; it was with tears of happiness that they saw John approach the communion rail.

Later, on their way home under the starry winter sky, he said: "This is my Christmas present to you. I had ceased to believe in God, but I saw Him living and walking again in the Toronto slums. You showed Him to me." All remained silent, for they knew what a great miracle had taken place, and that indeed the Christ Child had sent them a most wonderful gift—but they had done so little to deserve it.

Once more, they realized that the ways of God are incomprehensible, and they rendered thanks. Today, John works in a distant northern mining camp. He is a real apostle of Christ and the spirit of St. Francis lives in him. Many are the souls he has brought back to God.

Let us never forget that around us there are thousands of men like John, and that a kind word or a kind gesture might make the difference between a saved soul or a lost one. Let us therefore remember to love our fellow men as St. Francis used to love them, and leave the rest to God's grace.

The Other Wise Man

Henry Van Dyke (1852–1933)

"And those who would see wonderful things must often be ready to travel alone."

In this delightful tale, we follow the pilgrimage of the "other wise man," a fourth sage from the East that set out to find the Christ but missed the journey of the other three. We glimpse something of the ardor of natural philosophy, the nobility of the passionate quest, and the way that God's grace is open to all who seek with a true heart.

YOU KNOW the story of the Three Wise Men of the East, and how they travelled from far away to offer their gifts at the manger-cradle in Bethlehem. But have you ever heard the story of the Other Wise Man, who also saw the star in its rising, and set out to follow it, yet did not arrive with his brethren in the presence of the young child Jesus? Of the great desire of this fourth pilgrim, and how it was denied, yet accomplished in the denial; of his many wanderings and the probations of his soul; of the long way of his seeking and the strange way of his finding the One whom he sought—I would tell the tale as I have heard fragments of it in the Hall of Dreams, in the palace of the Heart of Man.

I

In the days when Augustus Caesar was master of many kings and Herod reigned in Jerusalem, there lived in the city of Ecbatana, among the mountains of Persia, a certain man named Artaban. His house stood close to the outermost of the walls which encircled the royal treasury. From his roof he could look over the seven-fold battlements of black and white and crimson and blue and red and silver and gold, to the hill where the summer palace of the Parthian emperors glittered like a jewel in a crown.

Around the dwelling of Artaban spread a fair garden, a tangle of flowers and fruit-trees, watered by a score of streams descending from the slopes of Mount Orontes, and made musical by innumerable birds. But all colour was lost in the soft and odorous darkness of the late September night, and all sounds were hushed in the deep charm of its silence, save the splashing of the water, like a voice half-sobbing and half-laughing under the shadows. High above the trees a dim glow of light shone through the curtained arches of the upper chamber, where the master of the house was holding council with his friends.

He stood by the doorway to greet his guests—a tall, dark man of about forty years, with brilliant eyes set near together under his broad brow, and firm lines graven around his fine, thin lips; the brow of a dreamer and the mouth of a soldier, a man of sensitive feeling but inflexible will—one of those who, in whatever age they may live, are born for inward conflict and a life of quest.

His robe was of pure white wool, thrown over a tunic of silk; and a white, pointed cap, with long lapels at the sides, rested on his flowing black hair. It was the dress of the ancient priesthood of the Magi, called the fire-worshippers.

"Welcome!" he said, in his low, pleasant voice, as one after another entered the room—"welcome, Abdus; peace be with you, Rhodaspes and Tigranes, and with you my father, Abgarus. You are all welcome. This house grows bright with the joy of your presence."

There were nine of the men, differing widely in age, but alike in the richness of their dress of many-coloured silks, and in the massive golden collars around their necks, marking them as Parthian nobles, and in the winged circles of gold resting upon their breasts, the sign of the followers of Zoroaster.

They took their places around a small black altar at the end of the room, where a tiny flame was burning. Artaban, standing beside it, and waving a barsom of thin tamarisk branches above the fire, fed it with dry sticks of pine and fragrant oils. Then he began the ancient chant of the Yasna, and the voices of his companions joined in the hymn to Ahura-Mazda:

We worship the Spirit Divine,
   all wisdom and goodness possessing,
Surrounded by Holy Immortals,
   the givers of bounty and blessing;
We joy in the work of His hands,
   His truth and His power confessing.

We praise all the things that are pure,
   for these are His only Creation
The thoughts that are true, and the words
   and the deeds that have won approbation;
These are supported by Him,
   and for these we make adoration.
Hear us, O Mazda! Thou livest
   in truth and in heavenly gladness;
Cleanse us from falsehood, and keep us
   from evil and bondage to badness,
Pour out the light and the joy of Thy life
   on our darkness and sadness.

Shine on our gardens and fields,
   shine on our working and waving;
Shine on the whole race of man,
   believing and unbelieving;
Shine on us now through the night,
Shine on us now in Thy might,
The flame of our holy love
   and the song of our worship receiving.

The fire rose with the chant, throbbing as if the flame responded to the music, until it cast a bright illumination through the whole apartment, revealing its simplicity and splendour.

The floor was laid with tiles of dark blue veined with white; pilasters of twisted silver stood out against the blue walls; the clear-story of round-arched windows above them was hung with azure silk; the vaulted ceiling was a pavement of blue stones, like the body of heaven in its clearness, sown with silver stars. From the four corners of the roof hung four golden magic-wheels, called the tongues of the gods. At the eastern end, behind the altar, there were two dark-red pillars of porphyry; above them a lintel of the same stone, on which was carved the figure of a winged archer, with his arrow set to the string and his bow drawn.

The doorway between the pillars, which opened upon the terrace of the roof, was covered with a heavy curtain of the colour of a ripe pomegranate, embroidered with innumerable golden rays shooting upward from the floor. In effect the room was like a quiet, starry night, all azure and silver, flushed in the cast with rosy promise of the dawn. It was, as the house of a man should be, an expression of the character and spirit of the master.

He turned to his friends when the song was ended, and invited them to be seated on the divan at the western end of the room.

"You have come to-night," said he, looking around the circle, "at my call, as the faithful scholars of Zoroaster, to renew your worship and rekindle your faith in the God of Purity, even as this fire has been rekindled on the altar. We worship not the fire, but Him of whom it is the chosen symbol, because it is the purest of all created things. It speaks to us of one who is Light and Truth. Is it not so, my father?"

"It is well said, my son," answered the venerable Abgarus. "The enlightened are never idolaters. They lift the veil of form and go in to the shrine of reality, and new light and truth are coming to them continually through the old symbols." "Hear me, then, my father and my friends," said Artaban, "while I tell you of the new light and truth that have come to me through the most ancient of all signs. We have searched the secrets of Nature together, and studied the healing virtues of water and fire and the plants. We have read also the books of prophecy in which the future is dimly foretold in words that are hard to understand. But the highest of all learning is the knowledge of the stars. To trace their course is to untangle the threads of the mystery of life from the beginning to the end. If we could follow them perfectly, nothing would be hidden from us. But is not our knowledge of them still incomplete? Are there not many stars still beyond our horizon—lights that are known only to the dwellers in the far south-land, among the spice-trees of Punt and the gold mines of Ophir?"

There was a murmur of assent among the listeners.

"The stars," said Tigranes, "are the thoughts of the Eternal. They are numberless. But the thoughts of man can be counted, like the years of his life. The wisdom of the Magi is the greatest of all wisdoms on earth, because it knows its own ignorance. And that is the secret of power. We keep men always looking and waiting for a new sunrise. But we ourselves understand that the darkness is equal to the light, and that the conflict between them will never be ended."

"That does not satisfy me," answered Artaban, "for, if the waiting must be endless, if there could be no fulfilment of it, then it would not be wisdom to look and wait. We should become like those new teachers of the Greeks, who say that there is no truth, and that the only wise men are those who spend their lives in discovering and exposing the lies that have been believed in the world. But the new sunrise will certainly appear in the appointed time. Do not our own books tell us that this will come to pass, and that men will see the brightness of a great light?"

"That is true," said the voice of Abgarus; "every faithful disciple of Zoroaster knows the prophecy of the Avesta, and carries the word in his heart. 'In that day Sosiosh the Victorious shall arise out of the number of the prophets in the east country. Around him shall shine a mighty brightness, and he shall make life everlasting, incorruptible, and immortal, and the dead shall rise again.'"

"This is a dark saying," said Tigranes, "and it may be that we shall never understand it. It is better to consider the things that are near at hand, and to increase the influence of the Magi in their own country, rather than to look for one who may be a stranger, and to whom we must resign our power."

The others seemed to approve these words. There was a silent feeling of agreement manifest among them; their looks responded with that indefinable expression which always follows when a speaker has uttered the thought that has been slumbering in the hearts of his listeners. But Artaban turned to Abgarus with a glow on his face, and said:

"My father, I have kept this prophecy in the secret place of my soul. Religion without a great hope would be like an altar without a living fire. And now the flame has burned more brightly, and by the light of it I have read other words which also have come from the fountain of Truth, and speak yet more clearly of the rising of the Victorious One in his brightness."

He drew from the breast of his tunic two small rolls of fine parchment, with writing upon them, and unfolded them carefully upon his knee.

"In the years that are lost in the past, long before our fathers came into the land of Babylon, there were wise men in Chaldea, from whom the first of the Magi learned the secret of the heavens. And of these Balaam the son of Beor was one of the mightiest. Hear the words of his prophecy: 'There shall come a star out of Jacob, and a sceptre shall arise out of Israel.'"

The lips of Tigranes drew downward with contempt, as he said:

"Judah was a captive by the waters of Babylon, and the sons of Jacob were in bondage to our kings. The tribes of Israel are scattered through the mountains like lost sheep, and from the remnant that dwells in Judea under the yoke of Rome neither star nor sceptre shall arise."

"And yet," answered Artaban, "it was the Hebrew Daniel, the mighty searcher of dreams, the counsellor of kings, the wise Belteshazzar, who was most honoured and beloved of our great King Cyrus. A prophet of sure things and a reader of the thoughts of the Eternal, Daniel proved himself to our people. And these are the words that he wrote." (Artaban read from the second roll.) "Know, therefore, and understand that from the going forth of the commandment to restore Jerusalem, unto the Anointed One, the Prince, the time shall be seven and threescore and two weeks."

"But, my son," said Abgarus, doubtfully, "these are mystical numbers. Who can interpret them, or who can find the key that shall unlock their meaning?"

Artaban answered: "It has been shown to me and to my three companions among the Magi—Caspar, Melchior, and Balthazar. We have searched the ancient tablets of Chaldea and computed the time. It falls in this year. We have studied the sky, and in the spring of the year we saw two of the greatest planets draw near together in the sign of the Fish, which is the house of the Hebrews. We also saw a new star there, which shone for one night and then vanished. Now again the two great planets are meeting. This night is their conjunction. My three brothers are watching by the ancient Temple of the Seven Spheres, at Borsippa, in Babylonia, and I am watching here. If the star shines again, they will wait ten days for me at the temple, and then we will set out together for Jerusalem, to see and worship the promised one who shall be born King of Israel. I believe the sign will come. I have made ready for the journey. I have sold my possessions, and bought these three jewels—a sapphire, a ruby, and a pearl—to carry them as tribute to the King. And I ask you to go with me on the pilgrimage, that we may have joy together in finding the Prince who is worthy to be served."

While he was speaking he thrust his hand into the inmost fold of his girdle and drew out three great gems—one blue as a fragment of the night sky, one redder than a ray of sunrise, and one as pure as the peak of a snow-mountain at twilight—and laid them on the outspread scrolls before him.

But his friends looked on with strange and alien eyes. A veil of doubt and mistrust came over their faces, like a fog creeping up from the marshes to hide the hills. They glanced at each other with looks of wonder and pity, as those who have listened to incredible sayings, the story of a wild vision, or the proposal of an impossible enterprise.

At last Tigranes said: "Artaban, this is a vain dream. It comes from too much looking upon the stars and the cherishing of lofty thoughts. It would be wiser to spend the time in gathering money for the new fire-temple at Chala. No king will ever rise from the broken race of Israel, and no end will ever come to the eternal strife of light and darkness. He who looks for it is a chaser of shadows. Farewell."

And another said: "Artaban, I have no knowledge of these things, and my office as guardian of the royal treasure binds me here. The quest is not for me. But if thou must follow it, fare thee well."

And another said: "In my house there sleeps a new bride, and I cannot leave her nor take her with me on this strange journey. This quest is not for me. But may thy steps be prospered wherever thou goest. So, farewell."

And another said: "I am ill and unfit for hardship, but there is a man among my servants whom I will send with thee when thou goest, to bring me word how thou farest."

So, one by one, they left the house of Artaban. But Abgarus, the oldest and the one who loved him the best, lingered after the others had gone, and said, gravely: "My son, it may be that the light of truth is in this sign that has appeared in the skies, and then it will surely lead to the Prince and the mighty brightness. Or it may be that it is only a shadow of the light, as Tigranes has said, and then he who follows it will have a long pilgrimage and a fruitless search. But it is better to follow even the shadow of the best than to remain content with the worst. And those who would see wonderful things must often be ready to travel alone. I am too old for this journey, but my heart shall be a companion of thy pilgrimage day and night, and I shall know the end of thy quest. Go in peace."

Then Abgarus went out of the azure chamber with its silver stars, and Artaban was left in solitude.

He gathered up the jewels and replaced them in his girdle. For a long time he stood and watched the flame that flickered and sank upon the altar. Then he crossed the hall, lifted the heavy curtain, and passed out between the pillars of porphyry to the terrace on the roof.

The shiver that runs through the earth ere she rouses from her night-sleep had already begun, and the cool wind that heralds the daybreak was drawing downward from the lofty snow-traced ravines of Mount Orontes. Birds, half-awakened, crept and chirped among the rustling leaves, and the smell of ripened grapes came in brief wafts from the arbours.

Far over the eastern plain a white mist stretched like a lake. But where the distant peaks of Zagros serrated the western horizon the sky was clear. Jupiter and Saturn rolled together like drops of lambent flame about to blend in one.

As Artaban watched them, a steel-blue spark was born out of the darkness beneath, rounding itself with purple splendours to a crimson sphere, and spiring upward through rays of saffron and orange into a point of white radiance. Tiny and infinitely remote, yet perfect in every part, it pulsated in the enormous vault as if the three jewels in the Magian's girdle had mingled and been transformed into a living heart of light.

He bowed his head. He covered his brow with his hands.

"It is the sign," he said. "The King is coming, and I will go to meet him."

II

All night long, Vasda, the swiftest of Artaban's horses, had been waiting, saddled and bridled, in her stall, pawing the ground impatiently, and shaking her bit as if she shared the eagerness of her master's purpose, though she knew not its meaning.

Before the birds had fully roused to their strong, high, joyful chant of morning song, before the white mist had begun to lift lazily from the plain, the Other Wise Man was in the saddle, riding swiftly along the high-road, which skirted the base of Mount Orontes, westward.

How close, how intimate is the comradeship between a man and his favourite horse on a long journey. It is a silent, comprehensive friendship, an intercourse beyond the need of words.

They drink at the same way-side springs, and sleep under the same guardian stars. They are conscious together of the subduing spell of nightfall and the quickening joy of daybreak. The master shares his evening meal with his hungry companion, and feels the soft, moist lips caressing the palm of his hand as they close over the morsel of bread. In the gray dawn he is roused from his bivouac by the gentle stir of a warm, sweet breath over his sleeping face, and looks up into the eyes of his faithful fellow-traveller, ready and waiting for the toil of the day. Surely, unless he is a pagan and an unbeliever, by whatever name he calls upon his God, he will thank Him for this voiceless sympathy, this dumb affection, and his morning prayer will embrace a double blessing—God bless us both, the horse and the rider, and keep our feet from falling and our souls from death!

Then, through the keen morning air, the swift hoofs beat their tattoo along the road, keeping time to the pulsing of two hearts that are moved with the same eager desire—to conquer space, to devour the distance, to attain the goal of the journey.

Artaban must indeed ride wisely and well if he would keep the appointed hour with the other Magi; for the route was a hundred and fifty parasangs, and fifteen was the utmost that he could travel in a day. But he knew Vasda's strength, and pushed forward without anxiety, making the fixed distance every day, though he must travel late into the night, and in the morning long before sunrise.

He passed along the brown slopes of Mount Orontes, furrowed by the rocky courses of a hundred torrents.

He crossed the level plains of the Nisaeans, where the famous herds of horses, feeding in the wide pastures, tossed their heads at Vasda's approach, and galloped away with a thunder of many hoofs, and flocks of wild birds rose suddenly from the swampy meadows, wheeling in great circles with a shining flutter of innumerable wings and shrill cries of surprise.

He traversed the fertile fields of Concabar, where the dust from the threshing-floors filled the air with a golden mist, half hiding the huge temple of Astarte with its four hundred pillars.

At Baghistan, among the rich gardens watered by fountains from the rock, he looked up at the mountain thrusting its immense rugged brow out over the road, and saw the figure of King Darius trampling upon his fallen foes, and the proud list of his wars and conquests graven high upon the face of the eternal cliff.

Over many a cold and desolate pass, crawling painfully across the wind-swept shoulders of the hills; down many a black mountain-gorge, where the river roared and raced before him like a savage guide; across many a smiling vale, with terraces of yellow limestone full of vines and fruit-trees; through the oak-groves of Carine and the dark Gates of Zagros, walled in by precipices; into the ancient city of Chala, where the people of Samaria had been kept in captivity long ago; and out again by the mighty portal, riven through the encircling hills, where he saw the image of the High Priest of the Magi sculptured on the wall of rock, with hand uplifted as if to bless the centuries of pilgrims; past the entrance of the narrow defile, filled from end to end with orchards of peaches and figs, through which the river Gyndes foamed down to meet him; over the broad rice-fields, where the autumnal vapours spread their deathly mists; following along the course of the river, under tremulous shadows of poplar and tamarind, among the lower hills; and out upon the flat plain, where the road ran straight as an arrow through the stubble-fields and parched meadows; past the city of Ctesiphon, where the Parthian emperors reigned, and the vast metropolis of Seleucia which Alexander built; across the swirling floods of Tigris and the many channels of Euphrates, flowing yellow through the corn-lands—Artaban pressed onward until he arrived, at nightfall on the tenth day, beneath the shattered walls of populous Babylon.

Vasda was almost spent, and Artaban would gladly have turned into the city to find rest and refreshment for himself and for her. But he knew that it was three hours' journey yet to the Temple of the Seven Spheres, and he must reach the place by midnight if he would find his comrades waiting. So he did not halt, but rode steadily across the stubble-fields.

A grove of date-palms made an island of gloom in the pale yellow sea. As she passed into the shadow Vasda slackened her pace, and began to pick her way more carefully.

Near the farther end of the darkness an excess of caution seemed to fall upon her. She scented some danger or difficulty; it was not in her heart to fly from it—only to be prepared for it, and to meet it wisely, as a good horse should do. The grove was close and silent as the tomb; not a leaf rustled, not a bird sang.

She felt her steps before her delicately, carrying her head low, and sighing now and then with apprehension. At last she gave a quick breath of anxiety and dismay, and stood stock-still,

THE OTHER WISE MAN

quivering in every muscle, before a dark object in the shadow of the last palm-tree.

Artaban dismounted. The dim starlight revealed the form of a man lying across the road. His humble dress and the outline of his haggard face showed that he was probably one of the Hebrews who still dwelt in great numbers around the city. His pallid skin, dry and yellow as parchment, bore the mark of the deadly fever which ravaged the marsh-lands in autumn. The chill of death was in his lean hand, and, as Artaban released it, the arm fell back inertly upon the motionless breast.

He turned away with a thought of pity, leaving the body to that strange burial which the Magians deemed most fitting—the funeral of the desert, from which the kites and vultures rise on dark wings, and the beasts of prey slink furtively away. When they are gone there is only a heap of white bones on the sand.

But, as he turned, a long, faint, ghostly sigh came from the man's lips. The bony fingers gripped the hem of the Magian's robe and held him fast.

Artaban's heart leaped to his throat, not with fear, but with a dumb resentment at the importunity of this blind delay.

How could he stay here in the darkness to minister to a dying stranger? What claim had this unknown fragment of human life upon his compassion or his service? If he lingered but for an hour he could hardly reach Borsippa at the appointed time. His companions would think he had given up the journey. They would go without him. He would lose his quest.

But if he went on now, the man would surely die. If Artaban stayed, life might be restored. His spirit throbbed and fluttered with the urgency of the crisis. Should he risk the great reward of his faith for the sake of a single deed of charity? Should he turn aside, if only for a moment, from the following of the star, to give a cup of cold water to a poor, perishing Hebrew?

"God of truth and purity," he prayed, "direct me in the holy path, the way of wisdom which Thou only knowest."

Then he turned back to the sick man. Loosening the grasp of his hand, he carried him to a little mound at the foot of the palm-tree.

He unbound the thick folds of the turban and opened the garment above the sunken breast. He brought water from one of the small canals nearby, and moistened the sufferer's brow and mouth. He mingled a draught of one of those simple but potent remedies which he carried always in his girdle—for the Magians were physicians as well as astrologers—and poured it slowly between the colourless lips. Hour after hour he laboured as only a skilful healer of disease can do. At last the man's strength returned; he sat up and looked about him.

"Who art thou?" he said, in the rude dialect of the country, "and why hast thou sought me here to bring back my life?"

"I am Artaban the Magian, of the city of Ecbatana, and I am going to Jerusalem in search of one who is to be born King of the Jews, a great Prince and Deliverer of all men. I dare not delay any longer upon my journey, for the caravan that has waited for me may depart without me. But see, here is all that I have left of bread and wine, and here is a potion of healing herbs. When thy strength is restored thou canst find the dwellings of the Hebrews among the houses of Babylon."

The Jew raised his trembling hand solemnly to heaven.

"Now may the God of Abraham and Isaac and Jacob bless and prosper the journey of the merciful, and bring him in peace to his desired haven. Stay! I have nothing to give thee in return—only this: that I can tell thee where the Messiah must be sought. For our prophets have said that he should be born not in Jerusalem, but in Bethlehem of Judah. May the Lord bring thee in safety to that place, because thou hast had pity upon the sick."

It was already long past midnight. Artaban rode in haste, and Vasda, restored by the brief rest, ran eagerly through the silent plain and swam the channels of the river. She put forth the remnant of her strength, and fled over the ground like a gazelle.

But the first beam of the rising sun sent a long shadow before her as she entered upon the final stadium of the journey, and the eyes of Artaban, anxiously scanning the great mound of Nimrod and the Temple of the Seven Spheres, could discern no trace of his friends.

The many-coloured terraces of black and orange and red and yellow and green and blue and white, shattered by the convulsions of nature, and crumbling under the repeated blows of human violence, still glittered like a ruined rainbow in the morning light.

Artaban rode swiftly around the hill. He dismounted and climbed to the highest terrace, looking out toward the west.

The huge desolation of the marshes stretched away to the horizon and the border of the desert. Bitterns stood by the stagnant pools and jackals skulked through the low bushes; but there was no sign of the caravan of the Wise Men, far or near.

At the edge of the terrace he saw a little cairn of broken

bricks, and under them a piece of papyrus. He caught it up and read: "We have waited past the midnight, and can delay no longer. We go to find the King. Follow us across the desert."

Artaban sat down upon the ground and covered his head in despair.

"How can I cross the desert," said he, "with no food and with a spent horse? I must return to Babylon, sell my sapphire, and buy a train of camels, and provision for the journey. I may never overtake my friends. Only God the merciful knows whether I shall not lose the sight of the King because I tarried to show mercy."

III

There was a silence in the Hall of Dreams, where I was listening to the story of the Other Wise Man. Through this silence I saw, but very dimly, his figure passing over the dreary undulations of the desert, high upon the back of his camel, rocking steadily onward like a ship over the waves.

The land of death spread its cruel net around him. The stony waste bore no fruit but briers and thorns. The dark ledges of rock thrust themselves above the surface here and there, like the bones of perished monsters. Arid and inhospitable mountain-ranges rose before him, furrowed with dry channels of ancient torrents, white and ghastly as scars on the face of nature. Shifting hills of treacherous sand were heaped like tombs along the horizon. By day, the fierce heat pressed its intolerable burden on the quivering air. No living creature moved on the dumb, swooning earth, but tiny jerboas scuttling through the parched bushes, or lizards vanishing in the clefts of the rock. By night the jackals prowled and barked in the distance, and the lion made the black ravines echo with his hollow roaring, while a bitter, blighting chill followed the fever of the day. Through heat and cold, the Magian moved steadily onward.

Then I saw the gardens and orchards of Damascus, watered by the streams of Abana and Pharpar, with their sloping swards inlaid with bloom, and their thickets of myrrh and roses. I saw the long, snowy ridge of Hermon, and the dark groves of cedars, and the valley of the Jordan, and the blue waters of the Lake of Galilee, and the fertile plain of Esdraelon, and the hills of Ephraim, and the highlands of Judah. Through all these I followed the figure of Artaban moving steadily onward, until he arrived at Bethlehem. And it was the third day after the three Wise Men had come to that place and had found Mary and Joseph, with the young child, Jesus, and had laid their gifts of gold and frankincense and myrrh at his feet.

Then the Other Wise Man drew near, weary, but full of hope, bearing his ruby and his pearl to offer to the King. "For now at last," he said, "I shall surely find him, though I be alone, and later than my brethren. This is the place of which the Hebrew exile told me that the prophets had spoken, and here I shall behold the rising of the great light. But I must inquire about the visit of my brethren, and to what house the star directed them, and to whom they presented their tribute."

The streets of the village seemed to be deserted, and Artaban wondered whether the men had all gone up to the hill-pastures to bring down their sheep. From the open door of a cottage he heard the sound of a woman's voice singing softly. He entered and found a young mother hushing her baby to rest. She told him of the strangers from the far East who had appeared in the village three days ago, and how they said that a star had guided them to the place where Joseph of Nazareth was lodging with his wife and her new-born child, and how they had paid reverence to the child and given him many rich gifts.

"But the travellers disappeared again," she continued, "as suddenly as they had come. We were afraid at the strangeness of their visit. We could not understand it. The man of Nazareth took the child and his mother, and fled away that same night secretly, and it was whispered that they were going to Egypt. Ever since, there has been a spell upon the village; something evil hangs over it. They say that the Roman soldiers are coming from Jerusalem to force a new tax from us, and the men have driven the flocks and herds far back among the hills, and hidden themselves to escape it."

Artaban listened to her gentle, timid speech, and the child in her arms looked up in his face and smiled, stretching out its rosy hands to grasp at the winged circle of gold on his breast. His heart warmed to the touch. It seemed like a greeting of love and trust to one who had journeyed long in loneliness and perplexity, fighting with his own doubts and fears, and following a light that was veiled in clouds.

"Why might not this child have been the promised Prince?" he asked within himself, as he touched its soft cheek. "Kings have been born ere now in lowlier houses than this, and the favourite of the stars may rise even from a cottage. But it has not seemed good to the God of wisdom to reward my search so soon and so easily. The one whom I seek has gone before me; and now I must follow the King to Egypt."

The young mother laid the baby in its cradle, and rose to minister to the wants of the strange guest that fate had brought into her house. She set food before him, the plain fare of peasants, but willingly offered, and therefore full of refreshment for the soul as well as for the body. Artaban accepted it gratefully; and, as he ate, the child fell into a happy slumber, and murmured sweetly in its dreams, and a great peace filled the room.

But suddenly there came the noise of a wild confusion in the streets of the village, a shrieking and wailing of women's voices, a clangour of brazen trumpets and a clashing of swords, and a desperate cry: "The soldiers! The soldiers of Herod! They are killing our children."

The young mother's face grew white with terror. She clasped her child to her bosom, and crouched motionless in the darkest corner of the room, covering him with the folds of her robe, lest he should wake and cry.

But Artaban went quickly and stood in the doorway of the house. His broad shoulders filled the portal from side to side, and the peak of his white cap all but touched the lintel.

The soldiers came hurrying down the street with bloody hands and dripping swords. At the sight of the stranger in his imposing dress they hesitated with surprise. The captain of the band approached the threshold to thrust him aside. But Artaban did not stir. His face was as calm as though he were watching the stars, and in his eyes there burned that steady radiance before which even the half-tamed hunting leopard shrinks, and the bloodhound pauses in his leap. He held the soldier silently for an instant, and then said in a low voice:

"I am all alone in this place, and I am waiting to give this jewel to the prudent captain who will leave me in peace."

He showed the ruby, glistening in the hollow of his hand like a great drop of blood.

The captain was amazed at the splendour of the gem. The pupils of his eyes expanded with desire, and the hard lines of greed wrinkled around his lips. He stretched out his hand and took the ruby.

"March on!" he cried to his men, "there is no child here. The house is empty."

The clamor and the clang of arms passed down the street as the headlong fury of the chase sweeps by the secret covert where the trembling deer is hidden. Artaban re-entered the cottage. He turned his face to the east and prayed:

"God of truth, forgive my sin! I have said the thing that is not, to save the life of a child. And two of my gifts are gone. I have spent for man that which was meant for God. Shall I ever be worthy to see the face of the King?"

But the voice of the woman, weeping for joy in the shadow behind him, said very gently:

"Because thou hast saved the life of my little one, may the Lord bless thee and keep thee; the Lord make His face to shine upon thee and be gracious unto thee; the Lord lift up His countenance upon thee and give thee peace."

IV

Again there was a silence in the Hall of Dreams, deeper and more mysterious than the first interval, and I understood that the years of Artaban were flowing very swiftly under the stillness, and I caught only a glimpse, here and there, of the river of his life shining through the mist that concealed its course.

I saw him moving among the throngs of men in populous Egypt, seeking everywhere for traces of the household that had come down from Bethlehem, and finding them under the spreading sycamore-trees of Heliopolis, and beneath the walls of the Roman fortress of New Babylon beside the Nile—traces so faint and dim that they vanished before him continually, as footprints on the wet river-sand glisten for a moment with moisture and then disappear.

I saw him again at the foot of the pyramids, which lifted their sharp points into the intense saffron glow of the sunset sky, changeless monuments of the perishable glory and the imperishable hope of man. He looked up into the face of the crouching Sphinx and vainly tried to read the meaning of the calm eyes and smiling mouth. Was it, indeed, the mockery of all effort and all aspiration, as Tigranes had said—the cruel jest of a riddle that has no answer, a search that never can succeed? Or was there a touch of pity and encouragement in that inscrutable smile—a promise that even the defeated should attain a victory, and the disappointed should discover a prize, and the ignorant should be made wise, and the blind should see, and the wandering should come into the haven at last?

I saw him again in an obscure house of Alexandria, taking counsel with a Hebrew rabbi. The venerable man, bending over the rolls of parchment on which the prophecies of Israel were written, read aloud the pathetic words which foretold the sufferings of the promised Messiah—the despised and rejected of men, the man of sorrows and acquainted with grief.

"And remember, my son," said he, fixing his eyes upon the face of Artaban, "the King whom thou seekest is not to be found in a palace, nor among the rich and powerful. If the light of the world and the glory of Israel had been appointed to come with the greatness of earthly splendour, it must have appeared long ago. For no son of Abraham will ever again rival the power which Joseph had in the palaces of Egypt, or the magnificence of Solomon throned between the lions in Jerusalem. But the light for which the world is waiting is a new light, the glory that shall rise out of patient and triumphant suffering. And the kingdom which is to be established forever is a new kingdom, the royalty of unconquerable love.

"I do not know how this shall come to pass, nor how the turbulent kings and peoples of earth shall be brought to acknowledge the Messiah and pay homage to him. But this I know. Those who seek him will do well to look among the poor and the lowly, the sorrowful and the oppressed."

So I saw the Other Wise Man again and again, travelling from place to place, and searching among the people of the dispersion, with whom the little family from Bethlehem might, perhaps, have found a refuge. He passed through countries where famine lay heavy upon the land, and the poor were crying for bread. He made his dwelling in plague-stricken cities where the sick were languishing in the bitter companionship of helpless misery. He visited the oppressed and the afflicted in the gloom of subterranean prisons, and the crowded wretchedness of slave-markets, and the weary toil of galley-ships. In all this populous and intricate world of anguish, though he found none to worship, he found many to help. He fed the hungry, and clothed the naked, and healed the sick, and comforted the captive; and his years passed more swiftly than the weaver's shuttle that flashes back and forth through the loom while the web grows and the pattern is completed.

It seemed almost as if he had forgotten his quest. But once I saw him for a moment as he stood alone at sunrise, waiting at the gate of a Roman prison. He had taken from a secret resting-place in his bosom the pearl, the last of his jewels. As he looked at it, a mellower lustre, a soft and iridescent light, full of shifting gleams of azure and rose, trembled upon its surface. It seemed to have absorbed some reflection of the lost sapphire and ruby. So the secret purpose of a noble life draws into itself the memories of past joy and past sorrow. All that has helped it, all that has hindered it, is transfused by a subtle magic into its very essence. It becomes more luminous and precious the longer it is carried close to the warmth of the beating heart.

Then, at last, while I was thinking of this pearl, and of its meaning, I heard the end of the story of the Other Wise Man.

V

Three-and-thirty years of the life of Artaban had passed away, and he was still a pilgrim and a seeker after light. His hair, once darker than the cliffs of Zagros, was now white as the wintry snow that covered them. His eyes, that once flashed like flames of fire, were dull as embers smouldering among the ashes.

Worn and weary and ready to die, but still looking for the King, he had come for the last time to Jerusalem. He had often visited the holy city before, and had searched all its lanes and crowded bevels and black prisons without finding any trace of the family of Nazarenes who had fled from Bethlehem long ago. But now it seemed as if he must make one more effort, and something whispered in his heart that, at last, he might succeed.

It was the season of the Passover. The city was thronged with strangers. The children of Israel, scattered in far lands, had returned to the Temple for the great feast, and there had been a confusion of tongues in the narrow streets for many days.

But on this day a singular agitation was visible in the multitude. The sky was veiled with a portentous gloom. Currents of excitement seemed to flash through the crowd. A secret tide was sweeping them all one way. The clatter of sandals and the soft, thick sound of thousands of bare feet shuffling over the stones, flowed unceasingly along the street that leads to the Damascus gate.

Artaban joined a group of people from his own country, Parthian Jews who had come up to keep the Passover, and inquired of them the cause of the tumult, and where they were going.

"We are going," they answered, "to the place called Golgotha, outside the city walls, where there is to be an execution. Have you not heard what has happened? Two famous robbers are to be crucified, and with them another, called Jesus of Nazareth, a man who has done many wonderful works among the people, so that they love him greatly. But the priests and elders have said that he must die, because he gave himself out to be the Son of God. And Pilate has sent him to the cross because he said that he was the 'King of the Jews.'"

How strangely these familiar words fell upon the tired heart of Artaban! They had led him for a lifetime over land and sea. And now they came to him mysteriously, like a message of despair. The King had arisen, but he had been denied and cast out. He was about to perish. Perhaps he was already dying. Could it be the same who had been born in Bethlehem thirty-three years ago, at whose birth the star had appeared in heaven, and of whose coming the prophets had spoken?

Artaban's heart beat unsteadily with that troubled, doubtful apprehension which is the excitement of old age. But he said within himself: "The ways of God are stranger than the thoughts of men, and it may be that I shall find the King, at last, in the hands of his enemies, and shall come in time to offer my pearl for his ransom before he dies."

So the old man followed the multitude with slow and painful steps toward the Damascus gate of the city. Just beyond the entrance of the guardhouse a troop of Macedonian soldiers came down the street, dragging a young girl with torn dress and dishevelled hair. As the Magian paused to look at her with compassion, she broke suddenly from the hands of her tormentors, and threw herself at his feet, clasping him around the knees. She had seen his white cap and the winged circle on his breast.

"Have pity on me," she cried, "and save me, for the sake of the God of Purity! I also am a daughter of the true religion which is taught by the Magi. My father was a merchant of Parthia, but he is dead, and I am seized for his debts to be sold as a slave. Save me from worse than death!"

Artaban trembled.

It was the old conflict in his soul, which had come to him in the palm-grove of Babylon and in the cottage at Bethlehem—the conflict between the expectation of faith and the impulse of love. Twice the gift which he had consecrated to the worship of religion had been drawn to the service of humanity. This was the third trial, the ultimate probation, the final and irrevocable choice.

Was it his great opportunity, or his last temptation? He could not tell. One thing only was clear in the darkness of his mind—it was inevitable. And does not the inevitable come from God?

One thing only was sure to his divided heart—to rescue this helpless girl would be a true deed of love. And is not love the light of the soul?

He took the pearl from his bosom. Never had it seemed so luminous, so radiant, so full of tender, living lustre. He laid it in the hand of the slave.

"This is thy ransom, daughter! It is the last of my treasures which I kept for the King."

While he spoke, the darkness of the sky deepened, and shuddering tremors ran through the earth heaving convulsively like the breast of one who struggles with mighty grief.

The walls of the houses rocked to and fro. Stones were loosened and crashed into the street. Dust clouds filled the air. The soldiers fled in terror, reeling like drunken men. But Artaban and the girl whom he had ransomed crouched helpless beneath the wall of the Praetorium.

What had he to fear? What had he to hope? He had given away the last remnant of his tribute for the King. He had parted with the last hope of finding him. The quest was over, and it had failed. But, even in that thought, accepted and embraced, there was peace. It was not resignation. It was not submission. It was something more profound and searching. He knew that all was well, because he had done the best that he could from day to day. He had been true to the light that had been given to him. He had looked for more. And if he had not found it, if a failure was all that came out of his life, doubtless that was the best that was possible. He had not seen the revelation of "life everlasting, incorruptible and immortal." But he knew that even if he could live his earthly life over again, it could not be otherwise than it had been.

One more lingering pulsation of the earthquake quivered through the ground. A heavy tile, shaken from the roof, fell and struck the old man on the temple. He lay breathless and pale, with his gray head resting on the young girl's shoulder, and the blood trickling from the wound. As she bent over him, fearing that he was dead, there came a voice through the twilight, very small and still, like music sounding from a distance, in which the notes are clear but the words are lost. The girl turned to see if some one had spoken from the window above them, but she saw no one.

Then the old man's lips began to move, as if in answer, and she heard him say in the Parthian tongue:

"Not so, my Lord! For when saw I thee hungered and fed thee? Or thirsty, and gave thee drink? When saw I thee a stranger, and took thee in? Or naked, and clothed thee? When saw I thee sick or in prison, and came unto thee? Three-and-thirty years have I looked for thee; but I have never seen thy face, nor ministered to thee, my King."

He ceased, and the sweet voice came again. And again the maid heard it, very faint and far away. But now it seemed as though she understood the words:

"Verily I say unto thee, Inasmuch as thou hast done it unto one of the least of these my brethren, thou hast done it unto me."

A calm radiance of wonder and joy lighted the pale face of Artaban like the first ray of dawn, on a snowy mountain-peak. A long breath of relief exhaled gently from his lips.

His journey was ended. His treasures were accepted. The Other Wise Man had found the King.

A Canadian Christmas

Ryan N. S. Topping

*"Once Advent begins, three activities
change the character of this household."*

The author recounts how one family keeps the traditions of Advent and Christmas alive and burning brightly in the cold of a Canadian winter.

I HAVE ALWAYS taken an interest in Christmas traditions. One cold, dark December evening, not long ago, the topic came up with an old bachelor friend. We were sipping something or other around the fire, musing over the sorry old state of the world. It was the longest night of the year. We both agreed that too many Christmases are cut short: gifts unwrapped by Christmas Eve, trees tossed by St. Stephen's, lights down by Our Lady's Feast. The whole bustle of December parties and shopping leaves many of us, we agreed, anxious and exhausted even before the great festivities begin, if begin they do at all. We lingered over such thoughts deep into the night. It was in this rather disturbed state of mind that my friend went on to tell me this story to cheer me up. He recalled a family he had stayed with some Christmases ago. These were cousins of his, also from Canada. He couldn't remember then the town in which they lived, nor do I recollect now their names—though I remember they can see northern lights there.

In any case, he told me that night of the long visit about ten years ago he had with these relatives and of how they celebrated Christmas in a way he thought jolly good. His story encouraged my melancholy soul. Since that time, we've since tried to keep up, in my own family, one or two of the traditions practiced in this one. I may not get all the details right. But, in case something of what I recall may encourage your family, I pass along here the substance of what my friend told me that evening:

"The whole affair really gets going," my friend paused to clear his throat, "long before December 25. The great feast of Christmas is paired, in this home, like other feasts of the Church, with a fast. This means that the days of December—that is to say, Advent—are actually a 'little Lent.' The fasting is not so harsh as during the real Lent. But you can feel the *purple* in the air, if you know what I mean. Parties are few. Everything about those weeks builds to the big night. In this spirit, preparations begin even before December, at least for the mother."

"Why only for mother?" I interrupted.

"Because she is the one who shops."

"I don't understand . . ." At this my friend began to chuckle. I hardly ever go into stores, as he knew. "I see," I nodded after a few more words of explanation. "The mother shops for gifts before December so she need not during Advent." He smiled; I didn't interrupt him again. And so he continued . . .

Once Advent begins, three activities change the character of this household. First, there is the writing of the annual Christmas circular. Next, the nightly Jesse Tree. Finally, a change in diet. The December Feasts give reason to bring out the sweets again—St. Lucy's, Our Lady of Guadalupe, St. Nicholas. The fast in this house is just enough, so I found, to keep the appetites a little unhappy.

The Jesse Tree deserves explanation. When the children were young and few, the mother made her own. It is an ancient devotion, they told me; one you can see on some medieval churches. Basically, it is a pictorial "family album" of the savior. Jesus is God's son, but he is also Jesse's. After Vespers, the household gathered around a sheet of cloth with an image of a tree sewn upon it. Each evening, a new felt image was pulled out of a calendar with twenty-four slots. The images were then placed upon the felt "tree" hanging on a wall in the dining room. The first day began with creation, the next with Adam and Eve, after that, the fall, the flood, and so on. Eventually, you arrived at Abraham, then Jesse, then King David, and Christ himself. By the end of Advent, the entire family, from the three-year-old to the thirteen-year-old had gained a good picture of salvation history. I only saw the last week or so of the ritual, but even I was surprised at how many centuries of turmoil and tears it took to bring Jesus into the manger!

Then there was the family circular. This also is mother's work, though father, and in their own way the children, helped too. No one in the family used Facebook. You might have thought that they had no friends. But that was not the case. A week before Christmas, I saw them mail some two hundred letters, each with a new photo of the family in their Sunday ties. And, as the days after Christmas trickled by, almost as many came in through their door. Not having children of my own, I didn't really grasp how much can change over a year, till I had read their letter for the first time. (I've since read many more.) Moves, jobs, books read, a book written, a birth, a death, each found its way into that letter. The best way I could describe their letter is as a "state of the union" report—except with cute pictures of the kids. I suppose they take the view that a family is like a kingdom.

A few other customs impressed me. One was the crèche. Somewhere near the end of the season, the family pulls out a small but lovely set of figurines including ox, ass, stable, some hay, and a miniature star. Jesus only arrived *after* Midnight Mass. The wise men only appeared well *after* Christmas day. Every year, evidently, these eastern sages remake their dusty pilgrimage along the bookshelves to trudge through the living room ever closer to the stable, and Epiphany.

During these days, baking appeared. Since mom was not at the mall, she had more time to devote to the kids, and the food. I was happy about this. The children baked too. This, of course, caused flour and sugar to ice the floor and stove; but there was good humor about it all. Even father got into the kitchen once or twice over these weeks.

One thing I did think was unfair. Almost as soon as the

colorful sugar bread men appeared from the oven, they were whisked away like convicts into their frozen cells in the garage. Some of the children were also not pleased. (One morning I overheard one of the older brothers trying to explain to the younger ones about "pleasure being heightened by delay," or something or other; I don't think anyone was convinced.)

I was pleased to hear there were a few extra days when they did get to eat treats. They told me in particular about what happens on December 6. I wasn't there yet, but a lot went on. That's the day when St. Nicholas appears. The night before, so they said, each child hangs up a stocking. Shoes are pulled out, even mom's and dad's. For the good, St. Nicholas will bring a reward of chocolate, an orange, and maybe some small toy, like a pencil. For the bad, something else.

Alas! Not all children are always good. Now my cousins *are* good children. But twelve months is a long time. It is not only St. Nicholas who arrives. Each child knows that another visitor lurches behind him, watching to see if anyone has been grouchy, run away from washing the dishes, or kept their clothes on the floor of their room, or . . . you get the idea. Only a few weeks ago, so they told me, one little boy *had* been visited by Black Peter. When the children told me how events unfolded I was, frankly, shocked at how lacking in sensitivity these parents could be. Instead of a bright orange in his stocking, this boy found something else in his shoe: a lump of dark coal! Everyone's cheeks reddened. The offending boy picked up the coal and threw it across the room as tears shot out of his face. Goodness swelled up among the brothers, they assured me. Sticks of chocolate were broken; orange slices were divided, and an intensely boyish sympathy was shared by all. But, as I say, that was a good week before I arrived.

So much for the weeks before Christmas.

Christmas Eve carried its own rituals, and these I did see. December 24 is the one night of the year when everyone, unless flirting with death, can stay awake long into the night. The house was mostly quiet. Father led the boys in cleaning the rooms. Mother made fish soup. The Christmas tree was now decorated. Everyone indulged in an afternoon nap. On the tree: I did wonder why they left this so late. No one told me the reason, but "everything in its place" seems to be the thinking. Whereas carols start bleeding out of shop speakers after Thanksgiving, my cousins said they were not keen to "spoil their appetite." Even so, the tree gets dressed rather late for my taste.

About the Masses, I don't really have much to say. Midnight Mass carries its own halo of mystery about it. The hushed walk to the church under the stars, the frozen air, the bells, the Gloria, the incense, the lusty carols and good wishes, I leave all of these aside.

As a boy, I remember always waking up early on Christmas day. These children slept late. I deduced two reasons for this. The most obvious was the party. After Midnight Mass, this after-event lasted till 3 or 4 a.m. The other reason is that presents come out like a trickle instead of a flood. My cousins had six or seven kids then, all boys—I think they have more now—and each one gets a gift each of the twelve days of Christmas. Even I grew impatient for the parents to come down from bed. When they finally did, out appeared trays of chocolate, sliced meats and cheeses, crackers and sparkling juice for yet another glorious reappearance. After all had grazed, we gathered. All cuddled near to the tree and the presents. Father read from St. Luke's Gospel. Then we had a carol. Only after that did the one gift of the day come out.

At first, as I say, I was a bit surprised at this routine, and the scarcity of gifts on Christmas Day. But over the next few days, I saw that a similar ritual was performed. Each of the twelve days, in fact, the children and adults were supposed to exchange one gift, however modest. Minimal chores were done. Father mostly stayed home from work. A few friends visited. During the afternoons, some portion of the family would skate, or play board games, or be busied with a new book or toy in some corner of the house. Dickens, I think, was a favorite for the father, and so was T. S. Eliot's *Murder in the Cathedral*. At night, the fireplace was stacked high with ready wood.

"Is this when you finally left," I wondered, shuffling the coals in our own sleepy fire.

"I only stayed the first six days of Christmas," he told me. "I had a new contract to begin and a long drive ahead."

"You must have been tired. Was there anything else you saw?" I now asked, amazed by my friend's story.

"Not that I saw," he continued. "But my cousins like to conclude the twelve days of Christmas with a party, so they said. I've not been to one, but they say it has a medieval theme . . . eating with your hands and such like. Oh yes, there is also an annual Christmas play, and the making and eating of gingerbread houses. But I wasn't there for these customs, and perhaps a few others."

And with that, dear reader, our own coals finally died.

I stretched and looked at the clock which was now past midnight. My friend took his hat and bid me farewell. The next morning I recounted to my wife what I could remember of this family's celebration. And since then, with this Canadian Christmas in our minds, we have tried in our home to keep better the festival of our Lord's birth.

PART II

Essays & Poems

Advent Calls Us to Silence

Pope Benedict XVI

"God is here, he has not withdrawn from the world."

Joy and hope are the twin notes which ring clearly through these weeks leading up to Christmas. Believers live in joy, Benedict XVI argues, because even now we can witness signs of our hope being fulfilled. In the Scriptures, in the liturgical year of celebrations, in the lives and prayers of the saints, in the beauty of creation, in the love of friends, and through the countless little favors the Lord grants us each day, we see the goodness of the God who will not fail to keep his promises.

WITH THIS celebration we are entering the liturgical season of Advent. In the biblical Reading we have just heard, taken from the First Letter to the Thessalonians, the Apostle Paul invites us to prepare for "the coming of our Lord Jesus Christ" (5:23), with God's grace keeping ourselves blameless. The exact word Paul uses is "coming", in Latin *adventus*, from which the term "Advent" derives.

Let us reflect briefly on the meaning of this word, which can be rendered with "presence", "arrival" or "coming". In the language of the ancient world it was a technical term used to indicate the arrival of an official or the visit of the king or emperor to a province. However, it could also mean the coming of the divinity that emerges from concealment to manifest himself forcefully or that was celebrated as being present in worship. Christians used the word "advent" to express their relationship with Jesus Christ: Jesus is the King who entered this poor "province" called "earth" to pay everyone a visit; he makes all those who believe in him participate in his Coming, all who believe in his presence in the liturgical assembly. The essential meaning of the word adventus was: God is here, he has not withdrawn from the world, he has not deserted us. Even if we cannot see and touch him as we can tangible realities, he is here and comes to visit us in many ways.

The meaning of the expression "advent" therefore includes that of visitatio, which simply and specifically means "visit"; in this case it is a question of a visit from God: he enters my life and wishes to speak to me. In our daily lives we all experience having little time for the Lord and also little time for ourselves. We end by being absorbed in "doing". Is it not true that activities often absorb us and that society with its multiple interests monopolizes our attention? Is it not true that we devote a lot of time to entertainment and to various kinds of amusement? At times we get carried away. Advent, this powerful liturgical season that we are beginning, invites us to pause in silence to understand a presence. It is an invitation to understand that the individual events of the day are hints that God is giving us, signs of the attention he has for each one of us. How often does God give us a glimpse of his love! To keep, as it were, an "interior journal" of this love would be a beautiful and salutary task for our life! Advent invites and stimulates us to contemplate the Lord present. Should not the certainty of his presence help us see the world with different eyes? Should it not help us to consider the whole of our life as a "visit", as a way in which he can come to us and become close to us in every situation?

Another fundamental element of Advent is expectation, an expectation which is at the same time hope. Advent impels us to understand the meaning of time and of history as a kairós, as a favourable opportunity for our salvation. Jesus illustrated this mysterious reality in many parables: in the story of the servants sent to await the return of their master; in the parable of the virgins who await the bridegroom; and in those of the sower and of the harvest. In their lives human beings are constantly waiting: when they are children they want to grow up, as adults they are striving for fulfilment and success and, as they advance in age, they look forward to the rest they deserve. However, the time comes when they find they have hoped too little if, over and above their profession or social position, there is nothing left to hope for. Hope marks humanity's journey but for Christians it is enlivened by a certainty: the Lord is present in the passage of our lives, he accompanies us and will one day also dry our tears. One day, not far off, everything will find its fulfilment in the Kingdom of God, a Kingdom of justice and peace.

However there are many different ways of waiting. If time is not filled by a present endowed with meaning, expectation risks becoming unbearable; if one expects something but at a given moment there is nothing, in other words if the present remains empty, every instant that passes appears extremely long and waiting becomes too heavy a burden because the future remains completely uncertain. On the other hand, when time is endowed with meaning and at every instant we perceive something specific and worthwhile, it is then that the joy of expectation makes the present more precious. Dear brothers and sisters, let us experience intensely the present in which we already receive the gifts of the Lord, let us live it focused on the future, a future charged with hope. In this manner Christian Advent becomes an opportunity to reawaken within ourselves the true meaning of waiting, returning to the heart of our faith which is the mystery of Christ, the Messiah who was expected for long centuries and was born in poverty, in Bethlehem. In coming among us, he brought us and continues to offer us the gift of his love and his salvation. Present among us, he speaks to us in many ways: in Sacred Scripture, in the liturgical year, in the saints, in the events of daily life, in the whole of the creation whose aspect changes according to whether Christ is behind it or whether he is obscured by the fog of an uncertain origin and an uncertain future. We in turn may speak to him, presenting to him the suffering that afflicts us, our impatience, the questions that well up in our hearts. We may be sure that he always listens to us! And if Jesus is present, there is no longer any time that lacks meaning or is empty. If he is present, we may continue to hope, even when others can no longer assure us of any support, even when the present becomes trying.

Dear friends, Advent is the season of the presence and expectation of the eternal. For this very reason, it is in a particular way a period of joy, an interiorized joy that no suffering can diminish. It is joy in the fact that God made himself a Child. This joy, invisibly present within us, encourages us to journey on with confidence. A model and support of this deep joy is the Virgin Mary, through whom we were given the Infant Jesus. May she, a faithful disciple of her Son, obtain for us the grace of living this liturgical season alert and hardworking, while we wait. Amen!

That Holy Thing

George MacDonald (1824–1905)

They all were looking for a king
 To slay their foes and lift them high:
Thou cam'st, a little baby thing
 That made a woman cry.

O Son of Man, to right my lot
 Naught but Thy presence can avail;
Yet on the road Thy wheels are not,
 Nor on the sea Thy sail!

My how or when Thou wilt not heed,
 But come down Thine own secret stair,
That Thou mayst answer all my need—
 Yea, every bygone prayer.

Rejoice, the Lord Is Near

Pope St. John Paul II (1920–2005)

"Rejoice in the Lord always."

Gaudete Sunday takes its name from the opening word of the liturgy appointed for the third Sunday of Advent. In the midst of this "little Lent," which is Advent, the Church sets before the faithful a summons to *rejoice*. As John Paul II reminds us, in these days, we gaze particularly upon the faith of Mary, Elizabeth, Zechariah, and John the Baptist.

"*GAUDETE IN Domino semper. Iterum dico: Gaudete! . . . Dominus prope.*" "Rejoice in the Lord always, again I will say, Rejoice. . . . The Lord is at hand" (Phil 4:4–5). It is from these words taken from St. Paul's letter to the Philippians, that this Sunday takes the liturgical name "Gaudete". Today the liturgy urges us to rejoice because the birth of the Lord is approaching: in fact it is only 10 days away.

In his Letter to the Thessalonians, the Apostle exhorts us thus: "Rejoice always, pray constantly, give thanks in all circumstances. . . . May the God of peace himself sanctify you wholly;

and may your spirit and soul and body be kept sound and blameless at the coming of our Lord Jesus Christ" (1 Thes 5:16-18; 23).

This is a typical *Advent exhortation*. Advent is the liturgical season that prepares us for the Lord's birth, but it is also the time of expectation for the *definitive return of Christ* for the last judgement, and St. Paul refers, in the first place, to this second coming. The very fact that the conclusion of the liturgical year coincides with the beginning of Advent suggests that "the beginning of the time of salvation is in some way linked to the "end of time". This exhortation typical of Advent always applies: "The Lord is at hand!"

In today's liturgy the prospect of Christ's coming at Christmas, so near now, seems to prevail. The echo of joy at the Messiah's birth resounds in the *Magnificat,* the canticle that wells up in Mary during her visit to the elderly wife of Zechariah. Elizabeth greets Mary with the words: "And why is this granted me, that the mother of my Lord should come to me? For behold, when the voice of your greeting came to my ears, the babe in my womb leaped for joy. And blessed is she who believed that there would be a fulfilment of what was spoken to her from the Lord" (Lk 1:43-45). Advanced in age and by now beyond all hope of possible motherhood, Elizabeth had realized that the extraordinary grace granted her was closely linked to the divine plan of salvation. The son who was to be born of her had been foreseen by God as the Precursor called to prepare the way for Christ (cf. Lk 1:76). And Mary replies with the words of the *Magnificat,* repeated in the responsorial psalm today: "My soul magnifies the Lord, and my spirit rejoices in God my Saviour, for he has regarded the low estate of his handmaiden.... He who is mighty has done great things for me, and holy is his name" (Lk 1:46-49).

John the Baptist is one of the most significant biblical figures we meet during this important season of the liturgical year. In the fourth Gospel we read: "There was a man sent from God whose name was John. He came for testimony, to bear witness to the light that all might believe through him. He was not the light, but came to bear witness to the light" (Jn 1:6-8). To the question "Who are you?", John the Baptist responds: "I am not the Christ", nor Elijah, nor any other of the prophets (cf. Jn 1:19-20). And faced with the insistence of those sent from Jerusalem, he says: "I am the voice of one crying in the wilderness, 'Make straight the way of the Lord'" (Jn 1:23).

With this quote from Isaiah, in a certain sense he reveals his identity and clarifies his special role in the history of salvation. And when the representatives of the Sanhedrin ask him why he is baptizing, although he is neither the Messiah, nor Elijah, nor any other prophet, he answers: "I baptize with water; but among you stands one whom you do not know, even he who comes after me, the thong of whose sandal I am not worthy to untie" (Jn 1:26-27).

John the Baptist's witness re-echoes in the Advent verse: "The Lord is at hand!" The different perspectives of the night of Bethlehem and the baptism in the Jordan converge in the same truth: we must shake off our inertia and prepare the way of the Lord who comes.

Dear brothers and sisters of the parish of Our Lady of Valme, I am pleased to celebrate the Eucharist with you on this Third

Sunday of Advent! I affectionately greet the Cardinal Vicar, the new Auxiliary Bishop of the Western Sector, Bishop Vincenzo Apicella, your parish priest and his assistants both priests and laity, of the *Obra de la Iglesia*. From its beginning your parish was entrusted to this religious family, whose foundress, Mother Trinidad Sanchez Moreno, I greet. This year, on 7 December, she celebrated her 50th anniversary of religious life.

This day of celebration permits us all to give thanks to God for this beautiful church, recently opened and dedicated to Our Lady of Valme. "Valme", as is well known, is an invocation in Spanish that dates to the 13th century, when King St. Ferdinand, in difficulty while attempting to re-conquer Seville, asked the heavenly Mother for assistance: "Valimi, Signora", "Help me, my Lady". Since then many of the faithful in Spain and in other parts of the world continue to repeat "Valimi", help me Mary, and be our support.

This morning we too turn with hope to the Blessed Virgin, entrusting her with the projects and hopes of your parish community. I am aware of your commitment in putting Mass and the adoration of the Eucharist at the centre of your parish life, as well as of your care for liturgical celebrations and your devotion to Mary, Mother of God and of the Church, which motivates you. I know the great faith that nourishes your heartfelt support of the Successor of Peter and your Bishops, as you strive to grow in fraternal charity and in the ardent desire to bring everyone the Gospel of Christ, the one Saviour of mankind.

I encourage you to continue on the path you have undertaken as I congratulate you, among other things, for the initiative called "Linking Apartments", an effective form of apostolic activity to make the inhabitants of your area feel the closeness of Jesus and of the ecclesial community.

This apostolic activity, as indeed all your other pastoral efforts, fits well into the city mission which involves all of Rome. Within the framework of its gradual development, it is planned that after Christmas every family in the city will be given a copy of Mark's Gospel. This Gospel contains the teachings of the Apostle Peter, of whom the Evangelist was the faithful disciple and interpreter right here in Rome. I have wished to accompany this gift with a letter in which I personally, as it were, offer this Gospel text to all Romans.

My hope is that the Good News of Christ will enter every home and help families to rediscover that only in Christ can man find salvation. In him it is possible to find the interior peace, hope and strength necessary to face life's various situations each day, even those most onerous and difficult. In the letter accompanying the Gospel, I recalled that Jesus is not a figure of the past. He is the Word of God who even today continues to shed light on man's path; his actions are the expression of the Father's love for every human being.

"The spirit of the Lord God is upon me, because the Lord has anointed me he has sent me to bring glad tidings to the lowly, to heal the broken-hearted, to proclaim liberty to the captives and release to the prisoners, to announce a year of favour from the Lord." (Is 61:12).

In the synagogue of Nazareth, at the moment of beginning his public ministry, Christ will apply these words of the prophet

Isaiah to himself. Today he repeats them for us during this liturgical assembly, and in repeating them he invites us to rejoice again with the words of Isaiah: "I rejoice heartily in the Lord, in my God is the joy of my soul; for he has clothed me with a robe of salvation, and wrapped me in a mantle of justice" (Is 61:10).

The prophet's joyful proclamation is echoed in what St. Paul writes in the passage from his Letter to the Thessalonians we have just heard. Isaiah affirms: "I rejoice heartily in the Lord" (Is 61:10), and Paul exhorts: "Rejoice! The Lord is at hand!" (cf. Phil 4:4-5; 1 Thes 5:16, 23).

The Lord Jesus is at hand at every moment of our life. He is at hand if we consider him in the perspective of Christmas, but he is also at hand if we look at him on the banks of the Jordan when he officially receives his messianic mission from the Father; lastly, he is at hand in the perspective of his return at the end of time.

Christ is at hand! He comes by virtue of the Holy Spirit to announce the Good News; he comes to cure and to set free to proclaim a time of grace and salvation, in order to begin, already on the night of Bethlehem, the work of the world's redemption.

Let us therefore rejoice and exult! The Lord is at hand; he is coming to save us.

Amen!

Moonless Darkness Stands Between

Gerard Manley Hopkins (1844–1889)

MOONLESS DARKNESS stands between.
Past, the Past, no more be seen!
But the Bethlehem-star may lead me
To the sight of Him Who freed me
From the self that I have been.
Make me pure, Lord: Thou art holy;
Make me meek, Lord: Thou wert lowly;
Now beginning, and alway:
Now begin, on Christmas day.

Great Is the Lord's Love for Us

Bernard of Clairvaux (1090–1153)

"What was not was created; what had perished was recreated."

In these Advent reflections, the great medieval mystic St. Bernard explores how the Incarnation fits within the larger pattern of God's goodness to the human family. What man had destroyed, God has repaired. Though body and soul now suffer a painful union, though creator and creation exist in uneasy friendship, God has taken the initiative. What greater promise of our dignity could God give us than to take on our nature!

"GREAT ARE the works of the Lord," (Ps. cx. 2.) says the Psalmist. Great indeed are all God's works, but the mysteries which chiefly excite our wonder and admiration are naturally those which concern our eternal salvation. Hence the same Prophet sings: "The Lord hath done great things for us." (Ps. cxxv. 3.) His munificent dealings with us are shown forth chiefly in our Creation, our present redemption, and our future glorification. O Lord, how greatly art Thou exalted in all Thy works! Do Thou proclaim their excellence to Thy people, and let us not be silent concerning them.

There is a threefold commingling to be considered in these three mysteries, most manifestly heavenly, most evidently the effect of the omnipotence of God. In the first of these mysteries, that of our creation, "God made man from the slime of the earth, and breathed into his face the breath of life." (Gen. ii. 7.) What a wonderful Creator, Who unites and commingles things so opposite! At His beck the slime of the earth and the spirit, or breath of life, are united, and make one being. The earth of which He made man had been previously created when "in the beginning God created the heavens and the earth." But the origin of the spirit was special, not common. It was not infused into the mass of matter, but is specially breathed into each individual of the human race.

O man, acknowledge your dignity! Recognize the glory of human nature! You have a body taken from this earth, for it was fitting that one who is the appointed lord of all visible creatures should bear a similarity to them. But you are at the same time more noble and more exalted than they; nor are they in any way to be compared to you. In you body and soul are closely united; the first is moulded and fashioned, the second is inspired. On which side lies the advantage? Which of the two is the gainer in this union? According to the wisdom of this world, where what is low and mean is associated with what is excellent, those who are in power lord it over their inferiors, and bend them to their will. The strong man tramples on him who is the weaker;

the learned man ridicules one who is unlearned; the crafty one deceives the simple; the powerful man despises the weak. It is not thus, O God, in Thy work, not thus in Thy commingling. It was not for such a purpose that Thou didst unite spirit with matter; what is exalted with what is lowly; a noble and excellent creature with the abject, worthless clay. Thou didst will the soul to rule; at the same time who does not see what dignity and advantage it thus confers on the body? Would not the body without the soul be senseless matter? From the soul it derives its beauty, from the soul its growth, from the soul the brightness of the eye and the sound of the voice. All the senses are animated by the soul. By this union charity is commended to me. I read of charity in the very history of my own creation. Not only is charity proclaimed in its first page; it is imprinted within me by the gracious hand of my Maker.

Great indeed is this union of body and soul; would that it had remained firm and unbroken! But, alas! though it had been secured by the Divine seal—for God made man to His own image and likeness—the union was marred, for the seal was broken and the likeness defaced. The worst of thieves approached, stealthily damaged the yet fresh seal, and so sadly changed the Divine likeness that man is now compared to senseless beasts, and is become like unto them.

God made man just, and of this his likeness to God it is written: "The Lord our God is righteous, and there is no iniquity in him." (Ps. xci. 16.) He made man just and truthful, as He Himself is justice and truth; nor could this union be broken while the integrity of the seal was preserved. But that forger came, and, while promising a better seal, broke, alas! that which had been stamped by the hand of God. "You shall be as gods," he said, "knowing good and evil." (Gen. iii. 5.) O malicious one! O crafty spirit! Of what use to that man and woman could the likeness of this knowledge be? Let them "be as gods" by all means, but let them be upright, truthful, like God, in Whom there is no sin. While this seal remained whole the union remained uninjured. Now we have a woeful experience of what we were persuaded to attempt by the devil's craft. The seal once broken, a bitter parting followed, a sad divorce. O wicked wretch! where is your promise, "You shall not die"? Behold, we all die. There is no man living that shall not taste death. What, then, will become of us, O Lord our God? Will no one repair Thy work? Will no one help to raise the fallen? None can remake but He Who first made. Therefore, "by reason of the misery of the needy, and the groans of the poor, now I will arise, saith the Lord. I will set him in safety: I will deal confidently in his regard." (Ps. xi. 6.) The enemy shall not prevail over him, nor the son of iniquity have any power to hurt him. Behold, I now make a new mixture, upon which I set a deeper and stronger seal. I will give to fallen man Him Who was not made to My likeness, but Who is the very image and splendour of My glory and the figure of My substance; not made, but begotten before all ages.

The first mixture was compounded of two things, earth and spirit. The second is made up of three, that from this fact we may learn to contemplate the mystery of the Blessed Trinity—the Word Who was in the beginning with God, and was God; the soul, which was created out of nothing, and had no previous existence; and the flesh, taken from corrupted nature without any corruption, separated and singled out by a Divine plan, as if it had not been a portion of mortal flesh; and these three are united together in one Person, our Lord and Saviour Jesus Christ. We have in these three a threefold exhibition of power. What was not was created; what had perished was recreated; and what was higher than all was made a little lower than the angels. Here are the three Gospel measures of meal which are, as it were, fermented, that they may become the bread of angels, in order that man may eat the bread which strengthens his heart. Happy Mary! blessed amongst women, in whose chaste womb that bread was prepared by the Holy Ghost Who came down upon thee! Yea, happy woman! who hid in these measures the leaven of thy own glorious faith; so that by faith thou didst conceive Him, by faith thou didst bring Him forth, and by thy faith those things were accomplished in thee which were spoken to thee by the Lord, and for believing which Elizabeth declared thee blessed.

And who need wonder when I say that the Word was united to human flesh through the faith of Mary, seeing that He received that same flesh from hers? There is nothing in the foregoing explanation opposed to our regarding the faith of Mary as a type of the kingdom of heaven; nor does it seem unfitting to compare her faith with the kingdom of heaven, since by that same faith its losses are repaired. This bond of union, this Trinity in Christ, no human power could wholly sever. The "prince of this world" had nothing in Him, the latchet of whose shoe the Baptist himself was unworthy to loosen. Yet it was necessary that this triad should in a certain way be dissolved; otherwise, what is not dissolved cannot be reconstructed. Of what use are bread unbroken, a treasure hidden, wisdom concealed? Well might St. John weep when no one was found to open the book and break its seals. Whilst it remained closed, no man amongst us could attain to its Divine wisdom. O Lamb of God! O truly meek Lamb! do Thou open the book. Open out Thy pierced hands and feet, that the treasure of salvation and the plentiful redemption hidden in them may come forth. Break Thy bread to the hungry. Thou alone canst break it to them, Who alone couldst stand firm and unshaken when the union between Thy Divine and human natures appeared broken in Thy passion. In this breaking Thou still hadst power to lay down Thy life and to take it up again. In Thy mercy Thou didst to a certain degree destroy this temple, but didst not wholly dissolve it. Let the soul be separated from the body, the Word will preserve that flesh from corruption and bestow a full liberty on the soul, that it alone of all human souls may be free among the dead, and lead forth from the prison-house those who were bound, those sitting in darkness and in the shadow of death. Let this holy and Divine soul lay down its immaculate flesh, that by dying it may conquer death; but let it resume that flesh on the third day, that by rising again it may raise us all from death to life. This has been done, and let us rejoice in the accomplishment of the mystery. By that death, death is destroyed, and by the Resurrection of Jesus Christ from the dead we are regenerated in the hope of life.

But who shall say what is to take place in the third and future union? "Eye hath not seen, ear hath not heard, nor hath it entered into the heart of man to conceive what God hath prepared for them that love Him." The consummation of the union will be when Christ shall have restored and given back the kingdom to God and the Father.

To sum up, in the first mixture, where man is made and composed of body and soul, we saw charity recommended. In the second mixture or union, the Incarnation, humility shines pre-eminent in the infinite condescension of God in assuming our human nature, whereby He teaches us that it is by humility alone we can repair the wounds of charity.

In the first union it is no result of humility that the rational soul is united to an earthly body, for it is not by any deliberate act of its own. The soul is immediately breathed into it by God.

It is otherwise in the second union, where the Uncreated Spirit, Himself the Sovereign Good, humbly drew nigh to our nature, and of His own will and choice assumed an unsullied body.

From both we learn that charity and humility are deservedly followed by glorification, for without charity nothing can profit us, and without humility none shall be exalted. In humility, then, is laid up for us the perfection of the beatitude which we expect and long for. May we be so blest as to attain it!

A Hymn on the Nativity of My Saviour

Ben Jonson (1572–1637)

I sing the birth was born tonight,
The Author both of life and light;
    The angels so did sound it,
And like the ravished shepherds said,
Who saw the light, and were afraid,
    Yet searched, and true they found it.

The Son of God, the eternal King,
That did us all salvation bring,
    And freed the soul from danger;
He whom the whole world could not take,
The Word, which heaven and earth did make,
    Was now laid in a manger.

The Father's wisdom willed it so,
The Son's obedience knew no "No,"
    Both wills were in one stature;

And as that wisdom had decreed,
The Word was now made Flesh indeed,
   And took on Him our nature.

What comfort by Him do we win?
Who made Himself the Prince of sin,
   To make us heirs of glory?
To see this Babe, all innocence,
A Martyr born in our defense,
   Can man forget this story?

Keeping Christmas Local

Joseph Pearce

*"I am happy to proclaim that Christ is very much
alive in the heart of small town America."*

Joseph Pearce is a contemporary writer and biographer of major Christian literary figures, including C. S. Lewis, J. R. R. Tolkien, Hilaire Belloc, Oscar Wilde, and Solzhenitsyn. In this essay, he reflects on how one small town's efforts at celebrating Christmas with gusto is helping to revive a local economy, local friendships, and a local network of families. In the ancient understanding, culture flows from cult; that is, from worship. In the rightly ordered celebration of Christmas, we both worship the King and renew our common culture.

ONE OF the most discouraging things about small town America is the way that corporate gigantism has ripped its heart out. This is made all too painfully evident when I drive on the back roads to Charlotte from my home in South Carolina, which is my preferred route when time permits. Taking these country roads, I pass through several small towns that have become like the ghost towns of the legendary West. People still live there, in an impoverished state, but the downtown area is deserted. Indeed, to put no finer point upon it, downtown is a desert devoid of all commercial activity. One sees old buildings, dignified even in their dilapidated state, empty and neglected, standing like tombstones commemorating the passing of a healthier culture. What is missing is the neighbourly heart of the local community in the local commerce that once beat there with the pulse of family life.

Such gloomy thoughts seem out of place as we approach Christmas, which, as the singer Andy Williams reminds us, is "the most wonderful time of the year". Mindful of this, and not wishing to be a veritable Scrooge in the midst of the seasonal cheer, or, even worse, a doom-monger who, like the White Witch of Narnia, declares that it is "always winter but never Christmas", I am happy to proclaim that Christ is very much alive in the heart of small town America and that He is breathing life back into downtown. This is never clearer than at Christmas when the little town in which I live beats as one with the little town of Bethlehem.

This past weekend, with the tree we had just purchased perched on the roof of the car, we parked outside the family-owned country store on Main Street, from which we buy the feed for our chickens and ducks and the raw milk for ourselves, the latter of which is delivered weekly to the store from a local dairy. (South Carolina, unlike most states, has not declared raw milk illegal.) The store itself was closed, its being Sunday, but we'd parked there in order to see the Christmas parade. Shivering in the chill breeze, we were warmed by the spectacle passing before us. For over an hour, half of the population passed in procession before us while the other half lined the streets to watch. Local businesses passed by, one after the other, employees tossing candy to the children while others waved and greeted the onlookers with the seasonal greeting of "Merry Christmas!" (and ne'er a "happy holidays" to be heard!).

To my delight, I noted several troops of American Heritage Girls, which was founded twenty years ago as a Christian alternative to the Girl Scouts after the latter had dropped God from their promise and had banned prayer. Beginning with only around 100 girls, when it was founded in small-town Ohio, AHG now has over 30,000 members around the United States. Clearly, if the evidence of my local Christmas parade is anything to go by, it has now effectively eclipsed the Godless Girl Scouts, at least here in the buckle of the Bible-Belt.

And speaking of the Bible-Belt, the parade was also blessed with the presence of many local churches, mostly Baptists, whose members greeted those lining the streets with the ubiquitous "Merry Christmas", handing out flyers giving details of their respective Christmas services, along with the equally ubiquitous candy. The presence of my Protestant brethren bearing public witness to Christ as "the reason for the season" warmed the cockles of my Catholic heart!

Another feature of the season is the annual Christmas concert, performed in the local theatre by the small-town's Chorale. Subscribing to Chesterton's adage that if a thing is worth doing, it is worth doing badly, I first attended this annual festive event with a somewhat supercilious fear that the quality of the performance would be woeful. I was pleasantly surprised. The quality of musicianship is high, as is the selection of music. The whole of the first half of this year's concert was a performance of Benjamin Britten's *Ceremony of Carols*, a cantata of eleven movements for three-part treble chorus, solo voices, and harp. The text consists of a series of mediaeval English poems, longtime favourites of mine, sung in the splendor of Chaucerian Middle English with a smattering of Latin.

After the intermission we moved into the twentieth century with a string of popular seasonal classics: *It's Beginning to Look a Lot Like Christmas*, *Deck the Hall with boughs of Holly*, the *Carol of the Bells*, *The Christmas Song* ("Chestnuts roasting on an open fire . . .") and a rousing rendition of *Joy to the World*. The climax, predictably and commendably enough, was a performance of Handel's *Hallelujah Chorus*. Who could ask for more?

And then, this year and in previous years, there are the local theatrical productions of *A Christmas Carol*, *A Charlie Brown Christmas*, and *It's a Wonderful Life*.

Christmas would not be Christmas without the Christmas shopping, of course, but even here I try to keep it local. I make my purchases, wherever possible, from local small stores, such as the aforementioned country store and those other new stores which are beginning to reappear on Main Street, and I try to buy locally produced gifts. The country store, for example, is well-stocked with local honey, or locally-made cooking sauces, pickles, chutneys and chow-chow, as well as local cook-books and books of local history. Speaking of books, I try to buy books from small publishers and I try to buy them directly from the publishers or from local bookstores, resisting (at least most of the time) the allure of the Almighty Amazon. The food we purchase for our Christmas feast will be local produce and, usually, local meat, including, when we have turkey, birds raised on a farm around the corner from where we live. The beer I drink will be locally craft-produced ale and, should I desire something stronger, the moonshine I imbibe will be made in the local distillery.

And lest anyone should think my way of doing Christmas shopping a little odd or eccentric, I would simply point out that strong local communities are only possible when there's a strong local economy. If I want the family-owned businesses to return to Main Street, resurrecting the ghost towns, I need to spend my money in those stores when they begin to reappear. And if this means that I have less to spend on the mass-produced junk from China on sale in Walmart, so much the better!

And on that jolly note, I raise a glass of locally-crafted ale and wish you all a truly Merrie Christmas!

The Burning Babe

Robert Southwell (1561–1595)

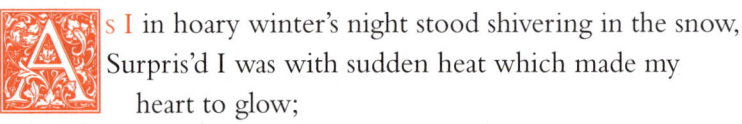

As I in hoary winter's night stood shivering in the snow,
Surpris'd I was with sudden heat which made my heart to glow;
And lifting up a fearful eye to view what fire was near,
A pretty Babe all burning bright did in the air appear;
Who, scorched with excessive heat, such floods of tears did shed
As though his floods should quench his flames which with his tears were fed.
"Alas!" quoth he, "but newly born, in fiery heats I fry,
Yet none approach to warm their hearts or feel my fire but I!
My faultless breast the furnace is, the fuel wounding thorns,
Love is the fire, and sighs the smoke, the ashes shame and scorns;
The fuel Justice layeth on, and Mercy blows the coals,
The metal in this furnace wrought are men's defiled souls,
For which, as now on fire I am to work them to their good,
So will I melt into a bath to wash them in my blood."
With this he vanish'd out of sight and swiftly shrunk away,
And straight I called unto mind that it was Christmas day.

The Rituals of Christmas

G. K. Chesterton (1874–1936)

"Let us show that the ancient culture ... still knows something about how real pictures are made."

Chesterton takes a failed modern ritual as a stepping stone from which to consider the meaning of rituals in general and of Christmas rituals in particular. The loss of ritual, in Chesterton's view, is a sign of the rise of barbarity. Lose ritual and you lose the sense of the sacred; lose the sacred and man loses his own soul.

CHRISTMAS, WITH its Christmas candles and its hundred shapes and patterns of fire, from the old legend of the log to the blue flames of Snapdragon and the sacred oblation of burning brandy (in the true tradition of sacrifice, which is the destruction of the most precious thing for the glory of the divine powers) has rather irrationally thrown my thoughts back to the flames of a torchlight procession which I saw on the last great ceremonial festival in this city. It was a ritual rather new and national than old and religious. But it was one with which

I have a special spiritual sympathy, and about which, at the time, I felt a certain sentiment and formed a certain opinion. I had a reason for not stating the opinion then; and I have a reason for stating the reason now.

I could not bring myself to criticise the Armistice celebrations immediately after Armistice Day; because it was just possible that any criticism, which was really critical, might be mistaken for a surrender to that most morbid and unmanly mood of reaction which I have noticed only too often throwing cold water upon those torches which those heroes will carry through history. I would rather join in any mummery, or tolerate any mistakes, than be for one moment mistaken for one of those "modern" persons who have gradually and cautiously, after the peril was over, plucked up courage to preach a religion of cowardice. We have had even poetry prostituted to the service of poltroonery. We have had lyrics loud with panic, of which the best we can say is that their healthiest excuse is shell-shock, but that it is a little difficult to remain charitable when the shocked claims popularity as the shocker. Mean little studies of neurotic paralysis have been put forward as the only realistic record of the one great proof that humanity has given to the heavens of the huge human equality in normal virility and valour. When to this dishonouring of the dead was added the vile indifference and injustice to the living, which has left thousands of the saviours of the world as drifting and desperate as so many old lags out of jail, the reaction to what many would call reason and "normalcy" is not one with which I desire to be connected or confused. And to express anything savouring of disappointment or doubt about the Armistice ceremonies might well have seemed like contributing to that contemptible coldness or striking the same note as did that dreary diminuendo. But now, as I say, when we shall soon be in a position to compare such ceremonial with the ancient ceremonials founded by our fathers, in the days when men had an instinct for such things, I think it worth while to remark on some of the memories, and even some of the mistakes, in the more modern formality in its more modern framework. If we are to have ceremonial, Armistice Day has a great deal to learn from Christmas Day, and especially from the days when the Christmas ritual was created.

All ceremony depends on symbol; and all symbols have been vulgarised and made stale by the commercial conditions of our time. This has been especially true since we have felt the commercial infection of America, and progress has turned London, not into a superior London, but into a very inferior New York. Of all these faded and falsified symbols, the most melancholy example is the ancient symbol of the flame. In every civilised age and country, it has been a natural thing to talk of some great festival on which "the town was illuminated." There is no meaning nowadays in saying that the town was illuminated. There is no point or purpose in having it illuminated for any normal and noble enthusiasm, such as the winning of a victory or the granting of a charter. The whole town is illuminated already, but not for noble things. It is illuminated solely to insist on the immense importance of trivial and material things, blazoned from motives entirely mercenary. The significance of such colours and such lights has therefore been entirely killed. It is no good to send up a golden and purple rocket for the glory of the King and Country, or to light a red and raging bonfire on the day of St. George, when everybody is used to seeing the same fiery alphabet proclaiming the importance of Tibbie's Tooth Paste or Giggle's Chewing Gum. The new illumination has not, indeed, made Tibbie and Giggle so important as St. George and King George; because nothing could. But it has made people weary of the way of proclaiming great things, by perpetually using it to proclaim small things. It has not destroyed the difference between light and darkness, but it has allowed the lesser light to put out the greater.

I was standing in the very heart of this holy town, opposite the Abbey, and within a stone's throw of the Thames, when I saw the torchlight procession turn the corner and take the road towards the Cenotaph. Now, a torchlight procession is one of the most magnificent of all those instinctive and imaginative institutions by which men have sought to express deep democratic passions of praise or triumph, or lamentation, since the morning of the world. Naturally, by all artistic instinct, they were held at night; and they were held in times and places which were lucky enough to retain a little night. They cannot be done in a garish and feverish civilisation which insists on turning night into day. In those older and simple societies, republics, or kingdoms, there would probably have been enough sense of public authority to command a Curfew, and force all citizens to put out all lights while the pageant of the sacred flames went by. But the modern mind is in an unfathomable muddle about all these things. Our streets are in a permanent dazzle, and our minds in a permanent darkness. It would be an intelligible process to abolish all ceremonies, as the Puritans did. But it is not intelligible to keep ceremonies and spoil them; and nothing in the literature of lunacy is weaker and wilder than the appearance of this wavering sort of lunatic, holding a lighted candle at noon.

A short time ago, the very section of the city in which I was standing was abruptly blotted out by total darkness, the electric light having gone wrong. I wish it had gone wrong at the moment when the marching men turned the corner with all their torches burning. One catastrophe of that sort would have saved the whole situation, and perhaps the whole memory and meaning of the Great War. Its glory would have got a good black background at last; and that moving conflagration would have burned red in men's memories until they died. That was the ceremony as our fathers planned it; and that is also how the ceremonies of Christmas were planned. If we are wise, we shall keep these latter also in the ancient manner, and according to plan. If we must be merely American in our business, let us at least be civilised in our pleasures. Let us understand, as the artists and the ancient priests and heralds have always understood, the meaning of contrast and the conception of a background. If Snapdragon burns with blue flames, do not let us kill it with a white light, with that enterprising spot-light which is so very decidedly a deathray. If we have the common-sense to see that red firelight looks redder in the twilight, let us have the courage to refuse the kind American gentleman's offer of an electric light ten times stronger than day-light. Let us show that the ancient culture, which has produced a picture or two in its time, still knows something about how real pictures are made; even if they are only picture postcards to be used as Christmas cards.

A Visit From St. Nicholas

Clement Clarke Moore (1779–1863)

'TWAS THE night before Christmas, when all through the house
Not a creature was stirring, not even a mouse;
The stockings were hung by the chimney with care,
In hopes that St. Nicholas soon would be there;
The children were nestled all snug in their beds;
While visions of sugar-plums danced in their heads;
And mamma in her 'kerchief, and I in my cap,
Had just settled our brains for a long winter's nap,
When out on the lawn there arose such a clatter,
I sprang from my bed to see what was the matter.
Away to the window I flew like a flash,
Tore open the shutters and threw up the sash.
The moon on the breast of the new-fallen snow,
Gave a lustre of midday to objects below,
When what to my wondering eyes did appear,
But a miniature sleigh and eight tiny rein-deer,
With a little old driver so lively and quick,
I knew in a moment he must be St. Nick.

More rapid than eagles his coursers they came,
And he whistled, and shouted, and called them by name:
"Now, *Dasher*! now, *Dancer*! now *Prancer* and *Vixen*!
On, *Comet*! on, *Cupid*! on, *Donner* and *Blitzen*!
To the top of the porch! to the top of the wall!
Now dash away! dash away! dash away all!"
As leaves that before the wild hurricane fly,
When they meet with an obstacle, mount to the sky;
So up to the housetop the coursers they flew
With the sleigh full of toys, and St. Nicholas too—
And then, in a twinkling, I heard on the roof
The prancing and pawing of each little hoof.
As I drew in my head, and was turning around,
Down the chimney St. Nicholas came with a bound.
He was dressed all in fur, from his head to his foot,
And his clothes were all tarnished with ashes and soot;
A bundle of toys he had flung on his back,
And he looked like a pedler just opening his pack.
His eyes—how they twinkled! his dimples, how merry!
His cheeks were like roses, his nose like a cherry!
His droll little mouth was drawn up like a bow,
And the beard on his chin was as white as the snow;
The stump of a pipe he held tight in his teeth,
And the smoke, it encircled his head like a wreath;
He had a broad face and a little round belly
That shook when he laughed, like a bowl full of jelly.
He was chubby and plump, a right jolly old elf,
And I laughed when I saw him, in spite of myself;

A wink of his eye and a twist of his head
Soon gave me to know I had nothing to dread;
He spoke not a word, but went straight to his work,
And filled all the stockings; then turned with a jerk,
And laying his finger aside of his nose,
And giving a nod, up the chimney he rose;
He sprang to his sleigh, to his team gave a whistle,
And away they all flew like the down of a thistle.
But I heard him exclaim, ere he drove out of sight—
"Happy Christmas to all, and to all a good night!"

A Remaining Christmas

Hilaire Belloc (1870–1953)

*". . . having in the whole of the complicated
affair a sacramental quality."*

After G. K. Chesterton and J. R. R. Tolkein, Belloc is perhaps the best known among the twentieth-century authors responsible for the Catholic literary revival in England. In this moving encomium to domestic rituals, Belloc describes the preparations and celebrations of the Christmas season in one traditional Catholic home.

A REMAINING CHRISTMAS: The world is changing very fast, and neither exactly for the better or the worse, but for division. Our civilization is splitting more and more into two camps, and what was common to the whole of it is becoming restricted to the Christian, and soon will be restricted to the Catholic half.

That is why I have called this article 'A Remaining Christmas'. People ask themselves how much remains of this observance and of the feast and its customs. Now a concrete instance is more vivid and, in its own way, of more value than a general appreciation. So I will set down here exactly what Christmas still is in a certain house in England, how it is observed, and all the domestic rites accompanying it in their detail and warmth.

This house stands low down upon clay near a little river. It is quite cut off from the towns; no one has built near it. Every cottage for a mile and more is old, with here and there a modern addition. The church of the parish (which was lost of course three and a half centuries ago, under Elizabeth) is as old as the Crusades. It is of the twelfth century. The house of which I speak is in its oldest parts of the fourteenth century at least, and perhaps earlier, but there are modern additions. One wing of it was built seventy years ago at the south end of the house, another at the north end, twenty years ago. Yet the tradition is so strong that you would not tell from the outside, and hardly from the inside, which part is old and which part is new. For, indeed, the old part itself grew up gradually, and the eleven gables of the house show up against the sky as though they were of one age, though in truth they are of every age down along all these 500 years and more.

The central upper room of the house is the chapel where Mass is said, and there one sees, uncovered by any wall of plaster or brick, the original structure of the house, which is of vast oaken beams, the main supports and transverses pieces half a yard across, morticed strongly into each other centuries, and smoothed roughly with the adze. They are black with the years. The roof soars up like a high pitched tent, and is supported by a whole fan of lesser curved oaken beams. There is but one window behind the altar. Indeed, the whole house is thus in its structure of the local and native oak, and the brick walls of it are only curtains built in between the wooden framework of that most ancient habitation. Beneath the chapel is the dining room, where there is a very large open hearth which can take huge logs and which is as old as anything in the place. Here wood only is burnt, and that wood oak.

Down this room there runs a very long oaken table as dark with age almost as the beams above it, and this table has a history. It came out of one of the Oxford colleges when the Puritans looted them 300 years ago. It never got back to its original home. It passed from one family to another until at last it was purchased (in his youth and upon his marriage) by the man who now owns this house. Those who know about such things give its date as the beginning of the seventeenth century. It was made, then, while Shakespeare was still living, and while the faith of England still hung in the balance; for one cannot say that England was certain to lose her Catholicism finally till the first quarter of that century was passed. This table, roughly carved at the side, has been polished with wax since first it began to bear food for men, and now the surface shines like a slightly, very slightly, undulating sea in a calm. At night the brass candlesticks (for this house is lit with candles, as the proper light for men's eyes) are reflected in it as in still brown water; so are the vessels of glass and of silver and of pewter, and the flagons of wine. No cloth is ever spread to hide this venerable splendour, nor, let us hope, ever will be.

At one end of the house, where the largest of its many outer doors (there are several such) swings massively upon huge forged iron hinges, there is a hall, not very wide; its length is as great as the width of the house and its height very great for its width. Like the chapel, its roof soars up, steep and dark, so that from its floor (which is made of very great and heavy slabs of the local stone) one looks up to the roof tree itself. This hall has another great wide hearth in it for the burning of oak, and there is an oaken staircase, very wide and of an easy slope, with an oaken balustrade and leading up to an open gallery above, whence you look down upon the piece. Above this gallery is a statue of Our Lady, carved in wood, uncoloured, and holding the Holy Child, and beneath her many shelves of books. This room is panelled, as are so many of the rooms of the house, but it has older panels than any of the others, and the great door of it opens on to the high road.

Now the way Christmas is kept in this house is this:

On Christmas Eve a great quantity of holly and of laurel is brought in from the garden and from the farm (for this house has a farm of 100 acres attached to it and an oak wood of ten acres). This greenery is put up all over the house in every room just before it becomes dark on that day. Then there is brought into the hall a young pine tree, about twice the height of a man, to serve for a Christmas tree, and on this innumerable little candles are fixed, and presents for all the household and the guests and the children of the village.

It is at about five o'clock that these last come into the house, and at that hour in England, at that date, it has long been quite dark; so they come into a house all illuminated with the

Christmas tree shining like a cluster of many stars seen through a glass.

The first thing done after the entry of these people from the village and their children (the children are in number about fifty—for this remote place keeps a good level through the generations and does not shrink or grow, but remains itself) is a common meal, where all eat and drink their fill in the offices. Then the children come in to the Christmas tree. They are each given a silver piece one by one, and one by one, their presents. After that they dance in the hall and sing songs, which have been handed down to them for I do not know how long. These songs are game songs, and are sung to keep time with the various parts in each game, and the men and things and animals which you hear mentioned in these songs are all of that countryside. Indeed, the tradition of Christmas here is what it should be everywhere, knit into the very stuff of the place; so that I fancy the little children, when they think of Bethlehem, see it in their minds as though it were in the winter depth of England, which is as it should be.

These games and songs continue for as long as they will, and then they file out past the great fire in the hearth to a small piece adjoining where a crib has been set up with images of Our Lady and St Joseph and the Holy Child, the Shepherds, and what I will call, by your leave, the Holy Animals. And here, again, tradition is so strong in this house that these figures are never new bought, but are as old as the oldest of the children of the family, now with children of their own. On this account, the donkey has lost one of its plaster ears, and the old ox which used to be all brown is now piebald, and of the shepherds, one actually has no head. But all that is lacking is imagined. There hangs from the roof of the crib over the Holy Child a tinsel star grown rather obscure after all these years, and much too large for the place. Before this crib the children (some of them Catholic and some Protestant, for the village is mixed) sing their carols; the one they know best is the one which begins: 'The First Good Joy that Mary had, it was the joy of One'. There are a half a dozen or so of these carols which the children here sing; and mixed with their voices is the voice of the miller (for this house has a great windmill attached to it). The miller is famous in these parts for his singing, having a very deep and loud voice which is his pride. When these carols are over, all disperse, except those who are living in the house, but the older ones are not allowed to go without more good drink for their viaticum, a sustenance for Christian men.

Then the people of the house, when they have dined, and their guests, with the priest who is to say Mass for them, sit up till near midnight. There is brought in a very large log of oak (you must be getting tired of oak by this time! But everything here is oaken, for the house is of the Weald). This log of oak is the Christmas or Yule log and the rule is that it must be too heavy for one man to lift; so two men come, bringing it in from outside, the master of the house and his servant. They cast it down upon the fire in the great hearth of the dining room, and the superstition is that, if it burns all night and is found still smouldering in the morning, the home will be prosperous for the coming year.

With that they all go up to the chapel and there the three night Masses are said, one after the other, and those of the household take their Communion.

Next morning they sleep late, and the great Christmas dinner is at midday. It is a turkey; and plum pudding, with holly in it and everything conventional, and therefore satisfactory, is done. Crackers are pulled, the brandy is lit and poured over the pudding till the holly crackles in the flame and the curtains are drawn a moment that the flames may be seen. This Christmas feast, so great that it may be said almost to fill the day, they may reprove who will; but for my part I applaud.

Now, you must not think that Christmas being over, the season and its glories are at an end, for in this house there is kept up the full custom of the Twelve Days, so that 'Twelfth Day', the Epiphany, still has, to its inhabitants, its full and ancient meaning as it had when Shakespeare wrote. The green is kept in its place in every room, and not a leaf of it must be moved until Epiphany morning, but on the other hand not a leaf of it must remain in the house, nor the Christmas tree either, by Epiphany evening. It is all taken out and burnt in a special little coppice reserved for these good trees which have done their Christmas duty; and now, after so many years, you might almost call it a little forest, for each tree has lived, bearing witness to the holy vitality of unbroken ritual and inherited things.

In the midst of this season between Christmas and Twelfth Day comes the ceremony of the New Year, and this is how it is observed:

On New Years' Eve, at about a quarter to twelve o'clock at

night, the master of the house and all that are with him go about from room to room opening every door and window, however cold the weather be, for thus, they say, the old year and its burdens can go out and leave everything new for hope and for the youth of the coming time.

This also is a superstition, and of the best. Those who observe it trust that it is as old as Europe, and with roots stretching back into forgotten times.

While this is going on the bells in the church hard by are ringing out the old year, and when all the windows and doors have thus been opened and left wide, all those in the house go outside, listening for the cessation of the chimes, which comes just before the turn of the year. There is an odd silence of a few minutes, and watches are consulted to make certain of the time (for this house detests wireless and has not even a telephone), and the way they know the moment of midnight is by the boom of a gun, which is fired at a town far off, but can always be heard.

At that sound the bells of the church clash out suddenly in new chords, the master of the house goes back into it with a piece of stone or earth from outside, all doors are shut, and the household, all of them, rich and poor, drink a glass of wine together to salute the New Year.

This, which I have just described, is not in a novel or in a play. It is real, and goes on as the ordinary habit of living men and women. I fear that set down thus in our terribly changing time it must sound very strange and, perhaps in places, grotesque, but to those who practise it, it is not only sacred, but normal, having in the whole of the complicated affair a sacramental quality and an effect of benediction: not to be despised.

Indeed, modern men, who lack such things, lack sustenance, and our fathers who founded all those ritual observances were very wise.

Man has a body as well as a soul, and the whole of man, soul and body, is nourished sanely by a multiplicity of observed traditional things. Moreover, there is this great quality in the unchanging practice of Holy Seasons, that it makes explicable, tolerable, and normal what is otherwise a shocking and intolerable and even in the fullest sense, abnormal thing. I mean, the mortality of immortal men.

Not only death (which shakes and rends all that is human in us, creating a monstrous separation and threatening the soul with isolation which destroys), not only death, but that accompaniment of mortality which is a perpetual series of lesser deaths and is called change, are challenged, chained, and put in their place by unaltered and successive acts of seasonable regard for loss and dereliction and mutability. The threats of despair, remorse, necessary expiation, weariness almost beyond bearing, dull repetition of things apparently fruitless, unnecessary and without meaning, estrangement, the misunderstanding of mind by mind, forgetfulness which is a false alarm, grief, and repentance, which are true ones, but of a sad company, young men perished in battle before their parents had lost vigour in age, the perils of sickness in the body and even in the mind, anxiety, honour harassed, all the bitterness of living—become part of a large business which may lead to Beatitude. For they are all connected in the memory with holy day after holy day, year by year, binding the generations together; carrying on even in this world, as it were, the life of the dead and giving corporate substance, permanence and stability, without the symbol of which (at least) the vast increasing burden of life might at last conquer us and be no longer borne.

This house where such good things are done year by year has suffered all the things that every age has suffered. It has known the sudden separation of wife and husband, the sudden fall of young men under arms who will never more come home, the scattering of the living and their precarious return, the increase and the loss of fortune, all those terrors and all those lessenings and haltings and failures of hope which make up the life of man. But its Christmas binds it to its own past and promises its future; making the house an undying thing of which those subject to mortality within it are members, sharing in its continuous survival.

It is not wonderful that of such a house verse should be written. Many verses have been so written commemorating and praising this house. The last verse written of it I may quote by way of ending:

"Stand thou for ever among human Houses, House of the Resurrection, House of Birth; House of the rooted hearts and long carouses, Stand, and be famous over all the Earth."

The House of Christmas

G. K. Chesterton (1874–1936)

THERE FARED a mother driven forth
Out of an inn to roam;
In the place where she was homeless
All men are at home.
The crazy stable close at hand,
With shaking timber and shifting sand,
Grew a stronger thing to abide and stand
Than the square stones of Rome.

For men are homesick in their homes,
And strangers under the sun,
And they lay their heads in a foreign land
Whenever the day is done.
Here we have battle and blazing eyes,
And chance and honor and high surprise,
But our homes are under miraculous skies
Where the yule tale was begun.

A Child in a foul stable,
Where the beasts feed and foam,
Only where He was homeless
Are you and I at home;
We have hands that fashion and heads that know,
But our hearts we lost - how long ago!
In a place no chart nor ship can show
Under the sky's dome.

This world is wild as an old wives' tale,
And strange the plain things are,
The earth is enough and the air is enough
For our wonder and our war;
But our rest is as far as the fire-drake swings
And our peace is put in impossible things
Where clashed and thundered unthinkable wings
Round an incredible star.

To an open house in the evening
Home shall men come,
To an older place than Eden
And a taller town than Rome.
To the end of the way of the wandering star,
To the things that cannot be and that are,
To the place where God was homeless
And all men are at home.

A Christmas Sermon

St. Augustine (354–430)

"Behold, we have the infant Christ; let us grow up in Him."

One of the greatest doctors of the Church, St. Augustine here in his Sermon 196 reflects on the marvel of Christ's descent into time. By faithfully living out our obligations, any Christian, in any state of life—marriage, widowhood, or holy orders—can reflect back the purity and goodness that Jesus brought down from heaven.

TODAY, THE birthday of our Lord Jesus Christ has dawned in festive splendor for us. It is His birthday, the day on which the Eternal Day was born. And hence it is this day because from this day forward the length of the day increases. Our Lord had two nativities: one divine, the other, human; both marvelous; the one without a woman as mother, the other without a man as father. Hence, the words of the Prophet Isaias may be applied to both generations: 'Who shall declare his generation?' Who would worthily tell of a God generating [His Son]? Who would worthily relate the parturition of a virgin? The former generation took place without the limits of time; the latter, on a definite day in time. Both happened without human calculation, and both are viewed with intense admiration. Consider that first generation: 'In the beginning was the Word, and the Word was with God; and the Word was God.' Whose Word? That of the Father Himself. What Word? The Son Himself. Never did the Father exist without the Son, yet He who was never without the Son generated that Son. He generated Him, yet the Son had no beginning, for there is no beginning for Him who was generated without beginning. Nevertheless, He is the Son and He was generated. Someone is going to say: 'How was He generated if He had ho beginning? If He was generated, He has a beginning; if he has no beginning, then, how was He generated?' I do not know how this happened. Do you ask me, a mere man, how God was generated? I am troubled by your question, but I have recourse to the words of the Prophet: 'Who shall declare his generation?' Come with me to [a consideration of] that human generation; come with me to that in which He 'emptied himself, taking the nature of a slave,' come, to see if we can comprehend it, to see if we can speak about it. For who would grasp the significance of: 'Who though He was by nature God, did not consider being equal to God a thing to be clung to?' Who would understand that? Who would worthily ponder it? Whose mind would dare to investigate it? Whose tongue would have the temerity to utter a decision concerning it? Whose thought can encompass it? Meanwhile, let us lay aside this problem as being too weighty for us. But, so that it would not be too weighty for us, He 'emptied himself, taking the nature of a slave and being made like unto men, 'Where? In the Virgin Mary. Then, let us say something if we have any power of utterance. The angel announces; the Virgin hears, believes, conceives, faith in her mind, Christ in her womb. A virgin has conceived you are amazed; a virgin has brought forth a child you are more amazed; after childbirth she has remained a virgin therefore 'Who shall declare his generation?'

I am going to say something that will please you, my very dear brethren. There are three states of life pursued by the members of the Church of Christ: marriage, widowhood, and virginity. Because those states, those different manifestations of purity, were destined to be found in the holy members of Christ, all three states of life gave witness to Christ. In the first place, the conjugal state bore this witness, for, when the Virgin Mary conceived, Elizabeth, the wife of Zachary, having already conceived, bore in her womb the herald of this Judge. Holy Mary came to Elizabeth to greet her cousin. Thereupon, the infant in Elizabeth's womb leaped for joy. He exulted; she prophesied. Here you have conjugal purity bearing witness to Christ. Where did the state of widowhood bear such witness? In the case of Anna. When the Gospel was read recently, you heard that Anna was a holy widow with prophetic powers who, having lived seven of her eighty-four years with her husband, was constantly in the Temple, worshiping in prayer both night and day. She, a widow, recognized Christ, She saw a tiny babe; she recognized the great God and she bore Him witness. You have, then, in her an illustration of the state of widowhood. In Mary herself we have an illustration of the virginal state. Let each one choose for himself which of these three states he will. Whoever has elected to live outside these states does not make provision for his inclusion in the members of Christ. Let not those women who are married say: 'We do not belong to Christ, for holy women have had husbands. Let not those women who are virgins boast; let them, rather, humble themselves in all things in proportion to their greatness.' You have all the instances of sanctification set before your eyes. Let no one turn aside from these bounds. Let no one turn away from his wife; it is better to be without a wife. If you seek conjugal chastity, you have Susanna; if chastity of widowhood, you have Anna; if virginity, you have Mary.

The Lord Jesus wished to become man for our sake. Wisdom lies upon this earth; let not His mercy become worthless. 'In the beginning was the Word, and the Word was with God; and the Word was God.' O Food and Bread of angels! The angels are filled by Thee; they are sated, yet they do not draw away from Thee. They live by Thee; they are wise in Thee; they are happy because of Thee. And where art Thou for my sake? In a narrow dwelling, in swaddling clothes, in a manger. For whom [dost Thou endure] all this? He who guides the stars is nourished at the breast, but He fills the angels; He speaks in the bosom of the Father, but He is silent in the womb of His Mother. As He advances in age, however, He will speak to us; He will finish the Gospel for us. For us He will suffer and die; He will rise again in token of our reward; He will ascend into heaven before the eyes of His disciples; He will come to the judgment from heaven. Behold, He who lay in the manger demeaned but did not destroy Himself; He took upon Himself what He was not but He remained what He was. Behold, we have the Infant Christ; let us grow up in Him.

Let these thoughts be sufficient for your Charity, because it is fitting for me to say something to the crowds whom I see gathered here for the feast. The first of January is near at hand. You are all Christians; by the grace of God, the state is Christian although there are two classes of people in it, that is, Christians and Jews. Let not those things be done which God hates: injustice in games, wickedness in jest. Let not men make themselves judges, lest they fall into the hands of the true Judge. Hearken, O Christians, you are the members of Christ. Consider what you are; ponder at what price you have been bought. . . .

The Shepherds Had an Angel

Christina Rossetti (1830–1894)

The shepherds had an angel,
The wise men had a star;
But what have I, a little child,
To guide me home from far,
Where glad stars sing together,
And singing angels are?

Lord Jesus is my Guardian,
So I can nothing lack;
The lambs lie in His bosom
Along life's dangerous track:
The wilful lambs that go astray
He, bleeding, brings them back.

Those shepherds thro' the lonely night
Sat watching by their sheep,
Until they saw the heav'nly host

Who neither tire nor sleep,
All singing Glory, glory,
In festival they keep.

Christ watches me, His little lamb,
Cares for me day and night,
That I may be His own in heav'n;
So angels clad in white
Shall sing their Glory, glory,
For my sake in the height.

Lord, bring me nearer day by day,
Till I my voice unite,
And sing my Glory, glory,
With angels clad in white.
All Glory, glory, giv'n to Thee,
Thro' all the heav'nly height.

A Few Words on Christmas

Charles Lamb (1775–1834)

"We go to bed sober; but we have forgotten their old devotions."

Best known for his retelling of Shakespeare's plays for children, Lamb here considers English customs, old and new, surrounding the celebration of Christmas. Writing at the beginning of the Romantic revival in literature and religion in England, Lamb calls his readers away from a cold, cerebral form of celebration, and looks back with nostalgia upon a time when his countrymen—prior to the Reformation—could enter into the central mystery of the faith with exuberant piety.

CLOSE THE shutters, and draw the curtains together, and pile fresh wood upon the hearth! Let us have, for once, an innocent *auto de fé*. Let the hoarded corks be brought forth, and branches of crackling laurel. Place the wine and fruit and the hot chestnuts upon the table.

And now, good folks and children, bring your chairs round to the blazing fire. Put some of those rosy apples upon your plates. We'll drink one glass of bright sherry "to our absent friends and readers," and then let us talk a little about Christmas.

And what is Christmas?

Why, it is the happiest time of the year. It is the season of mirth and cold weather. It is the time when Christmas-boxes and jokes are given; when mistletoe, and red-berried laurel, and soups, and sliding, and school-boys, prevail; when the country is illuminated by fires and bright faces; and the town is radiant with laughing children. Oranges, as rich as the fruit of the Hesperides, shine out in huge golden heaps. Cakes, frosted over (as if to rival the glittering snow) come forth by thousands from their summer (caves) ovens: and on every stall at every corner of every street are the roasted apples, like incense fuming on Pagan altars.

And *this* night is Christmas Eve. Formerly it was a serious and holy vigil. Our forefathers observed it strictly till a certain hour, and then requited their own forbearance with cups of ale and Christmas candles, with placing the *yule log* on the fire, and roaring themselves thirsty till morning. Time has altered this.

We are neither so good as our forefathers were—nor so bad. We go to bed sober; but we have forgotten their old devotions. Our conduct looks like a sort of compromise; so that we are not worse than our ancestors, we are satisfied not to be better: but let that pass. What we now call Christmas Eve—(there is something very delightful in old terms: they had always their birth in reason or sentiment) was formerly *Maedrenack*, or *The Night of Mothers*! How beautifully does this recall to one's heart that holy tale—that wonderful nativity, which the Eastern shepherds went by night to gaze at and adore—

(It was the winter wild,
When the heaven-born child
All meanly wrapp'd in the rude manger lay;)

a prodigy, which, had it been invention only, would have contained much that was immaculate and sublime; but, twined as it is with man's hopes and fears, is invested with a grand and overwhelming interest.

But to-night is Christmas Eve, and so we will be merry. Instead of toast and ale, we will content ourselves with our sherry and chestnuts; and we must put up with coffee or fragrant tea, instead of having the old *Wassail-bowl* which formed part of the inspiration of our elder poets. We were once admitted to the mysteries of that fine invention, and we respect it accordingly. Does any one wish to know its merits? Let him try what he can produce, on our hint, and be grateful to us for ever. The "Wassail-bowl" is, indeed, a great composition. It is not carved by Benvenuto Cellini (the outside *may*—but it is not material), nor shaped by Michael Angelo from the marble quarries of Carrara; but it is a liquor fit for the lips of the Indian Bacchus, and worthy to celebrate his return from conquest. It is made—for, after all, we must descend to particulars—it is made of wine, with some water (but parce, precor, precor!) with spices of various sorts, and roasted apples, which float in triumph upon its top. The proportions of each are not important—in fact, they should be adapted to the taste of the drinkers. The only caution that seems necessary is to "spare the water." If the Compositor should live in the neighbourhood of Aldgate, this hint may be deemed advisable;

though we mean no affront to either him or the pump.

One mark and sign of Christmas is the *music*; rude enough, indeed, but generally gay, and speaking eloquently of the season. Music, at festival times, is common to most countries. In Spain, the serenader twangs his guitar; in Italy, the musician allures rich notes from his Cremona; in Scotland, the bagpipe drones out its miserable noise; in Germany, there is the horn, and the pipe in Arcady. We too, in our turn, have our Christmas "*Waits*," who witch us at early morning, before cock-crow, with strains and welcomings which belong to night. They wake us so gently that the music seems to have commenced in our dreams, and we listen to it till we sleep again. Besides this, we have our songs, from the young and the old, jocose and fit for the time. What old gentleman of sixty has not his stock—his one, or two, or three frolicksome verses. He sings them for the young folks, and is secure of their applause and his own private satisfaction. His wife, indeed, perhaps says "Really, my dear Mr Williams, you should *now* give over these, &c."; but he is more resolute from opposition, and gambols through his "Flowery Meads of May," or "Beneath a shady bower," while the children hang on his thin, trembling, untuneable notes in delighted and delightful amaze.

The Oxen

Thomas Hardy (1840–1929)

CHRISTMAS EVE, and twelve of the clock.
"Now they are all on their knees,"
An elder said as we sat in a flock
By the embers in hearthside ease.

We pictured the meek mild creatures where
They dwelt in their strawy pen,
Nor did it occur to one of us there
To doubt they were kneeling then.

So fair a fancy few would weave
In these years! Yet, I feel,
If someone said on Christmas Eve,
"Come; see the oxen kneel

"In the lonely barton by yonder coomb
Our childhood used to know,"
I should go with him in the gloom,
Hoping it might be so.

What Christmas Is as We Grow Older

Charles Dickens (1812–1870)

"You shall hold your cherished places in our Christmas hearts, and by our Christmas fires."

In this encomium to the spirit of Christmas, Dickens summons readers to look upon the past year through the lens of mercy. Friends and enemies, the living and beloved dead, are all gathered around the family hearth of fellowship and remembrance to celebrate the festival of the birth of mercy.

TIME WAS, with most of us, when Christmas Day encircling all our limited world like a magic ring, left nothing out for us to miss or seek; bound together all our home enjoyments, affections, and hopes; grouped everything and every one around the Christmas fire; and made the little picture shining in our bright young eyes, complete.

Time came, perhaps, all so soon, when our thoughts overleaped that narrow boundary; when there was some one (very dear, we thought then, very beautiful, and absolutely perfect) wanting to the fulness of our happiness; when we were wanting too (or we thought so, which did just as well) at the Christmas hearth by which that some one sat; and when we intertwined with every wreath and garland of our life that some one's name.

That was the time for the bright visionary Christmases which have long arisen from us to show faintly, after summer rain, in the palest edges of the rainbow! That was the time for the beatified enjoyment of the things that were to be, and never were, and yet the things that were so real in our resolute hope that it would be hard to say, now, what realities achieved since, have been stronger!

What! Did that Christmas never really come when we and the priceless pearl who was our young choice were received, after the happiest of totally impossible marriages, by the two united families previously at daggers—drawn on our account? When brothers and sisters-in-law who had always been rather cool to us before our relationship was effected, perfectly doted on us, and when fathers and mothers overwhelmed us with unlimited incomes? Was that Christmas dinner never really eaten, after which we arose, and generously and eloquently rendered honour to our late rival, present in the company, then and there exchanging friendship and forgiveness, and founding an attachment, not to be surpassed in Greek or Roman story, which subsisted until death? Has that same rival long ceased to care for that same priceless pearl, and married for money, and become usurious? Above all, do we really know, now, that we should probably have been miserable if we had won and worn the pearl, and that we are better without her?

That Christmas when we had recently achieved so much fame; when we had been carried in triumph somewhere, for doing something great and good; when we had won an honoured and ennobled name, and arrived and were received at home in a shower of tears of joy; is it possible that THAT Christmas has not come yet?

And is our life here, at the best, so constituted that, pausing as we advance at such a noticeable mile-stone in the track as this great birthday, we look back on the things that never were, as naturally and full as gravely as on the things that have been and are gone, or have been and still are? If it be so, and so it seems to be, must we come to the conclusion that life is little better than a dream, and little worth the loves and strivings that we crowd into it?

No! Far be such miscalled philosophy from us, dear Reader, on Christmas Day! Nearer and closer to our hearts be the Christmas spirit, which is the spirit of active usefulness, perseverance, cheerful discharge of duty, kindness and forbearance! It is in the last virtues especially, that we are, or should be, strengthened by the unaccomplished visions of our youth; for, who shall say that they are not our teachers to deal gently even with the impalpable nothings of the earth!

Therefore, as we grow older, let us be more thankful that the circle of our Christmas associations and of the lessons that they bring, expands! Let us welcome every one of them, and summon them to take their places by the Christmas hearth.

Welcome, old aspirations, glittering creatures of an ardent fancy, to your shelter underneath the holly! We know you, and have not outlived you yet. Welcome, old projects and old loves, however fleeting, to your nooks among the steadier lights that burn around us. Welcome, all that was ever real to our hearts; and for the earnestness that made you real, thanks to Heaven! Do we build no Christmas castles in the clouds now? Let our thoughts, fluttering like butterflies among these flowers of children, bear witness! Before this boy, there stretches out a Future, brighter than we ever looked on in our old romantic time, but bright with honour and with truth. Around this little head on which the sunny curls lie heaped, the graces sport, as prettily, as airily, as when there was no scythe within the reach of Time to shear away the curls of our first-love. Upon another girl's face near it—placider but smiling bright—a quiet and contented little face, we see Home fairly written. Shining from the word, as rays shine from a star, we see how, when our graves are old, other hopes than ours are young, other hearts than ours are moved; how other ways are smoothed; how other happiness blooms, ripens, and decays—no, not decays, for other homes and other bands of children, not yet in being nor for ages yet to be, arise, and bloom and ripen to the end of all!

Welcome, everything! Welcome, alike what has been, and what never was, and what we hope may be, to your shelter underneath the holly, to your places round the Christmas fire, where what is sits open-hearted! In yonder shadow, do we see obtruding furtively upon the blaze, an enemy's face? By Christmas Day we do forgive him! If the injury he has done us may admit of such companionship, let him come here and take his place. If otherwise, unhappily, let him go hence, assured that we will never injure nor accuse him.

On this day we shut out Nothing!

"Pause," says a low voice. "Nothing? Think!"

"On Christmas Day, we will shut out from our fireside, Nothing."

"Not the shadow of a vast City where the withered leaves are lying deep?" the voice replies. "Not the shadow that darkens the whole globe? Not the shadow of the City of the Dead?"

Not even that. Of all days in the year, we will turn our faces towards that City upon Christmas Day, and from its silent hosts bring those we loved, among us. City of the Dead, in the blessed name wherein we are gathered together at this time, and in the Presence that is here among us according to the promise, we will receive, and not dismiss, thy people who are dear to us!

Yes. We can look upon these children angels that alight, so solemnly, so beautifully among the living children by the fire, and can bear to think how they departed from us. Entertaining angels unawares, as the Patriarchs did, the playful children are unconscious of their guests; but we can see them—can see a radiant arm around one favourite neck, as if there were a tempting of that child away. Among the celestial figures there is one, a poor misshapen boy on earth, of a glorious beauty now, of whom his dying mother said it grieved her much to leave him here, alone, for so many years as it was likely would elapse before he came to her—being such a little child. But he went quickly, and was laid upon her breast, and in her hand she leads him.

There was a gallant boy, who fell, far away, upon a burning sand beneath a burning sun, and said, "Tell them at home, with my last love, how much I could have wished to kiss them once, but that I died contented and had done my duty!" Or there was another, over whom they read the words, "Therefore we commit his body to the deep," and so consigned him to the lonely ocean and sailed on. Or there was another, who lay down to his rest in the dark shadow of great forests, and, on earth, awoke no more. O shall they not, from sand and sea and forest, be brought home at such a time!

There was a dear girl—almost a woman—never to be one—who made a mourning Christmas in a house of joy, and went her trackless way to the silent City. Do we recollect her, worn out, faintly whispering what could not be heard, and falling into that last sleep for weariness? O look upon her now! O look upon her beauty, her serenity, her changeless youth, her happiness! The daughter of Jairus was recalled to life, to die; but she, more blest, has heard the same voice, saying unto her, "Arise for ever!"

We had a friend who was our friend from early days, with whom we often pictured the changes that were to come upon our lives, and merrily imagined how we would speak, and walk, and think, and talk, when we came to be old. His destined habitation in the City of the Dead received him in his prime. Shall he be shut out from our Christmas remembrance? Would his love have so excluded us? Lost friend, lost child, lost parent, sister, brother, husband, wife, we will not so discard you! You shall hold your cherished places in our Christmas hearts, and by our

Christmas fires; and in the season of immortal hope, and on the birthday of immortal mercy, we will shut out Nothing!

The winter sun goes down over town and village; on the sea it makes a rosy path, as if the Sacred tread were fresh upon the water. A few more moments, and it sinks, and night comes on, and lights begin to sparkle in the prospect. On the hill-side beyond the shapelessly-diffused town, and in the quiet keeping of the trees that gird the village-steeple, remembrances are cut in stone, planted in common flowers, growing in grass, entwined with lowly brambles around many a mound of earth. In town and village, there are doors and windows closed against the weather, there are flaming logs heaped high, there are joyful faces, there is healthy music of voices. Be all ungentleness and harm excluded from the temples of the Household Gods, but be those remembrances admitted with tender encouragement! They are of the time and all its comforting and peaceful reassurances; and of the history that re-united even upon earth the living and the dead; and of the broad beneficence and goodness that too many men have tried to tear to narrow shreds.

Good King Wenceslas

John Mason Neale (1818–1866)

GOOD KING Wenceslas look'd out,
    On the Feast of Stephen;
When the snow lay round about,
   Deep, and crisp, and even:
Brightly shone the moon that night,
   Though the frost was cruel,
When a poor man came in sight,
   Gath'ring winter fuel.

"Hither page and stand by me,
   If thou know'st it, telling,
Yonder peasant, who is he?
   Where and what his dwelling?"
"Sire, he lives a good league hence.
   Underneath the mountain;
Right against the forest fence,
   By Saint Agnes' fountain."

GOOD KING WENCESLAS

"Bring me flesh, and bring me wine,
 Bring me pine-logs hither:
Thou and I will see him dine,
 When we bear them thither."
Page and monarch forth they went,
 Forth they went together;
Through the rude wind's wild lament,
 And the bitter weather.

"Sire, the night is darker now,
 And the wind blows stronger;
Fails my heart, I know now how,
 I can go no longer."
"Mark my footsteps, good my page;
 Tread thou in them boldly;
Thou shalt find the winter's rage
 Freeze thy blood less coldly."

In his master's steps he trod,
 Where the snow lay dinted;
Heat was in the very sod
 Which the Saint had printed.
Therefore, Christian men, be sure,
 Wealth or rank possessing,
Ye who now will bless the poor,
 Shall yourselves find blessing.

The Burden of Christmas

Charles Dudley Warner (1829–1900)

*"We have appropriated the English conviviality,
the German simplicity, the Roman pomp,
and we have added to it an element of expense."*

In this gentle remonstrance, delivered a century before Walmart and Amazon, Warner reflects on some of the excesses of the then-emerging modern American commercial habits surrounding Christmas and calls upon his readers to return to a simpler, (and we might add) more *sacred* celebration.

IT WOULD be the pity of the world to destroy it, because it would be next to impossible to make another holiday as good as Christmas. Perhaps there is no danger, but the American people have developed an unexpected capacity for destroying things; they can destroy anything. They have even invented a phrase for it—running a thing into the ground. They have perfected the art of making so much of a thing as to kill it; they can magnify a man or a recreation or an institution to death.

And they do it with such a hearty good-will and enjoyment. Their motto is that you cannot have too much of a good thing. They have almost made funerals unpopular by over-elaboration and display, especially what are called public funerals, in which an effort is made to confer great distinction on the dead. So far has it been carried often that there has been a reaction of popular sentiment and people have wished the man were alive. We prosecute everything so vigorously that we speedily either wear it out or wear ourselves out on it, whether it is a game, or a festival, or a holiday. We can use up any sport or game ever invented quicker than any other people. We can practise anything, like a vegetable diet, for instance, to an absurd conclusion with more vim than any other nation. This trait has its advantages; nowhere else will a delusion run so fast, and so soon run up a tree—another of our happy phrases. There is a largeness and exuberance about us which run even into our ordinary phraseology. The sympathetic clergyman, coming from the bedside of a parishioner dying of dropsy, says, with a heavy sigh, "The poor fellow is just swelling away."

Is Christmas swelling away? If it is not, it is scarcely our fault. Since the American nation fairly got hold of the holiday—in some parts of the country, as in New England, it has been universal only about fifty years—we have made it hum, as we like to say. We have appropriated the English conviviality, the German simplicity, the Roman pomp, and we have added to it an element of expense in keeping with our own greatness. Is anybody beginning to feel it a burden, this sweet festival of charity and good-will, and to look forward to it with apprehension? Is the time approaching when we shall want to get somebody to play it for us, like base-ball? Anything that interrupts the ordinary flow of life, introduces into it, in short, a social cyclone that upsets everything for a fortnight, may in time be as hard to bear as that festival of housewives called housecleaning, that riot of cleanliness which men fear as they do a panic in business. Taking into account the present preparations for Christmas, and the time it takes to recover from it, we are beginning—are we not?—to consider it one of the most serious events of modern life.

The Drawer[1] is led into these observations out of its love for Christmas. It is impossible to conceive of any holiday that could take its place, nor indeed would it seem that human wit could invent another so adapted to humanity. The obvious intention of it is to bring together, for a season at least, all men in the exercise of a common charity and a feeling of goodwill, the poor and the rich, the successful and the unfortunate, that all the world may feel that in the time called the Truce of God the thing common to all men is the best thing in life. How will it suit this intention, then, if in our way of exaggerated ostentation of charity the distinction between rich and poor is made to appear more marked than on ordinary days? Blessed are those that expect nothing. But are there not an increasing multitude of persons in the United States who have the most exaggerated expectations of personal profit on Christmas Day? Perhaps it is not quite so bad as this, but it is safe to say that what the children alone expect to receive, in money value would absorb the national surplus,

---

[1] "The Drawer" was the name of the column Warner edited in *Harper's Magazine*, where this essay originally appeared.

about which so much fuss is made. There is really no objection to this—the terror of the surplus is a sort of nightmare in the country—except that it destroys the simplicity of the festival, and belittles small offerings that have their chief value in affection. And it points inevitably to the creation of a sort of Christmas "Trust"—the modern escape out of ruinous competition. When the expense of our annual charity becomes so great that the poor are discouraged from sharing in it, and the rich even feel it a burden, there would seem to be no way but the establishment of neighborhood "Trusts" in order to equalize both cost and distribution. Each family could buy a share according to its means, and the division on Christmas Day would create a universal satisfaction in profit sharing—that is, the rich would get as much as the poor, and the rivalry of ostentation would be quieted. Perhaps with the money question a little subdued, and the female anxieties of the festival allayed, there would be more room for the development of that sweet spirit of brotherly kindness, or all-embracing charity, which we know underlies this best festival of all the ages. Is this an old sermon? The Drawer trusts that it is, for there can be nothing new in the preaching of simplicity.

A Christmas Carol

Sara Teasdale (1884–1933)

THE KINGS they came from out the south,
    All dressed in ermine fine;
They bore Him gold and chrysoprase,
    And gifts of precious wine.

The shepherds came from out the north,
    Their coats were brown and old;
They brought Him little new-born lambs—
    They had not any gold.

The wise men came from out the east,
    And they were wrapped in white;
The star that led them all the way
    Did glorify the night.

The angels came from heaven high,
    And they were clad with wings;
And lo, they brought a joyful song
    The host of heaven sings.

The kings they knocked upon the door,
   The wise men entered in,
The shepherds followed after them
   To hear the song begin.

The angels sang through all the night
   Until the rising sun,
But little Jesus fell asleep
   Before the song was done.

Why Do We Need Epiphany?

St. John Henry Newman (1801–1890)

"We view Him as an Object of our worship."

Each season has its glory. In the afterglow of the Christmas feast, the Church gives us Epiphany. During these days, we gaze upon the child Christ through the eyes of the wise men from the east—those first fruits of God's universal saving mission. With them, at Epiphany, we come neither to petition nor to enquire but simply to adore.

"This beginning of miracles did Jesus in Cana of Galilee, and manifested forth His glory; and His disciples believed in Him." John ii. 11.

THE EPIPHANY is a season especially set apart for adoring the glory of Christ. The word may be taken to mean the manifestation of His glory, and leads us to the contemplation of Him as a King upon His throne in the midst of His court, with His servants around Him, and His guards in attendance. At Christmas we commemorate His grace; and in

Lent His temptation; and on Good Friday His sufferings and death; and on Easter Day His victory; and on Holy Thursday His return to the Father; and in Advent we anticipate His second coming. And in all of these seasons He does something, or suffers something: but in the Epiphany and the weeks after it, we celebrate Him, not as on His field of battle, or in His solitary retreat, but as an august and glorious King; we view Him as the Object of our worship. Then only, during His whole earthly history, did He fulfill the type of Solomon, and held (as I may say) a court, and received the homage of His subjects; viz. when He was an infant. His throne was His undefiled Mother's arms; His chamber of state was a cottage or a cave; the worshippers were the wise men of the East, and they brought presents, gold, frankincense, and myrrh. All around and about Him seemed of earth, except to the eye of faith; one note alone had He of Divinity. As great men of this world are often plainly dressed, and look like other men, all but as having some one costly ornament on their breast or on their brow; so the Son of Mary in His lowly dwelling, and in an infant's form, was declared to be the Son of God Most High, the Father of Ages, and the Prince of Peace, by His star; a wonderful appearance which had guided the wise men all the way from the East, even unto Bethlehem.

This being the character of this Sacred Season, our services throughout it, as far as they are proper to it, are full of the image of a king in his royal court, of a sovereign surrounded by subjects, of a glorious prince upon a throne. There is no thought of war, or of strife, or of suffering, or of triumph, or of vengeance connected with the Epiphany, but of august majesty, of power, of prosperity, of splendour, of serenity, of benignity. Now, if at any time, it is fit to say, "The Lord is in His holy temple, let all the earth keep silence before Him." [Hab. ii. 20.] "The Lord sitteth above the waterflood, and the Lord remaineth a king for ever." "The Lord of Hosts is with us; the God of Jacob is our refuge." "O come, let us worship, and fall down, and kneel before the Lord our Maker." "O magnify the Lord our God, and fall down before His footstool, for He is Holy." "O worship the Lord in the beauty of holiness; bring presents, and come into His courts."

I said that at this time of year the portions of our services which are proper to the season are of a character to remind us of a king on his throne, receiving the devotion of his subjects. Such is the narrative itself, already referred to, of the coming of the wise men, who sought Him with their gifts from a place afar off, and fell down and worshipped Him. Such too, is the account of His baptism, which forms the Second Lesson of the feast of the Epiphany, when the Holy Ghost descended on Him, and a Voice from heaven acknowledged Him to be the Son of God. And if we look at the Gospels read throughout the season, we shall find them all containing some kingly action of Christ, the Mediator between God and man. Thus in the Gospel for the First Sunday, He manifests His glory in the temple at the age of twelve years, sitting among the doctors, and astonishing them with His wisdom. In the Gospel for the Second Sunday He manifests His glory at the wedding feast, when He turned the water into wine, a miracle not of necessity or urgency, but especially an august and bountiful act—the act of a King, who out of His abundance gave a gift to His own, therewith to make merry with their friends. In the Third Sunday, the leper worships Christ, who thereupon heals him; the centurion, again, reminds Him of His Angels and ministers, and He speaks the word, and his servant is restored forthwith. In the Fourth, a storm arises on the lake, while He is peacefully sleeping, without care or sorrow, on a pillow; then He rises and rebukes the winds and the sea, and a calm follows, deep as that of His own soul, and the beholders worship Him. And next He casts out Legion, after the man possessed with it had also "run and worshipped Him." [Mark v. 6.] In the Fifth, we hear of His kingdom on earth, and of the enemy sowing tares amid the good seed. And in the Sixth, of His second Epiphany from heaven, "with power and great glory."

Such is the series of manifestations which the Sundays after the Epiphany bring before us. When He is with the doctors in the temple, He is manifested as a prophet—in turning the water into wine, as a priest—in His miracles of healing, as a bounteous Lord, giving out of His abundance—in His rebuking the sea, as a Sovereign, whose word is law—in the parable of the wheat and tares, as a guardian and ruler—in His second coming, as a lawgiver and judge.

And as in these Gospels we hear of our Saviour's greatness, so in the Epistles and First Lessons we hear of the privileges and the duties of the new people, whom He has formed to show forth His praise. Christians are at once the temple of Christ, and His worshippers and ministers *in* the temple; they are the

Bride of the Lamb taken collectively, and taken individually, they are the friends of the Bridegroom and the guests at the marriage feast. In these various points of view are they presented to us in the Services during these weeks. In the Lessons from the prophet Isaiah we read of the gifts and privileges, the characteristics, the power, the fortunes of the Church—how widely spreading, even throughout all the Gentiles; how awful and high, how miraculously endowed, how revered, how powerful upon earth, how rich in temporal goods, how holy, how pure in doctrine, how full of the Spirit. And in the Epistles for the successive Sundays, we hear of the duties and distinguishing marks of her true members, principally as laid down in the twelfth and thirteenth chapters of St. Paul to the Romans; then as the same Apostle enjoins them upon the Colossians; and then in St. John's exhortations in his General Epistle.

The Collects are of the same character, as befit the supplications of subjects coming before their King. The first is for knowledge and power, the second is for peace, the third is for strength in our infirmities, the fourth is for help in temptation, the fifth is for protection, and the sixth is for preparation and purification against Christ's second coming. There is none which would suit a season of trial, or of repentance, or of waiting, or of exultation—they befit a season of peace, thanksgiving, and adoration, when Christ is not manifested in pain, conflict, or victory, but in the tranquil possession of His kingdom.

It will be sufficient to make one reflection, which suggests itself from what I have been saying.

You will observe, then, that the only display of royal greatness, the only season of majesty, homage, and glory, which our Lord had on earth, was in His infancy and youth. Gabriel's message to Mary was in its style and manner such as befitted an Angel speaking to Christ's Mother. Elisabeth, too, saluted Mary, and the future Baptist his hidden Lord, in the same honourable way. Angels announced His birth, and the shepherds worshipped. A star appeared, and the wise men rose from the East and made Him offerings. He was brought to the temple, and Simeon took Him in His arms, and returned thanks for Him. He grew to twelve years old, and again He appeared in the temple, and took His seat in the midst of the doctors. But here His earthly majesty had its end, or if seen afterwards, it was but now and then, by glimpses and by sudden gleams, but with no steady sustained light, and no diffused radiance. We are told at the close of the last-mentioned narrative, "And He went down with His parents, and came to Nazareth, *and was subjected unto them.*" [Luke ii. 51.] His subjection and servitude now began in fact. He had come in the form of a servant, and now He took on Him a servant's office. How much is contained in the idea of His subjection! and it began, and His time of glory ended, when He was twelve years old.

Solomon, the great type of the Prince of Peace, reigned forty years, and his name and greatness was known far and wide through the East. Joseph, the much-loved son of Jacob, who in an earlier age of the Church, was a type of Christ in His kingdom, was in power and favour eighty years, twice as long as Solomon. But Christ, the true Revealer of secrets, and the Dispenser of the bread of life, the true wisdom and majesty of the Father, manifested His glory but in His early years, and then the Sun of Righteousness was clouded. For He was not to reign really, till He left the world. He has reigned ever since; nay, reigned *in* the world, though He is not in sensible presence in it—the invisible King of a visible kingdom—for He came on earth but to show what His reign would be, after He had left it, and to submit to suffering and dishonour, that He *might* reign.

It often happens, that when persons are in serious illnesses, and in delirium in consequence, or other disturbance of mind, they have some few minutes of respite in the midst of it, when they are even more than themselves, as if to show us what they really are, and to interpret for us what else would be dreary. And again, some have thought that the minds of children have on them traces of something more than earthly, which fade away as life goes on, but are the promise of what is intended for them hereafter. And somewhat in this way, if we may dare compare ourselves with our gracious Lord, in a parallel though higher way, Christ descends to the shadows of this world, with the transitory tokens on Him of that future glory into which He could not enter till He had suffered. The star burned brightly over Him for awhile, though it then faded away.

We see the same law, as it may be called, of Divine Providence in other cases also. Consider, for instance, how the prospect of our Lord's passion opens upon the Apostles in the sacred history. Where did they hear of it? "Moses and Elias on the mountain appeared with Him in glory, and spake of His decease, which He should accomplish at Jerusalem." [Luke ix. 30, 31.]

That is, the season of His bitter trial was preceded by a short gleam of the glory which was to be, when He was suddenly transfigured, "and the fashion of His countenance was altered, and His raiment was white and glistering." [Luke ix. 29.] And with this glory in prospect, our Lord abhorred not to die: as it is written, "Who for the joy that was set before Him, endured the Cross, despising the shame."

Again, He forewarned His Apostles that they in like manner should be persecuted for righteousness' sake, and be afflicted and delivered up, and hated and killed. Such was to be their life in this world, "that if in this world only they had had hope in Christ, they had been of all men most miserable." [1 Cor. xv. 19.] Well then, observe, their trial too was preceded by a season of peace and pleasantness, in anticipation of their future reward; for before the day of Pentecost, for forty days Christ was with them, soothing, comforting, confirming them, "and speaking of the things pertaining unto the kingdom of God." [Acts i. 3.] As Moses stood on the mount and saw the promised land and all its riches, and yet Joshua had to fight many battles before he got possession, so did the Apostles, before descending into the valley of the shadow of death, whence nought of heaven was to be seen, stand upon the heights, and look over that valley, which they had to cross, to the city of the living God beyond it.

And so again, St. Paul, after many years of toil, refers back to a time when he had a celestial vision, anticipatory of what was to be his blessedness in the end. "I knew a man in Christ," he says, meaning himself, "about fourteen years ago, caught up to the third heaven.... And I knew such a man ... how that he was caught up into Paradise, and heard unspeakable words, which it is not lawful for a man to utter." [2 Cor. xii. 3, 4.] St. Paul then, as the twelve Apostles, and as our Lord before him, had his brief season of repose and consolation before the battle.

And lastly: the whole Church also may be said to have had a similar mercy vouchsafed to it at first, in anticipation of what is to be in the end. We know, alas, too well, that, according to our Lord's account of it, tares are to be with the wheat, fish of every kind in the net, all through its sojourning on earth. But in the end, "the saints shall stand before the throne of God, and serve Him day and night in His temple: and the Lamb shall feed them, and shall lead them unto living fountains of waters," and there shall be no more "sorrow nor pain, nor any thing that defileth or worketh abomination," "for without are dogs, and sorcerers, and whore-mongers, and murderers, and idolaters, and whosoever loveth and maketh a lie." Now was not this future glory shadowed forth in that infancy of the Church, when before the seal of the new dispensation was opened and trial began, "there was silence in heaven for half an hour;" and "the disciples continued daily with one accord in the temple, and in prayers, breaking bread from house to house, being of one heart, and of one soul, eating their meat with gladness and singleness of heart, praising God, and having favour with all the people;" [Acts ii. 46, 47.] while hypocrites and "liars," like Ananias and Sapphira, were struck dead, and "sorcerers," like Simon, were detected and denounced?

To conclude; let us thankfully cherish all seasons of peace and joy which are vouchsafed us here below. Let us beware of abusing them, and of resting in them, of forgetting that they *are* special privileges, of neglecting to look out for trouble and trial, as our due and our portion. Trial is our portion here—we must not think it strange when trial comes after peace. Still God mercifully does grant a respite now and then; and perhaps He grants it to us the more, the more careful we are not to abuse it. For all seasons we must thank Him, for time of sorrow and time of joy, time of warfare and time of peace. And the more we thank Him for the one, the more we shall be drawn to thank Him for the other. Each has its own proper fruit, and its own peculiar blessedness. Yet our mortal flesh shrinks from the one, and of itself prefers the other;—it prefers rest to toil, peace to war, joy to sorrow, health to pain and sickness. When then Christ gives us what is pleasant, let us take it as a refreshment by the way, that we may, when God calls, go in the strength of that meat forty days and forty nights unto Horeb, the mount of God. Let us rejoice in Epiphany with trembling, that at Septuagesima we may go into the vineyard with the labourers with cheerfulness, and may sorrow in Lent with thankfulness; let us rejoice now, not as if we have attained, but in hope of attaining. Let us take our present happiness, not as our true rest, but, as what the land of Canaan was to the Israelites,—a type and shadow of it. If we now enjoy God's ordinances, let us not cease to pray that they may prepare us for His presence hereafter. If we enjoy the presence of friends, let them remind us of the communion of saints before His throne. Let us trust in nothing here, yet draw hope from every thing—that at length the Lord may be our everlasting light, and the days of our mourning may be ended.

The Three Kings

Henry Wadsworth Longfellow (1807–1882)

THREE KINGS came riding from far away,
Melchior and Gaspar and Baltasar;
Three Wise Men out of the East were they,
And they travelled by night and they slept by day,
For their guide was a beautiful, wonderful star.

The star was so beautiful, large and clear,
That all the other stars of the sky
Became a white mist in the atmosphere,
And by this they knew that the coming was near
Of the Prince foretold in the prophecy.

Three caskets they bore on their saddle-bows,
Three caskets of gold with golden keys;
Their robes were of crimson silk with rows
Of bells and pomegranates and furbelows,
Their turbans like blossoming almond-trees.

And so the Three Kings rode into the West,
Through the dusk of the night, over hill and dell,
And sometimes they nodded with beard on breast,
And sometimes talked, as they paused to rest,
With the people they met at some wayside well.

"Of the child that is born," said Baltasar,
"Good people, I pray you, tell us the news;
For we in the East have seen his star,
And have ridden fast, and have ridden far,
To find and worship the King of the Jews."

And the people answered, "You ask in vain;
We know of no King but Herod the Great!"
They thought the Wise Men were men insane,
As they spurred their horses across the plain,
Like riders in haste, who cannot wait.

And when they came to Jerusalem,
Herod the Great, who had heard this thing,
Sent for the Wise Men and questioned them;
And said, "Go down unto Bethlehem,
And bring me tidings of this new king."

So they rode away; and the star stood still,
The only one in the grey of morn;
Yes, it stopped—it stood still of its own free will,

THE THREE KINGS

Right over Bethlehem on the hill,
The city of David, where Christ was born.

And the Three Kings rode through the gate and the guard,
Through the silent street, till their horses turned
And neighed as they entered the great inn-yard;
But the windows were closed, and the doors were barred,
And only a light in the stable burned.

And cradled there in the scented hay,
In the air made sweet by the breath of kine,
The little child in the manger lay,
The child, that would be king one day
Of a kingdom not human, but divine.

His mother Mary of Nazareth
Sat watching beside his place of rest,
Watching the even flow of his breath,
For the joy of life and the terror of death
Were mingled together in her breast.

They laid their offerings at his feet:
The gold was their tribute to a King,
The frankincense, with its odor sweet,
Was for the Priest, the Paraclete,
The myrrh for the body's burying.

And the mother wondered and bowed her head,
And sat as still as a statue of stone,
Her heart was troubled yet comforted,
Remembering what the Angel had said
Of an endless reign and of David's throne.

Then the Kings rode out of the city gate,
With a clatter of hoofs in proud array;
But they went not back to Herod the Great,
For they knew his malice and feared his hate,
And returned to their homes by another way.

Ring in the common love of good.
Ring out old shapes of foul disease;
   Ring out the narrowing lust of gold;
   Ring out the thousand wars of old,
Ring in the thousand years of peace.

Ring in the valiant man and free,
   The larger heart, the kindlier hand;
   Ring out the darkness of the land,
Ring in the Christ that is to be.

Epiphany in a Secular Age

Pope Benedict XVI

"Might we too sometimes see God as a sort of rival?"

In this piercing Epiphany homily, Pope Benedict XVI probes the meaning of the actions of both King Herod and the Magi for modern men and women. Herod is a practical atheist who has lost sight of God and so cannot see men as other than obstacles to his own autonomous rule. The magi, by contrast, are the seekers after truth, after the cause of all things, who find in nature and in Scripture the clue to that which they, and we, most seek.

IN THE Solemnity of Epiphany the Church continues to contemplate and to celebrate the mystery of the birth of Jesus the Saviour. In particular, this day stresses the universal destination and significance of this birth.

By becoming man in Mary's womb, the Son of God did not only come for the People of Israel, represented by the Shepherds of Bethlehem, but also for the whole of humanity, represented by the Magi. And it is precisely on the Magi and their journey in search of the Messiah (*cf.* Mt 2:1-12) that the Church invites us to meditate and pray today.

We heard in the Gospel that having arrived in Jerusalem from the East they asked: "Where is he who has been born king of the Jews? For we have seen his star in the East, and have come to worship him" (v. 2). What kind of people were they and what kind of star was it? They were probably sages who scrutinized the heavens, but not in order to try to "read" the future in the stars, possibly to profit by so doing. Rather, they were men "in search" of something more, in search of the true light that could point out the path to take in life. They were people certain that something we might describe as the "signature" of God exists in creation, a signature that man can and must endeavour to discover and decipher.

Perhaps the way to become better acquainted with these Magi and to understand their desire to let themselves be guided by God's signs is to pause to consider what they find on their journey, in the great city of Jerusalem.

First of all they met King Herod. He was certainly interested in the Child of which the Magi spoke; not in order to worship him, as he wished to make them believe by lying, but rather to kill him. Herod was a powerful man who saw others solely as rivals to combat. Basically, on reflection, God also seemed a rival to him, a particularly dangerous rival who would like to deprive men of their vital space, their autonomy, their power; a rival who points out the way to take in life and thus prevents one from doing what one likes.

Herod listened to the interpretations of the Prophet Micah's words, made by his experts in Sacred Scripture, but his only thought was of the throne. So God himself had to be clouded over and people had to be reduced to mere pawns to move on the great chessboard of power. Herod is a figure we dislike, whom we instinctively judge negatively because of his brutality.

Yet we should ask ourselves: is there perhaps something of Herod also in us? Might we too sometimes see God as a sort of rival? Might we too be blind to his signs and deaf to his words because we think he is setting limits on our life and does not allow us to dispose of our existence as we please?

Dear Brothers and Sisters, when we see God in this way we end by feeling dissatisfied and discontent because we are not letting ourselves be guided by the One who is the foundation of all things.

We must rid our minds and hearts of the idea of rivalry, of the idea that making room for God is a constraint on us. We must open ourselves to the certainty that God is almighty love that takes nothing away, that does not threaten; on the contrary he is the Only One who can give us the possibility of living to the full, of experiencing true joy.

The Magi then meet the scholars, the theologians, the experts who know everything about the Sacred Scriptures, who are familiar with the possible interpretations, who can quote every passage of it since they know it by heart and are therefore of valuable assistance to those who choose to walk on God's path.

However, St Augustine says, they like being guides to others, they point out the way; but they themselves do not travel, they stand stock-still. For them the Scriptures become a sort of atlas to be perused with curiosity, a collection of words and concepts for study and for learned discussion.

However, once again we can ask ourselves: is not there a temptation within us to consider the Sacred Scriptures, this very rich and vital treasure for the faith of the Church, as an object of study and of specialists' discussions rather than as the Book that shows us the way to attain life? I think, as I suggested in the Apostolic Exhortation *Verbum Domini*, that profound willingness must ceaselessly be born within them to see the words of the Bible interpreted in the Church's living Tradition (n. 18), as the truth that tells us what man is and how he can fulfil himself totally, the truth that is the way to take every day, with others, if we wish to build our lives on rock and not on sand.

And so we come to the star. What kind of star was the star the Magi saw and followed? This question has been the subject of discussion among astronomers down the centuries. Kepler, for example, claimed that it was "new" or "super-new", one of those stars that usually radiates a weak light but can suddenly and violently explode, producing an exceptionally bright blaze.

These are of course interesting things but do not guide us to what is essential for understanding that star. We must return to the fact that those men were seeking traces of God; they were seeking to read his "signature" in creation; they knew that "the heavens are telling of the glory of God" (Psalm 19 [18]:2); they were certain, that is, that God can be perceived in creation.

But, as sages, the Magi also knew that it is not with any kind of telescope but rather with the profound eyes of reason in search of the ultimate meaning of reality and with the desire for God, motivated by faith, that it is possible to meet him, indeed, becomes possible for God to come close to us.

The universe is not the result of chance, as some would like to make us believe. In contemplating it, we are asked to interpret in it something profound; the wisdom of the Creator, the inexhaustible creativity of God, his infinite love for us.

We must not let our minds be limited by theories that always go only so far and that—at a close look—are far from competing with faith but do not succeed in explaining the ultimate meaning of reality. We cannot but perceive in the beauty of the world, its mystery, its greatness and its rationality, the eternal rationality; nor can we dispense with its guidance to the one God, Creator of Heaven and of earth.

If we acquire this perception we shall see that the One who created the world and the One who was born in a grotto in Bethlehem and who continues to dwell among us in the Eucharist, are the same living God who calls us, who loves us and who wants to lead us to eternal life.

Herod, the Scriptural exegetes, the star: but let us follow the journey of the Magi to Jerusalem. Above the great city the star disappears, it is no longer seen. What does this mean? In this case too, we must interpret the sign in its depth. For those men it was logical to seek the new king in the royal palace, where the wise court advisors were to be found.

Yet, probably to their amazement, they were obliged to note that this newborn Child was not found in the places of power and culture, even though in those places they were offered precious information about him.

On the other hand they realized that power, even the power of knowledge, sometimes blocks the way to the encounter with this Child. The star then guided them to Bethlehem, a little town; it led them among the poor and the humble to find the King of the world.

God's criteria differ from human criteria. God does not manifest himself in the power of this world but in the humility of his love, the love that asks our freedom to be welcomed in order to transform us and to enable us to reach the One who is Love.

Yet, for us too things are not so different from what they were for the Magi. If we were to be asked our opinion on how God was to save the world, we might answer that he would have to manifest all his power to give the world a fairer economic system in which each person could have everything he wanted. Indeed, this would be a sort of violence to man because it would deprive him of the fundamental elements that characterize him. In fact neither our freedom nor our love would be called into question. God's power is revealed in quite a different way: in Bethlehem, where we encounter the apparent powerlessness of his love. And it is there that we must go and there that we find God's star.

Thus, a final important element of the event of the Magi appears to us very clearly: the language of creation enables us to make good headway on the path towards God but does not give us the definitive light. In the end, it was indispensable for the Magi to listen to the voice of the Sacred Scriptures: they alone could show them the way. The true star is the word of God which, amidst of the uncertainty of human discourses, gives us the immense splendour of the Divine Truth.

Dear brothers and sisters, let us allow ourselves to be guided by the star that is the word of God, let us follow it in our lives, walking with the Church in which the Word has pitched his tent. Our road will always be illumined by a light that no other sign can give us. And we too shall become stars for others, a reflection of that light which Christ caused to shine upon us. Amen.